NO ESCAPE

Arlene Hunt is an author and film reviewer. *No Escape* is her eleventh novel. A somewhat slow long-distance runner, when not writing, Arlene can usually be found halfway up a mountain with two German shepherds for company. She lives in Dublin.

Twitter: @arlenehunt
Facebook: Arlene Hunt
www.arlenehunt.com

ALSO BY ARLENE HUNT

Vicious Circle
False Intentions
Black Sheep
Missing Presumed Dead
Undertow
Blood Money
The Outsider
The Chosen (republished by Bookouture as *Last to Die*)
Last Goodbye

ARLENE HUNT

NO ESCAPE

HACHETTE
BOOKS
IRELAND

First published in Ireland in 2020 by HACHETTE BOOKS IRELAND

1

Cataloguing in Publication Data is available from the British Library

Trade paperback ISBN 978 1 47369 943 4
Ebook ISBN 978 1 47369 944 1

Typeset in Adobe Garamond by Bookends Publishing Services, Dublin

Printed and bound in Great Britain by Clays Ltd, Elcograf, S.p.A

Hachette Books Ireland policy is to use papers that are natural, renewable and recyclable products and made from wood grown in sustainable forests. The logging and manufacturing processes are expected to conform to the environmental regulations of the country of origin.

Hachette Books Ireland
8 Castlecourt Centre
Castleknock
Dublin 15, Ireland

A division of Hachette UK Ltd
Carmelite House, 50 Victoria Embankment, EC4Y 0DZ

www.hachettebooksireland.ie

To my parents

I

In an almost deserted car park fifty-six miles east of Cherbourg, France, a battered green van with a long wheelbase pulled in and drew alongside a Scania lorry with Irish registration plates. The driver of the van, a swarthy man with a bad complexion, got out, his movements rocking the van on threadbare tyres. He rubbed his back, scratched a buttock and lit a foul-smelling cigarillo with a wooden match.

The driver of the lorry also got out. He was in his early fifties, short, with a wiry build and a thin, pinched face that looked fox-like from a certain angle. His name was Murray.

The van driver shook Murray's hands, his breath pluming on the frigid air as he muttered a greeting in broken, halting English. He took a bulky Manila envelope from the dash of the van and stood to one side smoking while Murray checked the contents.

'This it?' Murray said, frowning. 'I thought I was collecting twenty.'

The van driver shrugged. 'This we got.'

Murray shook his head, resealed the envelope and climbed up into the cabin. He stowed it in the lockbox under the sleeping platform and jumped back down. 'Right, let's go.'

The van driver unlocked the rear door and barked an order. Murray stood a little way back, watching, as the six women and eight men climbed out and stood shivering on freezing tarmac.

Some carried rucksacks, some black plastic bags tied with elastic bands. The rest had little more than the clothes on their backs. Some of them would understand English, the majority, Murray knew, would not, not that it mattered.

Mixed bag, he thought sourly, sizing them up with a practised eye. Mostly Middle-Eastern, though not all. He squinted closely at the women and knew Arthur would bitch and moan about the selection. Not his problem, though, was it? At the end of the day his job was to get them into the country undetected, nothing more, nothing less. If Arthur had any objections he could do the next run himself, see how he fared.

He spat to one side, glanced at his watch, noted the time and motioned to the group to follow him to the rear of the lorry as the van rattled out of the car park and on into the night.

'English?' he asked.

A woman wearing a denim jacket with a fur-trimmed hood raised her hand slowly.

'Right,' Murray said. 'Tell them to take a piss now if they need to go. Once they're on board they stay put until we reach where we're going, got all that?'

The woman rattled off what he'd told her in her own language. The men understood immediately what was required of them and moved around to the other side of the lorry, but some of the women remained huddled together looking around them, confused and a little frightened.

Murray sighed. 'Jesus … there's some bushes over there if you're feeling delicate.' He pointed, then clapped his hands. 'Move it!'

When everyone was done he unlocked the rear doors of the lorry. The trailer was filled with fridges and washing machines in cardboard boxes, stacked to the roof. The bottom fridge on the right was a shell and easy to slide out, revealing a gap in the stacks that led to the front of the trailer. One by one, fourteen fully grown adults crawled through until they reached a space so tight there was barely room to stand, let alone sit. Murray came up the rear, carrying a torch in his mouth and a small drill in his right hand.

'Move in, move in, tighter.'

The group pressed tighter. He heard muttering and assumed the woman was relaying his words. A man he could not see retorted angrily.

'What did he say?'

'He say there is no room.'

'Yeah, well tell him this isn't fucking Shangri-La!'

Murray shoved the last person in, slid the wooden partition into place and drilled it shut, leaving them in pitch dark. He rapped on the wood with his knuckles.

'Tell them to be quiet, okay? Everyone needs to stay quiet.'

By the time the lorry rolled up the gangplank and onto the ferry some hours later, several of the fourteen had been sick and one woman had fainted from exhaustion and the unbearable heat.

Among the women were two sisters, one a teenager, the other a little older. The older girl was called Yulia. Yulia had stolen money and sold everything she owned to finance this journey, fleeing a past littered with violence and abuse. The younger girl, her sister, was called Celestine. She was mute.

Yulia hugged Celestine tight and whispered futures for them, ones full of hope and dignity. This was a test, she told Celestine, trying not to breathe the rancid air too deeply, a final hurdle before freedom.

'Don't be afraid,' Yulia said, stroking Celestine's hair. 'Everything is going to be all right. We will find our aunt, and we will work hard and stay out of trouble. You'll see, Celestine, I promised to take care of you and I will. No one will hurt us ever again.'

But she was wrong.

So very wrong.

2

Twenty-three hours later the same lorry rattled across a cattle grid and drove into a walled courtyard behind a single-storey stone farmhouse. The farmhouse was old and had stood for over two hundred years a quarter of a mile back from a secondary road that saw little traffic.

It had thick walls, small windows, a steeply pitched roof and two chimney stacks. From the outside it looked much the same as it had always done, but inside it had been modernised with no expense spared.

Francis 'Stonewall' McCabe watched the lorry on camera from inside the farmhouse. He was forty-five years old, massively built with broad, sloping shoulders and no real neck to speak of. In his bare feet he stood shy of six feet four, his hair was black/brown, thick and worn longer than was considered fashionable. His eyes were so dark in certain light they appeared black, evidence of the Spanish blood that ran through his veins from his maternal side.

He waited until Murray reversed the lorry into a huge concrete shed before he pushed back his chair. Immediately two dogs got to their feet.

They were Caucasian shepherds, bred to protect flocks of sheep from wolf and bear attack on high mountain terrains; intense creatures, loyal, territorial, fearsome. Stonewall doubted there would be any trouble with the delivery, but he was not a man who liked to leave things to chance. The very presence of the dogs often rendered even the most vociferous objectors silent.

He opened the back door as Rally, Murray's nephew, drove up in a Renault Trafic van with Duchy Ward in the passenger seat. The men got out, nodded to Stonewall and followed him across the yard into the shed.

'Where's Arthur?' Duchy asked, looking around.

Stonewall pulled the huge door shut. 'Your guess is as good as mine.'

A muscle bunched in Duchy's jaw. 'He should be here, taking care of business.'

Stonewall glanced at Murray, who got the message and unlocked the trailer. He crawled through and unscrewed the partition. Minutes later the 'cargo' emerged, blinking into the light. Stonewall looked them over. They were a sorry sight – soiled and stinking, dehydrated and weak.

'Any of them speak English?'

'The one with the hood,' Murray said. 'Maybe some of the others.'

'Tell them to hand over their phones.'

Murray told the woman with the hood and she translated to the group. Several of the men started talking angrily and waving their hands.

'Voz!' Stonewall snapped, and the dogs began to bark. The men fell silent, cowed.

'Par!' Stonewall said. The dogs stopped.

The display ended the discussion. Rally went around with a plastic bag and collected phones and a laptop. He handed the bag to Stonewall, who carried it to a metal cabinet on the far side of the shed and put it inside.

'I thought there was supposed to be twenty,' Duchy said. 'Where's the rest?'

Murray shrugged. 'This was all that turned up.'

'Fourteen ain't twenty.'

'I can count, Duchy, same as you,' Murray said, starting to feel hard done by. 'I collected what was there.'

Stonewall walked around the group, inspecting them like they were cattle at a mart, calculating. He singled out a blonde, who kept her eyes downcast, put his finger under her chin to lift her head. The kid standing next to her bared her teeth and growled.

Stonewall laughed. 'Relax, little wolf, I'm not going to hurt her.' He touched the blonde's face again. She had incredible green eyes and exquisite bone structure: cleaned up, she'd be worth more to them than the rest combined.

'I'll take this one to Lakeside,' he said.

'They should go for auction, the lot,' Duchy said.

'Arthur likes to take the pick of the litter.'

'Arthur ain't here, though, is he?'

'But I am.' Stonewall turned and looked at him, his voice carrying an edge. 'I'm taking this girl.'

Duchy took a step towards him. Instantly the dogs growled.

'If you have a problem,' Stonewall said, calm as you like, 'take it up with your brother.'

Duchy looked at the dogs, raised his hands and stepped backwards, a tight little smile on his lips. 'No, you're quite right, big man. No need for hostilities, is there?'

'All right.' Murray clapped his hands. 'You lot come with me, there's a shower and a toilet this way. If you have clean clothes you should change into them. Come on, let's get a move on.'

Stonewall reached for the blonde. Immediately she backed away, babbling ninety to the dozen. He glanced towards the woman with the hood. 'What is she cackling on about?'

'They are two.'

'Two what?'

'They are sisters, they want …' she clasped her hands together '… be together.'

Stonewall looked at the younger girl. She was fourteen, fifteen maybe? Heavy-set, with acne and dull sludge-coloured eyes that were watching him like a hawk.

'No,' he said. 'She stays here.'

The woman spoke rapidly to Yulia, who if anything became more frantic as Stonewall reached for her again. His fingers had barely brushed the fabric of her coat when the younger girl leaped at him, snarling and clawing.

Stonewall slapped her across the side of the head with an open hand. It was a hard, stinging blow and it all but flattened her. 'Take care of this,' he told Murray.

'On it.'

Yulia tried to keep hold of her sister. Stonewall, who had little patience for hysterics, grabbed the straps of her backpack and lifted her clean off her feet. He wrapped his arms around her waist and carried her to the door, kicking and screaming, with the dogs trotting at his heels. Rally opened it for him and he left.

'All right,' Murray said. 'Let's get—'

The girl was on her feet and running after Stonewall. Murray grabbed her and grunted in surprise as she smashed an elbow into this chest. Grimly he held on, but small as she was, she was like an animal, swinging her fists wildly. Murray managed to grab her wrists, but she sank her teeth into his left hand and clamped down hard.

'Rally!'

His nephew ran back.

'Grab her legs.'

Rally grappled with the girl's legs, getting several kicks for his trouble. He yanked them out from under her, throwing her onto the ground. Between them they managed to wrestle her onto her front and twist her arms behind her back.

'Get the tape.'

Rally ran to the workbench and returned with a roll of duct tape. They fastened her hands, her feet, and finally Murray slapped a piece of tape over her mouth, taking care to avoid her snapping teeth.

'You're bleeding,' Rally said, nodding to his arm.

'You think?' Murray said. 'She bit me!'

'Yeah?' Rally looked a little closer. 'You'll need to disinfect that. Did you know the human mouth is full of microbes and bacteria and all kinds of weird shit?' He looked absurdly proud of himself. 'Scientific fact, I read it.'

'Where?'

'Scientific journal of science,' Rally said, deadpan.

Murray glared. Somedays he wished he had never agreed to work for his uncle, Malachy Ward: somedays he wished he'd had the foresight to turn down the offer of easy money; because it wasn't easy, was it? There was nothing easy about this life, least not for the likes of him.

He dug his knee into the wriggling girl's spine until she stopped moving.

No, he thought, dragging her to her feet, there was nothing easy about this at all.

3

Mariposa Ward was playing a hand of patience in her office when she heard a car driving up the service road to the rear of Lakeside, the private members' club she ran with her husband, Arthur Ward.

She got up, looked out the window, left the office and went to the top of the stairs where she leaned over the balcony. 'Stefan?'

She heard scuffling from somewhere below and, moments later, Stefan, the mansion manager, wandered into view with a tea-towel draped over his shoulder. He was a small man, with loose jowls and perpetually watery eyes. He wore one of several toupees that fooled nobody, and if anyone were to enquire, he claimed he was fifty-five; and he had been, once.

'You bellowed?'

'Francis is pulling up round the back. Let him in, will you?'

'What did your last servant die of?'

'I stabbed him in the neck for giving me cheek.'

'It was a merciful release in that case.'

Mariposa laughed and went back to her office, changed quickly from her dressing gown into a bright silk kimono and reapplied her lipstick. She was older than her brother by less than a year. Like Francis – she refused point blank to call him Stonewall – she was tall, with masses of coarse dark air she dyed a shade darker still. She had a long face, with dark eyes set above a slightly hooked nose. She tilted her head back. She was still a handsome woman, she thought, patting her hair, in the right light, under the right circumstances.

She hurried downstairs and found Francis towering over Stefan, with a tiny blonde wearing a green backpack standing by his side. The girl was trembling and had clearly been crying. Mariposa recognised the look: fresh meat.

'Francis!' She stood on tiptoe and kissed his stubbly cheek. 'Where have you been hiding? I haven't seen you for weeks.'

'I've been around, here and there.'

She glanced at the woman, smiling. It was not a nice smile; Mariposa had many qualities, but she had never managed to pull off nice. 'And who do we have here?'

'This is Yulia. She arrived earlier today.'

'Does she speak English?'

'A little.'

'Yulia, such a pretty name.' She caught the sour whiff of Yulia's clothes and wrinkled her nose. 'Welcome to Lakeside, my name is Mariposa.'

Yulia stared at her, tearfully.

'Well, you must be exhausted from your travels. Stefan, why don't you show Yulia upstairs, help her get settled in and I'll be right behind you. Pop her in with Jade, maybe.'

She waited until Stefan had hustled Yulia away before she turned her attention back to her brother. 'What's up with her?'

'There was a kid with her, I had to split them up.'

Mariposa pressed her hand to her chest. 'A baby?'

Stonewall shook his head. 'Younger sister.'

'Oh.' Mariposa waved her hand, losing interest immediately. 'Come have a drink.'

'It's three o'clock in the afternoon.'

'Exactly, so it's bound to be cocktail hour somewhere.'

She led him to the lounge and threw open the doors. It was dark inside, the heavy velvet drapes pulled against the fading daylight, and traces of cigar smoke still lingered in the air from the night before. Mariposa switched on the lamps behind the bar and waved her hands at the mirrored shelves. 'Name your poison.'

'I'll have a beer.'

Stonewall removed his coat and sat down on a stool. Mariposa plucked a bottle of Heineken from a fridge beneath the counter, opened it and set it on the bar before him. Next, she dropped a square cube of ice into a wine glass, added a generous helping of gin and a dash of lime juice.

'Salut,' Stonewall said.

'Salut.'

Mariposa took a hefty gulp and coughed. She had been a bit heavy-handed with the gin. She put the glass down and leaned both hands on the counter, a wolfish grin on her scarlet lips. 'So,' she said. 'Any gossip?'

'Gossip?'

'Yes, Francis, news. How are things out there in the great beyond?'

'Same as it ever was.'

She narrowed her eyes. Honestly, sometimes it was like pulling teeth. 'How is Duchy settling back into civilian life?'

Stonewall tilted his head backwards to look at her. 'Like you care.'

'I never said I cared.'

'Yeah, I know, but you should have gone to his welcome home party. People noticed you weren't there. He noticed you weren't there.'

'So?' Mariposa took another sip, smaller this time. 'I'm supposed to forget everything he's said about me over the years?' she said sourly, feeling a spark of indignation.

Like his younger brother Arthur, Duchy had been a career criminal from the time he was old enough to walk. His career stalled when the van he was driving broke down outside Birmingham, puttering to a smoking stop on the hard shoulder of the A38. Unfortunately for Duchy it was stuffed full of illegal Chinese immigrants at the time, two of them heavily pregnant. The judge, a son of second-generation immigrants himself, took one look at the police photographs and tossed the book squarely at his head so Duchy spent eight of a fourteen-year sentence as a guest of HM Prison Birmingham, during which time he'd managed to get himself stabbed in the guts and almost died.

Now he was back on Irish soil, with a mousy English wife called Cally, who, Mariposa heard, had an arse so wide you could land a helicopter on it.

'Duchy reckons he's a changed man,' Stonewall said. 'He told everyone at the party a priest was called to give him last rites in prison – he reckons it's what saved his life.'

Mariposa patted her pockets, located her cigarette case, snapped it open and put one between her teeth. She lit it and inhaled the smoke as deeply as her lungs allowed before she spoke again. 'Bollocks,' she said. 'Francis, come on, you don't believe any of that dog and pony show, do you? Duchy bloody Ward? The man's an out-and-out thug.'

Stonewall shrugged and sipped his beer.

'What about you?'

'What about me?'

'Christ, Francis, it's a simple enough question.'

Her brother put the beer down and studied his massive hands. The backs were hopscotched with scars and old puckered injuries, long faded, never forgotten.

'Francis?'

'I don't know,' he said after an extended silence. 'Some days I'm okay.'

'And others?'

'Not as much.' He looked at her. 'I've been thinking maybe I should go see Belle?'

'Belle?' Mariposa was surprised. Belle was their grandfather's sister, a wizened old crone living in squalor on the outskirts of the city. 'What for?'

'She might be able to do something about the dreams. Chester used to say she had powers.'

'Chester was a drunk and she's a fraud, Francis. I'd rather eat glass than spend an afternoon with that old bag.'

'Maybe you're right.' Stonewall stood up. 'I got to go. Tell Arthur I said hello.'

'Tell him yourself. You see him more than I do these days,' Mariposa said, tapping her nails against the side of her glass.

Stonewall put on his coat and left.

Mariposa drained her drink. Belle, Christ, what was he thinking? People said time heals all wounds, but not for Mariposa; for Mariposa time was fertile ground for all manner of hatred and resentment.

She left the glass on the counter and went upstairs to the third floor. Stefan had put the girl in a room at the end of the hall, next to the linen closet. She was sitting on the bed, with her hands in her lap, her bag open on the floor by her feet.

'All right?' Mariposa asked Stefan, who shrugged.

'Clothes, an iPod, nothing else.'

'Yulia, is it?' Mariposa said. 'We need to get a few things straight here, all right? This is a private members' club – that means I set the rules and you follow them. You work for me now, all right?'

'Please … Celestine?'

'Her sister,' Stefan said. 'She keeps asking about her sister.'

'Oh, don't worry about her, she's … she's going to work same as you. Well, not the same as you but—'

Yulia sprang off the bed and made a break for the door. Mariposa reacted fast; she caught her by her hair and swung her into the wall so hard she crumpled onto the floor.

'Listen to me, sweetheart,' Mariposa said. 'I'm a very nice lady and this is a very nice place. If you play by the rules you can make some good money here. If you don't play by the rules, well, there are other places I can send you, places that don't understand the true value of a pretty face.'

She squatted over the girl and grabbed her face, her blood-red nails digging into the girl's skin. Yulia's terrified eyes met her own.

'You're mine now, you understand? You're my property.' The grip tightened. 'I treat my property well, I look after it. You behave yourself, you earn your keep and you'll earn your freedom. You'll even get to see that sister of yours from time to time. Think of this as an opportunity and behave yourself. You don't want me as an enemy, my girl, best keep that in mind.'

She patted Yulia on the cheek, stood up and left the room.

Stefan helped Yulia to her feet and tutted when he saw marks on her skin. She had such a pretty face, he'd hate to see it bruised.

'Come on, lovey,' he said. 'Let's go get you cleaned up. What size do you think you are? A six? Come on, come with Stefan and let's see what we have.'

4

'I'm leaving you.'

Leo Kennedy lifted his head from the pillow and squinted at the Amy-shaped shadow standing in the door of their bedroom. She was dressed, fully dressed he noted, and wearing an expression he had recently grown accustomed to, one of mild disdain with a hint of despair.

Not a good look for a fiancée.

'What?'

'I'm leaving you, Leo, it's over.' She put her hands on her hips. 'I can't do this anymore.'

Under normal circumstances, a man hearing this combination of words might react by, say, getting to his feet and pleading his case. But Leo had worked seventy hours plus that week in the bowels of a packed, sweltering hotel kitchen and had barely slept four hours, having passed out at around three a.m. following a mammoth drinking session with several Ecuadorean colleagues.

Taking all this into consideration, his options seemed limited, so he took what he thought was the right one and certainly the easiest.

He lowered his head to his pillow and went straight back to sleep.

As it turned out, Amy was also considering her options. Glaring at her lover, she took his snores as a sign, a sign that she couldn't fix the wild, dark-haired Irishman she had fallen in love with and only a fool would keep trying.

Amy Bradley was no fool.

Later that day, she cancelled their Sky subscription and allowed Drew, the senior vice-president of the firm, to take her to lunch. She cried prettily over her Cobb salad, dabbing her eyes with a handkerchief whenever she felt the moment warranted it, and by the time Drew had paid – using a platinum credit card – she agreed that she had done all she could to salvage her relationship, and yes she would be delighted to accept his generous offer of a spare room in his ultra-modern penthouse while she 'sorted things out'.

'Thank you, Drew.' She reached across the starched linen to place her hand on his. 'You've been such a wonderful friend these last few weeks.'

Drew, who had a whole lot more than friendship on his mind, beamed at her (his orthodontist had been expensive but worth every penny).

'Amy, you deserve so much more than that bog Paddy can give you.'

Amy agreed in principle. She pretended she didn't hear the 'bog Paddy' part.

'I'm keeping the ring,' she told a bewildered, monstrously hungover Leo when she called later that day. 'I've earned it.'

Leo was standing in his boxer shorts in the hallway of their flat. He said nothing. He was staring at his reflection in the mirror by the coat rack. He looked ghastly, but that was to be expected and it didn't help that the mirror was old and flecked in places. He wondered where it had come from. Was it new? He couldn't remember ever noticing it before now.

'Leo!' Amy's voice was like a gunshot in his ear. 'Are you even listening to me?'

'Sure.' He scratched his belly. 'You're keeping the ring, you've earned it.'

'Is that all you have to say?'

'What do you want me to say to that?'

'My God, you're such a heartless bastard.' She hung up.

Leo listened to the dial tone for a moment, turned and walked down the hall into the living room. It was getting dark outside, but he didn't bother switching on any lamps. He already felt like death warmed up: what good would light do?

In a strange way he was relieved Amy had been the one to pull the plug. At least this way he didn't have to tell her he'd been sacked from the hotel for threatening Nigel, the floor manager, with a filleting knife. Didn't have to see the look on her face or hear the withering contempt in her voice.

Didn't have to keep pretending he loved her.

Best not to think about love. Best not to think about that at all. Best not to think about Nigel either. Best not to think about his terrified face, or the sudden bloom of urine on his trouser legs. The obnoxious twerp had pushed Leo to the limit, there was no doubt about that. But pinning him to the tiles with a knife pressed against his carotid artery wasn't … well, in hindsight, it wasn't a good decision.

But then, a little voice in his head reminded him, he wasn't making good decisions these days, was he?

Least not ones he could remember making.

He grabbed a bottle of Widow Jane from the gold hostess trolley (where had that come from?) and carried it to the sofa. No need for a glass, he decided, no need for anything really.

He knew he could have killed Nigel. A millimetre more and he'd have blood on his hands. It had been tempting, oh so tempting, and that's what scared him the most.

He shivered and opened the bottle.

He drank. And drank. And drank.

Woke up to the cold light of dawn on the street outside a Morrisons supermarket, barefoot, no watch, no wallet.

Shit.

'You okay, mate?'

Shielding his eyes, Leo looked up at a figure that fuzzed and blurred before it became whole in the shape of a man in a security uniform.

'Peachy,' he mumbled. His tongue felt too big for his mouth.

'You can't sleep here, mate, it's private property.'

Leo crawled towards a metal pillar and used it to pull himself upright. The ground swayed beneath his feet; the air punched him senseless.

'You live around here?'

'Depends,' Leo said. 'Where's here?'

'You're on Hanover Park, mate.'

'Hanover?' He staggered forward and fell down again. This time he kept a firm grip on the metal pillar when he stood up. Hanover, what the hell was he doing on Hanover?

'Mate, you don't look so good,' the security guard and master of understatement said. 'You got someone you can call to come get you?'

'Nah,' Leo managed truthfully. Carefully he released the metal pillar and lurched off down the street.

Fortunately, his downstairs neighbour, Mr Patel, had not yet gone to work.

'Hello,' Leo said shakily, clinging to the doorjamb. 'Do you still have the spare key for the flat?'

Mr Patel peered at him over the top of his glasses, then looked down. 'Where are your shoes?'

'I'm not wearing any.'

'I can see that. Wait here, please.' He went inside and came back a moment later with the spare key. He passed it over. 'You look rough, old boy, if you don't mind my saying so.'

Leo nodded, waved his thanks and dragged himself upstairs.

The flat was still and quiet, the bourbon bottle lying empty on the floor by the coffee table. Leo sat on the couch with his head in his hands, feeling sick, grimy and disgusted with himself. He heard a buzzing sound and found his phone down the side of the sofa. It was his alarm. There were no messages, not a single one.

Figured.

Persona non grata.

It took a while, but eventually he managed a shower and was getting out when he heard someone knocking at the flat door. Half hoping it was Amy – though why wouldn't she use her keys? – he wrapped a towel around his waist and hobbled down the hall to open it. On the landing stood a leather-clad man with a motorbike helmet balanced precariously atop his head. He was holding a large brown envelope in one hand and a metallic box in the other.

'Leo Kennedy?'

'Yes.'

'Sign here.'

Leo took the electronic pen and scrawled something that looked like his signature in the window of the hand-held device. The courier handed him the envelope and left.

Slightly curious, Leo closed the door, hobbled to the kitchen and put the kettle on. While he waited for it to boil he opened the envelope and removed the two pages from inside. The first was a headed letter from a firm of Irish solicitors he'd never heard of. The second was a photocopy of the last will and testament of one Gina Marsh, née Kennedy, a great-aunt on his father's side of the family. According to the letter, Gina had passed away two months before after a 'short illness', and Leo was to scatter her ashes over the waters of Dublin's Grand Canal, under moonlight.

Leo read the words a second time. He'd only met Gina twice; the first time on the day he'd made his Holy Communion, the second when they'd buried his mother. He recalled a small woman, stuffed inside a fur coat that reeked of perfume. On both occasions she had told him to stand up straight and stop slouching. Certainly nothing in their brief exchanges suggested she cared a whit for him, but now – he read the letter and the photocopy again – it appeared she had left him her entire estate.

Leo sat down heavily on a kitchen stool.

Outside the sky darkened and the air grew thick and oppressive as storm clouds gathered. If Leo had been in any fit state to notice such things, he might have considered it a sign, a foreshadowing of things to come.

But he was not, and he didn't.

5

The fight began, as many fights often do, long before a single punch was thrown.

It was a Saturday and the Clampton Hotel in Blanchardstown was hosting a twenty-first birthday party for a pretty girl named Shelly Astor in the lower function room.

The night started well enough. Shelly's family and friends arrived in high spirits, laden down with gifts for the birthday girl. The younger women wore short dresses, high heels, fake tan and glitter; the lads dressed sharp to match their dates, in slim suits and waistcoats, all groomed to within an inch and not a hair out of place. The music was loud, the DJ imported from the UK for the night and for the first hour or two assistant manager Caroline Staunton genuinely thought she had everything under control.

Tony Wright, the head of hotel security, had a different view. He beckoned her out into the lobby for a 'quiet word'. 'We have a problem.'

'What is it?'

He led her to the internal courtyard of the hotel. Through the smoked glass they could see into the function room, both the dance floor and the bar area.

'See them?'

Caroline followed his finger. Tony was pointing to a group of men standing at the bar, drinking tequila from shot glasses. They were young, mid-twenties, dressed expensively, coiffed, she thought, like the young men on that television show about gangsters in Birmingham.

'See the one with the beard?'

'Yes.'

'That's Liam Kennedy.'

'Who?'

'Kennedy, he's trouble.'

'What do you mean he's trouble?'

'Got busted last year on a drugs charge, got busted this year for GBH, beat a kid so badly he put him in the hospital for four weeks.'

'Is he a guest?'

'He's here, isn't he?' Tony turned slightly. 'Now, see him, the man in the white shirt?'

Again, she followed his finger and saw an older man skirting the dance floor. He was late forties, wearing designer jeans and a snow-white shirt opened two buttons too many. He looked like a less plastic version of Simon Cowell. A girl followed, clinging to his hand. She was leggy, dark-haired, wearing a green dress that barely covered what the Good Lord had bounteously given. She also looked young enough to be his daughter.

'That's Arthur Ward.'

'Who?'

Tony gave an exasperated sigh. 'Ward. You must have heard of the Wards.'

'Assume I don't know everyone in the city, Tony, and take it from there.'

'Arthur Ward is *known* to the guards. Will that cover it?'

'Oh.'

'See the girl with him? That's Marcy Dunne.' Tony held up a hand when he saw Caroline's mouth opening. 'And before you ask who, she's Liam Kennedy's ex-bird and Arthur Ward's current squeeze.'

'Really?' Caroline was horrified. 'But she's hardly more than a child and that man must be—'

'That man is connected.'

'To what?'

Tony goggled at her. Okay, Caroline came from Carlow, and was therefore, by default, a culchie, but there was simply no excuse for this kind of ignorance.

'To trouble, Caroline. He's connected to trouble, the kind of trouble we don't want to tangle with.'

'How do you know all of this?'

'It's my job to know.'

'Right.' Caroline frowned. 'Well, should we ask them to leave?'

'Not a good idea.'

'Then what?'

'Can you close the bar early?'

She shook her head. 'Private function, two a.m. cut-off. There would be a riot.'

Tony calculated. Two a.m., that left three hours' drinking time and things were already starting to get messy. Earlier, he'd caught two lads filling glasses from bottles of vodka hidden in the flowerbeds outside and he knew, without question, there was more than booze being shared about. The party was a tinderbox: one spark and it would catch fire.

'I need you to call Marko and ask him to come in.'

'But it's his night off.'

Tony watched Liam Kennedy chase the tequila with a shot of Jägermeister and slam the glass on the counter to the raucous cheers of his sycophantic friends.

'We'll need him,' he said gravely. 'And if I were you I'd put a call into the Blanch cops and ask them to be on standby.'

'The guards?' Caroline shook her head in disbelief. 'Absolutely not. Now look, I appreciate you're being proactive, but there's no need for that kind of unpleasantness.'

'Call Marko then.'

'All right, I'll ask if he's available. Until then … try to keep an eye on things.'

And keep an eye Tony did, but it was like trying to juggle and tap dance at the same time. By midnight, many of the younger guests were drunk to the point of insensibility and there was an unmistakable air of tension building.

Trouble struck at four minutes past midnight when Marcy Dunne got up to dance with the birthday girl. Immediately, Kennedy pushed off the bar and stalked across the room, cutting directly through the crowd. People got out of his way. Kennedy was short, five eight, no more, no less, but what he lacked in height he more than made up for in brawn and was known to spend several days a week in the gym pumping iron with his crew. He moved light on his feet, jaw up, a bristling little bruiser.

Tony was dealing with a minor scuffle between two girls over a spilled drink when he saw Kennedy grab Marcy around the waist, and he knew with absolute certainty the shit was about to hit the fan. This was confirmed when he clocked Kennedy's entourage moving to surround Ward, who was sitting at a table talking with Shelly's father and two of her uncles, none of whom seemed particularly intimidated by the younger group of hard chaws. When Ward glanced towards the dance floor, one of the younger men tried to block his view, standing with his arms out, head tilted in the universal language of being a gobshite. Ward got to his feet. Shelley's uncles got to their feet too and now the tables were turning, too fast, too hard. Tony started towards them and was very relieved to see Marko enter from the lobby wearing his uniform.

'Marko!' he called. 'Watch that lot.' Tony nodded to the table and pushed through the crowd, eyeballing Kennedy who was jabbing his finger into Marcy's face. Shelly Astor was trying to get between them, but Kennedy shoved her to one side so hard he almost knocked her down.

'What's going on here?' Tony said.

Marcy looked at him, her eyes huge, pleading. She was a stunning girl, almost perfect in every way. No wonder the kid was acting like a fool.

'He won't leave me—'

'Stay out of this,' Kennedy said. 'We're having a private conversation.'

'Step away from her.'

Kennedy ignored him and grabbed Marcy's hand. 'I only want to talk, why won't you—?'

Tony loosened his stance. The kid was strong, with a low centre of gravity. Best thing to do was go for a choke hold, get him limp and drag him outside to cool off, get Marko to babysit while he rounded up the rest of the posse. It might get a bit hairy, but at least they'd be off the premises. Least the girl would be safe.

Yeah, that was a plan, that might work.

He darted forward and wrapped his arm around Kennedy's neck, leaned back and lifted the kid's feet off the ground. It was a good move, one he'd mastered over the years, but something wasn't … something didn't …

His eyes watered. Kennedy had dropped his hand, caught him between the legs and was squeezing his balls so hard they felt like they were going to pop.

'Let go,' Kennedy hissed.

Marcy fled. The pressure on Tony's testicles increased. Slivers of intense agony splintered upwards across his lower stomach. He couldn't take the pain any longer. He let go and staggered backwards, cupping his throbbing testicles in both hands.

'Dirty bastard,' he managed.

Liam Kennedy retched and spluttered, puce-faced. It was alarming how quickly he recovered, a gleam of sheer savagery in his eyes as he shoved through the crowd after Marcy.

Tony shuffled after him, wincing with every agonising step. The DJ blasted Avicii and everyone was stomping and cheering when Marcy, crying hysterically, fell into Arthur Ward's arms and all hell broke loose.

6

Stonewall McCabe heard his mobile phone vibrate, threw back the covers and got out of bed.

He found his jeans on the floor, dug his phone out of the back pocket, read the message on his screen and swore under his breath. It was late, and he was bone tired. He could, he supposed, ignore the message, but … dammit, there was always bloody something with Arthur.

He dressed quickly, let the dogs out into the courtyard and drove into the city, reaching North Strand forty minutes later. He parked opposite the main gates of Marcy Dunne's apartment building and sent a text, telling Arthur he was outside. Arthur came out a few minutes later, talking on his phone and smoking. When he got into the passenger seat, he hung up and slammed the door. Stonewall noted the bruising on his face, the blood on his shirt.

'What happened?'

Arthur rubbed his forehead, looking grim. 'I was at a party earlier, had a bit of a run-in with some gobshite, we had words.'

'Looks like you had more than words.'

'The little prick sucker-punched me.' Arthur was in bullish form, his blood high. He reeked of sex and cheap perfume. Stonewall noticed a love bite on the side of his neck, a ridiculous look for a man of his years.

'Where's your car?'

'At the Clampton. I had to leave it in the car park cause the bloody cops were crawling all over the place.'

'Whose party was it?'

Arthur shrugged, suddenly coy.

'Whose party?' Stonewall asked again.

'Some friend of Marcy's.'

A kid's party, then, Stonewall thought; plenty of mouths, witnesses, mobile phone footage. The fight was probably all over YouTube already. He felt his hands tighten on the steering wheel. This was reckless, stupid behaviour at a time when they didn't need any more attention. With Duchy home the cops were already sniffing around the gang. Rally had been pulled over a few weeks before; fortunately his cargo was legit. But it was a worry. Stonewall did not believe in chance or coincidence.

'Where do you want to go?'

'Is it okay if I crash with you tonight, brother?' Arthur reached one arm across the seats and squeezed the back of Stonewall's massive head, suddenly smiling, all charm. 'I'd go home, but I don't want to disturb Mariposa. Your sister needs her beauty sleep.'

Stonewall absorbed the insult and said nothing. He put the car in gear, drove down the street and turned onto the North Strand Road, heading out of town. Though he tolerated his brother-in-law's proclivities, he made no secret of the fact he found them distasteful. Skirt was skirt at the end of the day and Arthur had access to more than his fair share, so what was he doing tangled up with this particular young one, Marcy? It made him look stupid, it made him look weak; a man led by his dick was no man at all.

They drove through Fairview. Arthur put on the radio, channel-surfed until he found an eighties station and leaned back in his seat with a sigh.

As they passed The Yacht, Stonewall glanced in the rear-view mirror. There had been a car on their tail since they'd left Nottingham

Street. Might be nothing but whenever Stonewall slowed, the distance remained the same between them, which suggested it was hanging back.

'You drop that money in to Duchy like I asked?' Arthur's voice was soft and full of sleep.

'Yeah.'

'How was he?'

Stonewall considered this. How was Duchy? A good question. He had taken the money and counted it in front of Stonewall (an insult if ever there was one). Didn't say thank you, didn't offer Stonewall a drink, didn't ask about Arthur, didn't seem anything other than cold, angry. Bitter.

'He was grand, Arthur.'

'It's good to have him home again, isn't it? Like old times.'

'Sure.'

Arthur glanced at him. 'You know it's different this time, Francis.'

Stonewall watched the car in the rear-view mirror. He couldn't remember the last time Arthur had used his Christian name and wasn't sure he liked hearing it on his lips.

'I mean with this girl, Marcy, she's not like the—'

'It's none of my business, Arthur.'

'I mean it, she's special.'

'They're always special, until they're not,' Stonewall said, cutting him off as quickly as possible. This was not a conversation he wanted to have, not now, not ever. Mariposa was his sister and, whatever her quirks, he loved her. Whatever 'arrangement' Arthur and Mariposa had was between them, and it was none of his affair. Though it confirmed something he'd always known: at this stage in his life he'd rather chew off his own foot than marry.

His eyes flicked to the rear-view mirror again. The car behind was still there, still hanging back. Stonewall looked ahead and saw the traffic lights turn orange and tapped the brakes to indicate he was stopping. At the last second, he stepped on the accelerator and shot through on the red. The car behind them did the same, causing a taxi turning at the junction to slam on its brakes and blare its horn.

'What are you doing?' Arthur asked. 'Slow down.'

'We've got company.'

Arthur turned in his seat and saw the gaining lights. 'You carrying a weapon?'

'No.'

'Shit.'

Both cars tore along Clontarf Road, speed climbing. At the junction by St Anne's Park Stonewall overtook a line of traffic, spun the wheel, hung a hard left and shot up Watermill Road, tyres screaming.

'Head for Raheny,' Arthur said. 'I'll call Rally and tell him we need—'

A taxi pulled out of All Saints Road right in front of them. Stonewall veered and slammed on the brakes, but it was too late to stop. He tried to overtake, clipped the rear bumper and went spinning across the street before crashing into a row of parked cars.

Dazed, Stonewall shook his head. He'd bitten his tongue in the impact and his mouth was full of blood. He spat. Arthur had hit the passenger side window and cracked it with his skull. There was blood running down his face.

Stonewall groped for him. 'Arthur?'

The taxi driver was out, yelling and waving his arms. Stonewall heard a double pop, turned his head and saw the taxi driver sprinting away.

Two men were walking towards them; they wore black clothes and baseball caps. The nearest one had a gun in in his left hand, held low by his hip. He raised it.

The windscreen exploded, spraying glass everywhere. Stonewall ducked. He got the car started again, stepped hard on the accelerator and shot onto the road, careening wildly. Arthur roared as a muzzle flashed; Stonewall felt something whizz by his face and screamed as his right leg went white hot and useless. Bullets thunked off steel, something punched through the driver's window.

Stonewall slumped across the steering wheel. Uncontrolled, the car veered off the road, crumpled around a tree and came to a dead stop.

The gunman approached the car. He bent down, looked at Stonewall, then looked across him to where Arthur was trapped in the passenger seat with his hands raised.

'No!' Arthur said. 'Wait!'

7

Mariposa leaped from the moving car, sprinted across the car park and burst through the main doors of the A&E department. Despite the hour – or perhaps because of it – the place was packed to the rafters, with the worse for wear sleeping and the injured sitting slack-faced and sullen on rows of plastic seats. Several sets of eyes watched her rush up to the reception desk and shove a man aside so hard he almost fell. She was a welcome distraction to the monotony of waiting.

'I'm looking for Francis McCabe,' she said, her voice loud, hysteria barely reined in. More heads turned her way. 'He was brought here by ambulance earlier. Where is he? I need to see him.'

The receptionist cradled the phone under her chin and looked up. 'Okay, if you take a seat someone will be with you shortly.'

'Yeah,' the man she'd pushed said, aggrieved. 'I was here first.'

Mariposa ignored him. The gallop across the car park had loosened her hair and thick strands fell about her face. She looked quite mad. 'Francis McCabe.' She spelled the surname out in hard letters. 'He was brought in by ambulance and—'

'Listen to me, you *need* to wait your turn. Take a seat and someone will be with you in a moment.'

'I don't want a bloody seat.' Mariposa slammed her hands on the counter, bracelets jingling. 'God damn you, where is my brother?'

The receptionist dropped her left hand and pressed a button under the counter. It was twenty after three in the early hours of Saturday morning, she was three-quarters way through a twelve-hour shift and her back was killing her. She was certainly in no mood for hysterics.

A security man appeared. 'Is everything okay?'

'Could you explain to this … lady,' the receptionist pronounced the word with an edge suggesting she thought Mariposa was no such thing, 'that she needs to either take a seat or she will have to leave.'

The security man turned to Mariposa, who backed up sharply.

'Don't put your fucking hands on me.'

'Okay, you need to calm down.'

'Don't you dare touch me!'

'Mrs Ward?'

Two men were approaching. Mariposa knew before they flashed their IDs they were guards. Could tell by the cut of them. The first man was tall, handsome, with close-cut salt-and-pepper hair, more salt than pepper. The second man was shorter, balding, with rounded cheeks and pink, plump lips that she thought repellent.

Mariposa waved the ID away, unlooked at. She had little time for authority and none at all for the law. The first man shrugged, unoffended, and put it back into the inside pocket of his jacket. The second man offered Mariposa his hand. She ignored it.

'My name is Detective Inspector David Maken,' the first man said. 'This is Detective Sergeant Seamus Flood.'

'You're the one who phoned.'

'That's right, is there somewhere we can talk?' He directed this to the security man.

'I don't want to talk,' Mariposa said. 'I want to see my brother.'

'Mrs Ward, if you please.'

Stiff-legged, she allowed herself to be shepherded through the waiting room and into a small consultant's room off the main corridor. The moment she was inside Flood closed the door behind them; Mariposa was instantly overcome by a wave of claustrophobia.

'Will you have a seat?' Maken asked.

'I prefer to stand.' She leaned with her back against the wall. 'Arthur's dead, isn't he?'

'I'm afraid so.'

'What happened?'

'Initial reports suggest—'

'I'm not interested in suggestions, I want to know what happened.'

'There was a car chase, there was a crash.' He looked at Flood, then back to her. 'Two men; one of them shot your husband from close range.'

She sagged, lowered her head.

'My condolences to you, Mrs Ward,' Maken continued, in the same calm vein. 'I'm very sorry for your loss.'

The note of genuine pity almost undid her. Mariposa controlled her features and fixed her gaze on the ugly shoes Flood was wearing. When she was sure of her composure she raised her head again. 'I need to go.'

Maken had taken a card from his wallet and was writing on the back. His hands, she noticed, were good hands, big, square, strong-looking. She stared at his neatly cut nails, at the yellow wedding band on the ring finger of his left hand, and immediately formed a picture of his life. Mrs Maken would be a teacher or something wholesome like that; they'd have three children, two boys and a girl, and live in a neat suburban house with a front and back garden. There was probably a dog, a rescue of some kind. They'd go on a foreign holiday once a year and get slightly sunburned despite the health warnings; they'd stretch the family budget carefully, saving up for little things: the occasional night out, a weekend away, take the children to the cinema once every six or eight weeks.

And this man pitied *her*?

She felt a surge of rage and welcomed it. Rage was preferable to fear. Rage gave her clarity. Rage was the fuel that powered Mariposa's engine.

Maken put the pen away and proffered the card, letting it hang in the air between them. After a moment, Mariposa took it and put it in her handbag.

'Mrs Ward,' Maken said. 'Can you think of anyone, anyone at all, who might have wanted to hurt Arthur?'

'No.'

'Was he—?'

She drew herself up to her full height. 'Quentin Cullen is my solicitor, if you have more questions you can address them to him.'

Flood looked annoyed, Maken resigned.

'Mrs Ward, we are not your enemy.'

Mariposa gave him a withering look and left. She went back to the waiting room where Stefan stood, looking flustered and out of breath. Because they had come directly from Lakeside, he was dressed in an iridescent waistcoat over a scarlet blouson and his evening toupee, a flashy winged number with frosted tips. None of this looked out of place at the mansion, but under the waiting-room lights he might as well have been a peacock among pigeons.

'My god!' he cried when he saw her, oblivious to the stares. 'I practically parked in the next county.'

'Arthur's dead.'

'No!' He pressed his hands to his mouth, eyes wide. 'I don't believe it … are you … are you okay?'

'Of course not. Look, Francis is here somewhere too. I need to find him.'

'Of course.' He gave her arm a squeeze. 'I'm so terribly sorry.'

Mariposa nodded grimly and set off.

The receptionist was not any friendlier when she sidled up a second time. 'Don't make me call security again.'

'I'm sorry about earlier.' Mariposa held up her hands. 'Please, I need you to help me. My husband has been shot, murdered.'

The receptionist's expression softened a little.

'My brother was with him, Francis McCabe. He's been shot too. My husband is dead, but … I need to know …' Mariposa clasped her hands together. 'I need to know if Francis is okay.'

The receptionist tapped the keyboard in front of her. 'Francis?'

Mariposa nodded, not trusting her voice.

'Okay … well, your brother is in surgery.' She looked up. 'That's really all I can tell you right now. He's in surgery.'

Mariposa closed her eyes. Surgery meant he was alive.

'I'll let them know you're here, okay?' the receptionist said. 'I promise, someone will be down to talk to you shortly.' She cleared her throat. 'I'm sorry for your loss.'

Mariposa nodded and retreated. On the way back to Stefan she made a quick detour, pressed fifty euros into a porter's hand and got directions to the morgue.

The morgue was in the basement, the last set of doors beyond the lifts. There was nobody on duty when she entered and she could find no bell or call button, so she pushed open another door and found herself in a wide green room with a rubber floor. There were six gurneys, three lined up against the facing walls, four of them occupied.

Mariposa stared at them. She was not a squeamish woman, but suddenly, standing here in this chilly room, her feet felt as though they were rooted to the floor.

The door opened behind her, and she turned around to face an older man wearing a long white coat. A lanyard dangling from his neck identified him as Dr E. Collins.

He looked surprised to see her. 'You can't be in here.'

'I'm looking for my husband.' She waved her hand towards the gurneys. 'He's one of them.'

'Oh.' He walked across the floor and lifted a chart from where it hung on the wall. 'Were you called to identify him?'

'Yes,' she lied.

'What was his name?'

'Ward. Arthur Ward.'

He ran his finger down the chart, checked the tab on the first gurney, the one nearest Mariposa, then went to the next, then the third. 'This is him.'

Mariposa approached, fingers linked, her handbag dangling from her elbow. The air in the room was so cold she could see her breath on it.

'Are you ready?'

She nodded.

Collins pulled the zip midway down and peeled the plastic back.

Mariposa gripped her handbag hard to stop her hands from shaking and leaned forward.

Arthur's head was tilted at a strange angle, both eyes partially open. Most of his jaw was shattered, and jagged streaks of blood criss-crossed his face. There was a hole in his skull above his right eyebrow. It didn't look like much, but Mariposa, who had seen plenty of injuries in her time, recognised it for what it was. A bullet had entered here at close range and exited elsewhere, destroying all in its path.

She stepped back. She had seen enough.

'Sorry for your loss,' Collins said, mistaking her silence for grief.

'Did he suffer?'

He glanced at the dead man. 'I don't think so.'

Mariposa turned on her heel and left the morgue. She went outside and lit a cigarette.

The same security guard from before materialised next to her. 'There's no smoking on the hospital grounds.'

'Who's going to stop me?' She looked at him over her shoulder. 'You?'

Mariposa drew the smoke deep into her lungs and stared at him as she exhaled, daring him to say something else.

The security man shook his head and walked away. He wasn't paid enough for the bullshit he had to endure in this crazy place.

While Mariposa smoked, two floors above her a surgeon removed a bullet from Stonewall's thigh and dropped it into a metal tray.

'How's his pressure?' he asked the anaesthetist.

'Holding steady.'

'He's a lucky man,' the surgeon said. 'The bullet missed the femoral artery by centimetres.' He looked at the laceration on Stonewall's skull where a second bullet passed through his hair, taking some of his scalp but somehow missing his brain.

'A very lucky man.'

8

Stefan and Mariposa drove back to Lakeside in shocked silence. Dawn was visible on the horizon and they were both shattered. The only thing Mariposa wanted to do was crawl into bed, but when she saw the cars parked on the gravel outside the mansion she knew sleep would have to wait.

'The vultures are circling,' she muttered under her breath.

Stefan pretended he didn't hear her.

Doug, the mansion bouncer, opened the front door and let them in. 'They've been here since five.'

Doug was softly spoken, his voice barely audible at times. Nobody made fun of him about it though, at least not to his face. Not if they knew what was good for them.

'All right, Doug.' Stefan patted the huge man's arm as Mariposa carried on through to the lounge. 'You head on home, get some rest,' he said, before hurrying after her.

Murray, Rally and Duchy were waiting in the lounge with the lights low, drinking. Duchy was sitting at a table by himself; Murray and Rally shared a sofa, grim-faced and serious.

'Mariposa.' Duchy stood up and walked towards her. Mariposa stood rigid in his arms until he let her go. As soon as she was free she went behind the bar and tried to assemble a drink. Her hands were shaking so badly Stefan had to step in and take over.

'Is it true?' Murray's voice was hoarse from smoking and exhaustion. 'Is Arthur dead?'

'Yes.'

'What about Stonewall?'

She shook her head, unable to speak.

'He's been moved to the ICU,' Stefan said. He handed Mariposa her drink, led her around the bar and made her sit on a stool. 'We spoke briefly to the surgeon before we left. He said they removed a bullet from his leg. Another grazed his skull, but the damage was minimal.'

'Jesus Christ.' Murray put his fist to his mouth. He looked sick.

'He's a fighter,' Rally said, wringing his hands. 'Toughest man I know.'

'Shot in the leg?' Duchy asked, and there was something in his voice that made Murray turn to look at him. Stefan too.

'The bullet almost hit his femoral artery.' Mariposa's voice sounded strange, like it was coming from far away. 'He would have bled out in seconds.'

'But it didn't.'

'He got lucky,' Stefan said, taking Mariposa's free hand in his. 'He's going to be all right.'

'He's a fighter,' Rally said again, as if this somehow settled it.

'Were there cops there?' Duchy asked.

'Two,' Stefan said. 'A detective called Maken and another one called Flood.'

'Maken?' Murray and Rally exchanged a look. 'Isn't he the one who hauled you in for questioning earlier this year?'

'That's him.' Rally sat forward, linked his fingers together. 'Did he ask anything about us, Mariposa?'

'He asked if I knew who'd want to hurt Arthur.' She looked squarely at Duchy. 'I don't, do you?'

'Me? What would I know? I'm only home a wet weekend.'

Murray got up and stepped between them. He patted Mariposa awkwardly on the upper arm. 'Cops, no decency, asking you shit at a time like this.'

Mariposa burst into tears. Startled, Stefan took the drink from her and put it on the counter, untouched. He looked at the men. 'It's been a very long night, I think we should all try and get some rest.'

'We'll find the bastard who did this, you have my word, Mariposa,' Murray said. 'We won't rest until we find them. We'll tear this city apart if we have to.'

'They'll regret the day they were born,' Rally said, 'so they will.'

Duchy tossed back the last of his drink and jerked his head towards the door.

When they were gone, Stefan led Mariposa upstairs to the small set of rooms she kept on the east wing of the building. He prepared her night-clothes while Mariposa went to the bathroom. When she came back he saw that she had washed her face, but her hair was still tangled up in whatever bands and clips she had tamed it with earlier that evening.

She collapsed onto the bed.

'No, dear, not like this.'

She sat up and allowed Stefan to untangle her hair. When he was done he helped her undress, put her nightdress on and pulled back the sheets.

'In you get.'

She got in, complacent as a child.

'Drink.' He handed her a glass of water. 'You need to try and get some sleep, there's going to be a difficult few days ahead.'

She drank, passed the glass back, leaned her head against the pillows and closed her eyes. 'Arthur was engaged to another woman when we met, did you know that?'

'No.' Stefan sat on the side of the bed. 'I had no idea.'

'A nurse, some friend of Sylvia's.' Sylvia was Arthur and Duchy's younger sister. She opened her eyes to slits. 'Rosemary, pasty little thing. I saw her once, standing outside the old Carlton cinema. She was waiting for him.'

'What happened to her?'

'She died.'

Stefan pulled the covers up to her bony collarbones. He sat with her until she dozed off, then he crossed the hall to his own bedroom.

Normally the space delighted him. Over the years he had turned it into a sumptuous mini palace, filled with plush chairs, antiques and paintings. The long window was dressed in gold damask curtains that would not have looked out of place in the Palace of Versailles, but that night Stefan had barely the energy to lock the door behind him.

He sat at his dressing table and put his head in his hands, exhausted and afraid. Mariposa was a lot of things, but stable wasn't one of them. He dreaded to think what the coming weeks would bring.

Sighing, he removed his wig, cleaned his face, applied a lavish layer of night cream and climbed into his four-poster bed. He pulled a lavender-scented mask down over his eyes and snuggled under the covers. He doubted he'd get to sleep, but as with most things, he was wrong about that too.

9

While Stefan slept, upstairs on the third floor in the 'staff quarters' Yulia was testing the window of the bedroom she shared with another girl, Jade.

As she worked, she tried not to let her teeth chatter from the cold. She was dressed, but the rooms up here were damp and the roof poorly insulated. There was no central heating either so the condensation on the inside of the glass trickled down constantly, forming pools of water that had rotted the wooden frames over time.

Yulia, using a knife she had stolen from the kitchen, had been chipping away at the soft wood around the latch for two days. Now she could wedge the tip under the metal catch and push.

At first nothing happened, then she heard a soft 'pap' and the latch came up on one side. Once it was free, she put the knife aside, twisted the latch towards her and pressed down until the other side snapped up and the lock was useless.

She glanced at the twin bed across the room where Jade was sleeping under several blankets, her head turned to face the wall. No, not Jade, she thought, Louisa. The girl's real name, not one of the stupid names Mariposa made them say they were called. Louisa was from Belarus and she was sweet and kind, and terrified that she would die here, or that Mariposa would send her someplace where the men were not as kind or as generous as the men who came to Lakeside. Louisa told Yulia she had heard stories of this place and knew of several girls who Mariposa considered 'spent' and sent on their way, never to be heard from again. Louisa was terrified of everything and everyone and cried herself to sleep every night.

Yulia didn't give a shit about going to another place. This place, Lakeside, might have some cheap glitz, but it was a prison like any other. In fact it was worse because at least in a prison you had rights, you had some chance of going to bed at night unmolested.

It sickened her: the place, the work, the attitude of the other girls. Not all of them, of course, but some of them, Ruby and Topaz in particular, like turkeys guarding the Christmas stock; stupid, fearful, watching. Always watching. They were so terrified of Mariposa they'd rat out anyone who might cause her to be angry, and twice now Yulia had felt the sting of Mariposa's ire directly because of them. Locked up in the cellar for three days at a time, with no food, only water, no company but the spiders and the sounds from above. Mariposa was hard, yes, but she was also crazy; Yulia knew it would not be beyond her to stretch three days to a week or a month … more if she felt so inclined.

She had to get out of this place, she had to find her aunt, she had to find Celestine.

She looped a hairband around the lock so that it would not rattle, caught the two grips and pulled. At first the window would not budge an inch, but gradually it gave, making a hellishly loud sucking sound as the ancient paint and wood parted ways. Colder air rushed in and made the curtain flutter. Yulia pulled harder, her muscles straining as she gained one inch, then another.

When it was a third of the way she let go carefully and breathed a sigh of relief when it stayed in place. She bent down and peered through the gap, squinting as she tried to work out the distance from her window to the pitched roof of the back porch. Ten, twelve feet maybe? Too far to jump, but she could climb out and use the drainpipe to get to the roof, and there had to be a way down from there. If she could—

Suddenly hands grabbed her waist and her legs and dragged her inside and threw her on the ground.

Yulia fought, bit, kicked and yelled, until someone wrapped a blanket around her and pinned her arms. Blows reigned down, kicks too. Yulia tried to curl, to protect her head. Someone stood on her ankle; she screamed beneath the wool until a blow to the side of her head silenced her.

Dazed, dizzy, breathless, she flopped onto her back, felt the rush of freezing air as the blanket was whipped away. The overhead lights came on. She tried to raise her head – God, it hurt – and saw Jade sitting up in bed, pale and teary-eyed. Mariposa was standing by the door. Topaz and Ruby stood over her, each girl breathing heavily.

'You were right, Jade,' Mariposa said, her eyes glittering horribly in her pale face. 'Our little bird was getting ready to fly.'

'Please …' Yulia winced and pressed her hand to her ribs where someone, Topaz if she had to guess, had landed a painful kick. 'I need leave, I need find my sister, I need find Celestine.'

'Girls?' Mariposa said. 'Try not to mark the goods … too badly.'

Topaz made a fist. 'You did this,' she hissed, and punched Yulia in the stomach. 'You did this.'

IO

In the grey light of daybreak, Murray gave Duchy a lift back to the house in Castleknock. The house had belonged to Duchy's father, Malachy, and remained much as it had when the old man had passed from this world into the next.

It was late – or early, depending on how you looked at it – and both of them were exhausted, so he was surprised when Duchy asked him to come inside.

Murray followed Duchy down the hall into a large L-shaped kitchen that overlooked a small unadorned garden to the rear of the house. The kitchen was good quality, but dated and cold, even a little damp, not that Duchy seemed to notice. He had five years on Arthur, but he might have had ten or more. His skin was grey, his hair thin. Years of prison life had taken its toll: the results were written on his flesh.

'What did she mean by that?' Duchy demanded; his voice was a curious blend of accents, Dublin with a twang of the English Midlands. 'Do I *know* someone who would hurt Arthur. What did she mean?'

'She was upset.'

'I don't like it.' He walked in a tight circle, his hands on his head. 'That's a dangerous insinuation, is what it is.'

Murray stifled a yawn, rubbed a hand over his face, and found Duchy was staring at him with a look that made him nervous.

'Am I boring you?'

'What? Of course not.'

'Because I've got questions, cuz, like why my brother was shot in the head and her brother was shot only in the leg. Convenient that, eh?'

'And the head.'

'They *missed* his head.'

Duchy whirled around to the counter, put the kettle on and made them two cups of instant coffee. Murray, who detested coffee, muttered thanks and sat down at the table.

'What would Arthur be doing in Clontarf at that hour?'

Murray had a fair idea, but it was tricky, laying a man's business out to be picked over, even by his brother.

'Well?'

On the other hand, Arthur was not in a position to object. 'He has … had a girlfriend, she lives in North Strand.'

Duchy shook his head, disgusted. 'Of course he did. What's her name?'

'Marcy.'

'Marcy what?'

'I don't know.'

'Does Mariposa know?'

'About the girl?' Murray considered the question. 'I don't know. Maybe. Arthur wasn't always discreet.'

Duchy slammed his hand down and knocked his cup from the table with a swoop. It smashed against the wall tiles, spraying coffee everywhere.

Floorboards creaked overhead. 'Duchy, is that you, darlin'?'

The voice belonged to Cally, Duchy's wife. Hearing her, Duchy's expression softened. The anger vanished as quickly as it came.

'Be right there, love,' he called, his voice as light and sparkly as a woodland sprite. Murray tried not to notice the weird pitch – the day was strange enough already.

'May the Lord have mercy on his soul,' Duchy said quietly, and got to his feet. 'I appreciate the lift, Murray. It's better to hear bad tidings with family. You'll have to excuse me now. I've got to tell Cally the news.' He shook his head. 'This is going to break her heart.'

'Do you want me to call Sylvia?'

'No, I'll call her. She should hear it from me.' He looked at Murray. 'Find out if he was with this girl, find out what he was doing tonight. I want to know everything, every detail. Who've we got on the ground?'

'Not as many as we used to. Kids mostly.'

'What do you mean, "kids"?'

'I mean, these last few years …' Murray didn't want to be disloyal, especially not now and especially not in front of Duchy, but the truth was the truth: apart from the haulage, Lakeside, the illegals and a couple of fences, the business was pretty low-key. But from the look on Duchy's face, Murray was full sure the light of Christian compassion was waning, so he finished with a noncommittal, 'You know.'

'Yeah, I reckon I do. I reckon I know exactly.'

The murderous gleam was back.

Murray took the hint and got to his feet. The men shook hands, and Duchy waited in the doorway, with the hall light behind him, as Murray reversed back out onto the road.

At the next set of traffic lights, Murray lit a cigarette and smoked it in silence, mulling things over. He remembered the old days when Duchy Ward strode the land in his pomp. Days when it seemed there would be no end to the bloodshed, to the tit-for-tat wars fought on street corners and driveways.

He still remembered how it felt to pull up outside your house and scan every parked car for signs of an ambush, how terrifying it was to stop for a red light in case this was the moment a man would walk up to your window and put two in your head.

He remembered the sweaty weight of a bulletproof vest under his shirt, the sound of women crying over crisped bodies found in burnt-out cars. He remembered the haunted faces of loved ones who lost family members.

When Duchy was arrested Arthur pulled back from the brink. Forged new alliances and safeguarded their continued existence by brokering peace, backed up ably by Stonewall, no slouch when it came to hammering home a finer point. Okay, they lost the serious clout, and some of the dissatisfied took up with bigger, harder gangs. But the nucleus of the family? They'd dropped back, off the radar. It wasn't overnight, and it wasn't perfect, but they were still here.

With Arthur dead, all the cards were off the table.

Murray felt this knowledge in the pit of his stomach, in the roots of his hair, in his skin, in his teeth.

In his gut.

The shit was going to hit the fan.

He needed to be sure he was on the right side of the fan when it did so.

II

Pat Kennedy was drinking green tea from a flask and reading a fire inspector's report when he heard footsteps on the metal steps leading up to the prefabricated office overlooking the construction yard. Out of habit, he reached under the desk, his fingers brushing the pistol taped there. He did not expect to use it, certainly not here at the site, but it was always better to have a gun and not need one than need one and not have it.

The door opened and Tommy Doherty, his right-hand man, wearing a bright yellow hard hat, poked his head in. 'We have a problem.'

Pat brought his hand back to the table. 'What is it?'

Tommy took the hat off, came in and closed the door. 'Liam was arrested last night.'

'Again?'

'Yeah, apparently he was involved in some brawl out in the Clampton Hotel. One of the security guards was stabbed.'

'Where did you hear this?'

'Mate of mine works there, he called me ten minutes ago.'

Pat considered a moment. 'Liam doesn't use a knife.'

'No, but apparently he bit one of the guards on the hand when he was being arrested.'

Pat pinched the bridge of his nose. *Of course he did*, he thought, *the stupid hot-headed idiot.* Assault on a garda, resisting arrest, causing a public disorder, sure it was all in a day's work for Liam. 'The security guard, was he badly injured?'

'I'm told he'll live.' Tommy shrugged. 'What do you want me to do? I can call the solicitor and have Liam out in an hour.'

'No, leave him stew in his juices for a bit, at least this way we know where he is.' Pat frowned. 'What was the fight about?'

'No idea.'

'Find out the name of the garda and what station they work in.' Pat rubbed his forehead. 'Can you also get the security guard's name and address?'

'Shouldn't be too hard, leave it with me.'

Tommy grabbed his hat and left. Pat tried to go back to his reading, but found it was all but impossible to concentrate. Liam was his youngest brother, a good kid when he was sober, which was … well, hardly ever these days. He'd need to get on top of the situation before their father, Frank, got wind of it. That was the last thing any of them needed.

Time to clean up the mess, again.

First things first, he phoned The Elms, the grand country house where his father and step-mother lived. While waiting for an answer he pushed his chair back, walked to the window and looked out. It was a dry day, bright and crisp. The kind of day a man should be out on a golf course somewhere, chipping and hacking the beautiful game into submission. That's what businessmen did, wasn't it? Golf?

Agnes, the housekeeper, answered.

'Good morning, Agnes,' Pat said. 'Is Frank home?'

'He's asleep, Pat. Would you like me to—?'

'No, that's fine, leave him rest. Is Jackie around?'

'One moment.'

He waited, tapping the fingers of his free hand against his hip impatiently.

'Hello?'

'Jackie, it's Pat.'

'Well, what a pleasant surprise.'

'I wish it was,' Pat said. 'I need you to call Ambrose.'

'Oh, for heaven's sake, what's he done now?'

'Fighting, resisting arrest in the Clampton Hotel last night. It's possible a garda was bitten—'

'Oh, Pat.'

'Unfortunately, a security guard was also stabbed in the melee.'

'Stabbed?'

'Yes. But Liam doesn't use a knife, Jackie, you know that.'

'Do I know that? Do you know that for certain?'

Pat exhaled. 'We need to make sure the garda doesn't press charges for assault. The rest of it is … a minor skirmish.'

'Apart from the stabbing, you mean.'

'Jackie, I wouldn't ask if—'

'All right, I'll call Ambrose, but between you and me, Pat, I feel that particular friendship is starting to wane.'

'Bolster it up with a donation to a charity of his choice.'

'And who is going to make this donation?'

'I'll do it.'

'I see,' she said. 'I don't wish to be crass, but—'

'Four figures, Jackie. Cash. For a simple phone call.'

'Pat, Liam needs some kind of intervention.'

'I'll talk to him.'

'He's escalating. We've seen this happen before.'

'I'll talk to him.' Pat closed his eyes and quickly changed the subject. 'How is dad?'

'He's tired, this last round of chemo has been hard. You should come down and spend some time with him. I don't think he's fully on-board with retirement.'

'I will. I'll call in over the weekend.'

'He'd like that. Pat?'

'Yes, Jackie?'

'Have you spoken to Leo yet?'

'No.'

'You know he's coming home.'

'I know, I heard he accepted the carrot.'

'Patrick.'

Pat gripped the phone a little tighter. She had a way of saying his full name that made him feel like a bold child.

'What?'

'We can't let Frank know about the fight. He needs to concentrate all his energies on getting well.'

'I'm not an idiot, Jackie.'

'Please don't be angry.'

'I'm not angry.' That was a blatant lie; there was a knot of tension between his shoulder blades like a lump of concrete. He wasn't angry: he was stone-cold furious.

'Will you call him?'

'Who?'

'Leo.'

'If you like.'

She laughed. It always surprised him, her laugh. It was a tinkly sound, like you'd imagine a fairy making, and nothing at all like her throaty speaking voice.

'You don't have to do anything dramatic, but extend the olive branch. It would mean a lot to me – it would mean a lot to your father to have all his boys together again.'

'Then consider it done.'

'Thank you. I'll call Ambrose straight away, see if we can get this … misunderstanding cleared up.'

'Tell the superintendent I said hi.'

She laughed her tinkly laugh and hung up.

Pat let his arm drop and continued to look out the window, seeing nothing, seething quietly.

12

The Ryanair flight from Birmingham was on time. A woman exited the plane and made her way down the metal stairs, taking her time, careful not to step too close to the man in front of her. She was late thirties, five foot eight, very lean in a black slim-fitting suit under a black trench coat. Her hair was white-blonde, cut short around the back and sides, leaving a longer, sweeping fringe. Her face was plain, angular, with high cheekbones and a strong jaw. Her eyes were pale blue. The woman travelled light, carrying only a single duffle bag that had served her well for many years.

She presented her passport to the guard behind the glass at customs and stood composed and polite as he looked from the genuine photo to her genuine face.

'Purpose of visit?'

'Relaxation and recreation,' she replied. 'With friends.'

He looked at the photo again. The woman remained relaxed; the forgery was an excellent one and she knew it would take more than this lump of human-shaped wax to see through it.

'Enjoy your stay,' he said, sliding it back to her. She noticed he chewed his nails; they were bitten to the quick.

'Thank you. I will.' She took her passport, wasted a smile and went on through to arrivals.

Outside, it was misty, threatening rain. She tightened the belt of her mackintosh and followed the signs to the taxi rank. It was

Sunday and the queue was minimal. It moved quickly and it was not long before a taxi pulled in and the driver hopped out, offering to take her bag. Bemused, she let him have it and climbed into the back seat. The interior was clean and smelled of air freshener: lavender.

The driver got behind the wheel and shut the door. 'Bitter out there,' he said.

'Bitter?'

'Cold.'

'Bitter is a taste.'

The driver glanced in the rear-view mirror to see if she was pulling his leg; but she was not smiling and her expression held no trace of warmth. One of those, he thought to himself, and started the car. 'Where to, love?'

'Directly to this address.' She passed him a slip of paper. He read it and handed it back, checked the wing mirror and pulled away from the rank.

'Looks like this rain will be down for the day.'

She made no response: she was typing something on a smartphone.

'Do you mind if I listen to the radio?'

Again, she made no reply. He put it on, turning it up slightly louder than he normally did, to fill the silence. He drove faster than usual too, taking shortcuts, breaking questionable orange lights. He dropped her off at the hospital, decided to call it a day and went home.

*

At reception the blonde woman asked for and was directed to a private room along a quiet corridor on the third floor. She took the lift, and as she approached his room, a young man rose from a chair and deliberately blocked her path.

'Woah now, who are you?'

'That is not your concern.'

'Yeah? I can make it my bleedin' concern if you like.'

The blonde was standing eye to eye with him. She tilted her head back and inhaled deeply, calculating. This man was young, mid-twenties, gym strong. His body language was deliberately menacing, suggesting he was prepared to fight, which interested her because she could tell he was inexperienced at close-quarter combat. She could also tell he was afraid, which he was right to be. Even without the tools of her trade she could have incapacitated him in seconds.

Duchy had been right to call her.

'Call Duchy. Tell him Corrine has come.'

'How do you know Duchy?'

Such a stupid question did not deserve an answer, so she walked past him and sat down on the chair he had vacated. She put her bag on the ground and sat upright, knees together, staring straight ahead.

A little unnerved, the man got his mobile and stood blocking the door to Stonewall's room in case this was some kind of trick.

Duchy answered. 'What?'

'It's Rally, there's some woman here. She asked for you by name, she said to tell you Corrine has come.'

'Stonewall awake?'

'Barely.'

'Let her talk to him, then bring her directly here.'

'Okay.' Rally glanced at her again. 'Who is she?'

Duchy had already hung up.

13

Later that day Leo Kennedy grabbed his luggage from the carousel, walked through the sliding doors and out into arrivals at Dublin Airport.

'Hey, Bosco, over here!'

A tall woman with purple hair wearing skinny jeans, a ripped T-shirt and a leather biker jacket stood waving at him from behind the barrier. Her name was Eddie Lynch and she was Leo's oldest – and only – friend. When he'd mentioned he was coming home she'd insisted he stay with her for a few days until he got things sorted.

'You didn't have to come all the way out. I could have caught a bus.'

'Bus my eye.' She opened her arms. 'Bring it in.'

They embraced warmly.

'You've lost weight, Bosco,' she said, poking him in the ribs. 'Not a good look for a chef.'

'Only a little.' It was true, he'd had to bore another hole into his belt the day before. He hadn't had a drink in weeks and he had taken up walking, lots of walking, mostly at night when he should have been sleeping. But it helped to quiet the voice in his head.

She looked at his bag. 'Where's the rest of your luggage?'

'This is it.'

'What about all your furniture and stuff?'

'I let Amy keep it.'

'All of it?'

'It wasn't worth fighting over. I kept my knives and my clothes.'

Eddie's expression suggested she had opinions about that, but mercifully she kept them to herself.

'Come on, let's go, the parking here is mad expensive.'

He grabbed the handle of his suitcase and followed her across the concourse, walking fast to keep up with Eddie's weird distance-gobbling stride.

'So,' Eddie said. 'Do *they* know you're coming?'

Leo's lips twitched. Somehow Eddie always managed to make any reference to his family sound like it hurt her teeth. He didn't blame her. Eddie's old man had been part of Frank Kennedy's crew back in the day when his father wasn't pretending to belong to the landed gentry. He'd gone out one evening and never come back. Nobody knew where he went and there was never a body to bury, but Eddie had ideas of her own, ideas Leo found pretty credible.

'Jackie does.'

'Well, if her ladyship knows, they all do.'

'Yeah, probably.'

They stopped at the pay machines. Eddie put in her ticket, cursed when she saw how much they'd charged her for fifteen minutes and paid.

'You sure it's okay me crashing with you?' Leo asked as they reached Eddie's ancient purple Micra parked on the next level.

Eddie gave her best 'Eddie' shrug and got in behind the steering wheel.

'Eddie?'

'It's cool, Leo. Don't worry about it.'

Leo put his belt on. It very clearly was not cool, not cool at all, and he guessed why. Dom.

Dom was Eddie's girlfriend. They'd met on a holiday in Venice five years before and had fallen head over heels for each other. Half Brazilian, half French, Dom was a dancer and yoga teacher.

She detested Leo.

Eddie started the engine. 'So, what's the plan?'

'I have to go to the solicitor's in Sligo the day after tomorrow and collect the keys and her ashes, sign the paperwork and as far as I know that's about it.'

Eddie reversed out, spun the wheel and they were off. 'Does she really expect you to scatter her ashes over the canal?'

'Under a full moon.'

'That's mad. How well did you know her?'

'I met her twice and I don't think she really liked me.'

'She liked you enough to leave you a bloody building on Aungier Street.'

'Yeah, there is that,' Leo said, scratching his head. He was still wrapping his head around that one.

'What's it like?'

'I don't really remember. I was there a few times as a kid, but …' He shrugged. 'My memory's not what it used to be.

'Do you know the address?'

He told her.

'Want to swing by and have a gawk?'

'If you have time.'

'My time is my own, Bosco, you know that.'

He grinned. 'How's the great work going?'

'It's taking shape.' Eddie put the ticket in the machine, waited for the arm to rise and shot out of the car park at alarming speed. 'Madison thinks she has a buyer lined up.'

'Oh yeah?'

'Some restaurant in San Francisco, she reckons they love the vibe of Celtic abstract.' She changed lanes. 'Imagine how chuffed Ma would be if she was still alive. Selling art to the heathens … she'd dine out on bragging rights for years.'

'She'd be proud of you, Ed. I am.' He looked over at her. 'You never once wavered, did you?'

'Wavered about what?'

'Never once thought about packing it all in.'

'Sure I did,' Eddie said, overtaking a taxi and a Mercedes, the little purple Micra rattling as it went over seventy. 'Let's face it, art is not exactly an easy way to make a living.'

'But you did it.'

'Wait until the fat lady sings, Bosco, she's only warming her throat at the moment.'

They flew into town against the flow of evening traffic, and less than twenty-five minutes later Eddie pulled up on Aungier Street, opposite the address Leo had given her. They gazed at the three-storey building, taking in the peeling paint, the graffiti-strewn walls and the weeds growing out of the boarded-up windows of the upper floors.

'Is that it?'

Leo nodded, speechless.

'It's … er … a bit of a fixer-upper, yeah?'

Leo leaned forward, rested his forehead on the dashboard and closed his eyes. Eddie looked at him with some alarm. 'Are you okay?'

He didn't say anything. She heard him take a deep breath and let it out very slowly again, then another. She put her hand on his shoulder. He was having a moment. She wasn't surprised.

'I blew it up, Eddie,' he said after a while, his eyes still closed. 'All of it … Amy, work, I blew it sky high.'

Eddie patted him. 'It's okay. It's going to be okay. You've got to break some eggs to make an omelette. Come on, let's go home, get some food, get some rest.'

She put the indicator on and pulled out after a number nine bus. Halfway down the street she switched the radio on and caught Coldplay crooning 'Fix You'.

She reached for the dial, thought better of it and let the song play. She knew it had been Amy who'd left Leo and that she had left him for another man, a man she didn't love, but who she could at least understand (this was, according to Leo, what she told him as she was packing her bags). Eddie knew that Leo hadn't tried to stop her or change her mind. She knew this because she knew Leo. The project had failed, long live the project.

Amy had never stood a chance.

Chis Martin's voice soared as he hit the chorus. *Fix you?* Eddie thought as she navigated the traffic. *Good luck with that, pal. There are some people who can't be fixed.*

14

Under grey skies, Arthur Ward's funeral cortège made its way from the church to the graveyard at a snail's pace. Four black horses with feathered plumes pulled the ornate carriage up the winding hill, as onlookers gawked and pointed. It was quite a sight: Arthur's coffin was jet black and covered in white roses. Mourners were dressed to the hilt, suits and overcoats, matching ties.

Arthur would have approved of the drama, Mariposa thought.

She walked behind the carriage with Duchy, wearing a long velvet coat and a pillbox hat atop her head with a veil drawn over her face. She kept her head down, unwilling to make eye contact with anyone. To the curious onlookers she appeared dignified, though mired in grief. Stonewall was still in the hospital, his release delayed by some unforeseen infection that all but wiped him out.

Behind Mariposa, Sylvia, Arthur's sister, was sobbing and wailing at the top of her lungs. Mariposa tried not to feel aggrieved by this display of over-the-top grief. Her sister-in-law lived in Enniscorthy and owned an estate agent's there with her husband, a bland-looking locally grown turnip named James. There was no love lost between the two women and never had been. Mariposa thought Sylvia was a proper lady muck with a head full of notions, the type who liked to distance herself from her roots lest her roots take hold and strangle her. Between the wailing and an outfit that looked like she was about to take a turn on *Dancing with the Stars*, Sylvia had become the centre of attention, which of course was exactly where the silly cow liked to be.

Mariposa would be glad when this day was over, glad when the Wards went back to their own lives and forgot about her.

At the graveyard, she stood straight and still, barely listening to the priest, allowing her eyes to roam for the first time. In the distance she saw several photographers with long lenses. To be expected, of course, but she cursed them all the same. Under a barren chestnut tree, she caught a glimpse of a blonde woman in black standing alone, observing the crowd. There was something about her Mariposa found unnerving, but before she could ask anyone who she was, the blonde had walked off with her hands in her pockets.

When the funeral was over, Duchy invited all and sundry back to the Phoenix Inn for the afters. The crowd would be big, Mariposa thought with a grimace. Hangers-on and liggers, a free bar would see to that.

She rode back to the pub with Murray in a limousine.

'How are you holding up?'

She looked out the window. 'If I'm honest, I can't believe he's really gone.'

Murray leaned across and put his hand on hers. She resisted the urge to yank it away.

'He was a good man, we'll all miss him.'

Mariposa lowered her head.

Would this day never end?

As predicted, the pub was packed to the rafters. Face after face swam into her personal space, offering condolences, hand-wringing, bloated speeches. Mariposa nodded and said thank you, nodded again. Her back hurt, her feet hurt. She wanted to leave, to get back to Lakeside where Stefan was holding the fort.

But this was the final curtain, this was Arthur's swansong. Nod, and thank you, nod, and thank you. Best face forward.

She moved through the crowd, listening to slivers of conversations. Snippets, really. There was a general consensus, it seemed, relating to the shooting. And as the evening turned to night, and the songs grew louder and rowdier, speculation began to harden to fact.

She overheard a name mentioned several times.

Liam Kennedy.

She made a mental note of it.

Rally got drunk and weepy, so much so that Murray had to take him outside. Duchy moved from group to group, like a cat on a hot tin roof, talking, shaking hands, slapping shoulders. *The king is dead*, Mariposa thought, watching him, *long live the king*. His wife, Cally, was parked in the throng of women, talking, making friends. They had warmed to her, the collective mares, in a way they had never taken to Mariposa. She didn't mind. It was easier to jettison trash when you weren't attached to it.

She turned her head a fraction and caught Sylvia staring at her. Mariposa tried to muster a smile, but it fell short. There was a strange, sour look on her sister-in-law's face, one that Mariposa didn't like, not one bit.

Behind her, the familiar opening bars of 'Danny Boy' rippled through the crowd, Duchy's voice rising high and clear. Cally shushed everyone, her pink, round face proud and shiny. Mariposa turned to watch, and when she looked back Sylvia was gone.

15

Tony Wright lived on the ground floor of a nondescript block of apartments in Phibsboro, and he, all twenty-odd stone of him, was home when Pat and Tommy came knocking.

He was older than Pat had expected him to be, for some reason – late fifties or early sixties; big, beefy running towards fat. Bad blood pressure too, if his complexion was anything to go by. He answered the door wearing shapeless grey tracksuit pants, a T-shirt that had seen better days and flip-flops. His feet were swollen and shiny red, like vinyl. The expression on his face could not be called welcoming.

'Mr Wright?'

'Who's asking?'

'My name's Pat Kennedy and this is my associate Tommy Doherty. I was hoping to talk to you about the … incident last Friday, the party at the Clampton Hotel.'

'I've nothing to say about any of it so you can sling your hook.'

'Is there some reason you don't want to talk to me?'

'Yeah, a big one.' He made a fist.

'There's no need for that,' Pat said coolly. 'I'm not here to cause you any trouble. Quite the opposite, in fact.' He leaned forward a little. 'I would consider it a favour if you spoke with me.'

With the poorest of grace, Tony opened the door and motioned to them to come inside. They followed him down the hall and into a narrow kitchen that smelled of grease and faintly of curry. A black and white cat was asleep in a basket by the back door; it woke, looked at them without a shred of interest, yawned and went straight back to sleep.

'Sit down. Do you want a tea or a coffee or something?'

'We're grand, thanks,' Tommy said.

Pat pulled up a chair at the kitchen table, while Tommy remained standing, next to the sleeping cat, his hands clasped before him.

Tony glanced at him.

'I prefer to stand.'

Tony pulled out a second chair, turned it around so that the back was against his chest and lowered himself into it with care, wincing slightly.

'How bad is it?'

Tony hesitated before lifting his shirt to reveal a row of staples criss-crossing a livid scar that ran from his armpit to his navel. It wasn't the only scar his torso carried, but it was by far the freshest.

'You should be in a hospital.'

'Nah.' Tony lowered the T-shirt. 'Not as bad as it looks, it's not that deep.'

'Did you see who stabbed you?'

'No.'

'Commendable,' Pat replied. 'So how about you tell me what *did* happen?'

'Why don't you ask your brother?'

If Pat was surprised, it didn't show. 'Liam is . . .' He paused. 'My relationship with my brother is complicated, Mr Wright. I'm not sure I'd get any answer, let alone a straight one.'

Tony sighed heavily. 'Look, he was acting the maggot, okay? Him and his mates, things got out of hand.'

'Acting the maggot how exactly?'

'Marcy Dunne was there.'

'I see.' Pat glanced at Tommy. 'Alone?'

'No.'

Pat leaned back in his chair, his expression thoughtful. Now it was starting to make sense. Marcy Dunne, Liam's ex-girlfriend. They'd been dating for over a year until she abruptly called it off. The split had sent Liam on one of his entirely predictable benders. His brother did not take rejection well.

'My brother is a lot of things, Mr Wright, but he is not the type that would stab a man. Bludgeon you to death with his bare hands, possibly. But a knife? That's not his style.'

'I know, he nearly made pulp out of my nuts.'

'Now that sounds like Liam,' Pat said. He reached into the inside of his coat, took a brown envelope from it and placed it on the table.

'What's that?'

'A little something towards your medical costs.'

Tony Wright looked into Pat's eyes. He didn't look grateful, he didn't look hurt, he just looked tired, very sore and tired. 'All right,' he said after a while. 'Thanks.'

Pat got to his feet, eager to be gone. 'I appreciate you taking the time to see me, Mr Wright. Please, don't get up, we can see ourselves out.'

'He got lucky, didn't he?' Tony Wright said. 'Your brother.'

Pat paused, looked down. 'In what sense?'

'Arthur Ward, dying the way he did.'

Pat looked at Tommy, who frowned and gave a little shake of his head.

'Arthur Ward?' Pat said. 'What about him?'

'That's who your boy was fighting. Marcy was going out with Arthur Ward.'

'And he's dead?'

'Do you not watch the news?' Tony winced as he turned to look at him. 'Arthur Ward was shot dead the same night I was stabbed, the same night your brother gave him a right pasting.'

'I see,' Pat said, feeling a familiar coldness on his spine. 'Like I said, my brother does not use weapons in his disputes.'

Tony Wright shook his head. 'You don't need to convince me, son, I'm not the one needs telling. Liam made a lot of noise that night, made a lot of threats. Goes without saying, rumours are flying.'

'Rumours,' Pat said. 'Where would we be without rumours?'

16

The solicitor was a very small, very droll man in an ill-fitting pinstripe suit. He made Leo sign, here and here, here and here, and then here and here and the business was concluded.

He stood up and offered Leo a limp handshake from across the desk.

'Your great-aunt was a very singular woman,' he said. 'I am sorry for your loss.'

Leo nodded and picked up the cardboard box containing Gina's ashes.

'You'll need these, of course,' the solicitor said, opening a drawer and handing Leo a second set of keys.

Leo took them. 'What are these for?'

'Her car, it's at the Nolen family garage across town. I'll let Miggy know you're on your way to collect it.'

Leo pocketed the keys, said his thanks and stepped outside into a wind coming off the Garavogue River that could slice a person in half. Eddie was sitting in the Micra, bundled up in a parka, a woolly hat and several layers of scarfs. He battled across the car park, got in and let the wind slam the door behind him.

'Is that her?' Eddie nodded to the box.

'Yep.'

'I thought she'd be in an urn or something fancier.'

'Apparently she didn't believe in waste.'

'Practical, a woman after my own heart. Now what?'

'Now we find the Nolen family garage, collect whatever banger she left me, sell it and hit the road.'

'What do you reckon it is?'

'She was an old lady, probably something like this.'

'Hey!' Eddie started the engine. 'Make sure you keep a good grip on that box. Don't let Gina spill all over my Fanny.'

'Excuse me?'

Eddie tapped the dash. 'Fanny.'

'You named your car Fanny?'

'Uh, yeah.' Eddie reversed and pulled out of the car park. 'It's good to name things.'

Leo laughed, but held the box in a death grip until they located the garage, just in case.

The owner of the Nolen family garage was waiting on the forecourt for them when they arrived. Miggy Yates was in his late fifties, had a beard old Saint Nick would have envied and was wearing a short-sleeved T-shirt under a pair of dungarees.

'He's not even wearing a coat,' Leo said. 'Why is he not wearing a coat?'

'Hardy folk,' Eddie replied. 'I've heard of this phenomenon, not like us city petals.'

'It's minus two degrees.'

'Balmy.'

'There you are now,' Miggy said when Leo got out. 'You must be Gina's lad.'

'Her great-nephew, yes.' Leo shook a hand the size of a dinner plate and tried not to let his teeth chatter too loudly.

'You have the look of her.'

'I do?'

'In the eyes.' Miggy cocked his head. 'She was a grand woman, one of a kind.'

'Yes,' Leo said. 'A singular woman.'

'She was that!' Miggy threw back his head and laughed.

Leo got the distinct impression his great-aunt had made a fairly indelible mark on the pretty town and would have liked to know more about her. Someday he'd come back to Sligo and see what he could find out about her life there – he'd pick summertime to do it, though, definitely summer.

'So, about the car?'

'Oh, right. Hold on there now and I'll bring her out for you.'

'Do you need these?' Leo held out the keys, which only made Miggy laugh again.

'No no, no need, I have a set.' He winked at Leo. 'Sure half the town probably had at one stage or another.'

Leo blinked.

Miggy noticed his confusion and leaned in, suddenly serious. 'She wasn't herself the last few years, you know, before she went into the nursing home.'

'Sure.'

'Sometimes she'd drive places and forget where she was going or how she got there or where she parked. A few of us formed a little relay team, you might say, took it in turns to collect her and make sure she got home safely.'

'That was very good of you.'

'Ah sure, that's what you do.'

Leo looked at the ground. Strangers had looked after Gina, showed her kindness, minded her in her twilight years. He felt a slow burn of shame on the back of his neck.

'Be right back.'

Leo stood, with his hands buried deep in his pockets, wondering why, if Gina's mind had been slipping, had she left things to him, of all people. It didn't make any real sense. He heard Eddie exit the Micra, her footsteps clip-clopping on the concrete. She slipped an arm through his.

'You okay?'

'Yep.'

'How long did Gina live here, do you know?'

'I think since the early nineties.' He shrugged. 'I'm not really sure, to be honest.'

They heard the sound of an engine start nearby.

'That does not sound like an old lady's car,' Eddie said.

Seconds later, Miggy drove Gina's car around the corner and pulled up alongside them.

'Wow,' Eddie said.

Leo gasped.

Miggy let down the window and hung an arm out. 'What do you think? Don't make them like this anymore, eh?'

'It's beautiful,' Eddie said. 'Leo, what do you think?'

'This was great-aunt Gina's car?'

'Three hundred miles on the clock, would you believe it?'

'Bloody hell.'

'Service history in the glove compartment. She's been sitting in a garage since Gina went into the home, so there's hardly a mark on her.' Miggy got out and patted the roof. 'Be sorry to see her go. You know now, if you wanted to sell her I'd give you a fair price.'

'No,' Leo said softly. 'She's not for sale.'

Eddie snorted and elbowed him in the ribs. 'So, what are you going to call *her*?'

'Bellisa.'

'Bellisa?'

'It was Gina's middle name.'

Miggy clapped him on the shoulder. 'A fine name, Gina would have approved. Come on inside and we'll finish up the paperwork.'

In a daze, Leo followed him into the little office and came out fifteen minutes later, the proud owner of a black 1984 Ford Capri, 2.8 injection, rear-wheel-drive classic.

He got into the driver's seat and sat there, holding the steering wheel, feeling tears prickle at the back of his eyes, though he had no idea what he had to cry about.

'You okay?' Eddie bent down and looked at him.

'I don't know,' Leo said, gripping the wheel. 'I feel like … like this is happening to the wrong person or something.'

'How do you mean?'

'Gina … why did she want me to have all this?'

'I guess you made an impression on her.'

'I don't know, Eddie. It doesn't feel right to me.'

'Well,' Eddie said, shivering, 'this is one gift horse you shouldn't look in the mouth. Right, let's hit the road. Last one to the M50 has dinner made for them.'

17

Marcy Dunne hadn't stopped crying in days, and as much as she loved her daughter, Irene Dunne was growing sick to the teeth of it.

Of course she understood the poor girl was devastated, of course she understood the pain Marcy was going through, of course it was all terribly sad, but that was life, wasn't it? One body blow after another until you reached the grave.

Besides, she told her sister over their third glass of wine, red for her, white for Emer, she'd never really liked Arthur Ward, had always thought he was too superficial, too slick. 'And he was old enough to be her father.'

'Way too old.' Emer nodded in full agreement. 'Did you read all that business in the paper about the gangs and stuff?'

'Didn't surprise me,' Irene said, though it had. 'I knew he was a bad one, knew the first minute I clapped eyes on him.'

'Did you know he had a wife?'

'I had a feeling,' she said. 'Though Marcy said he told her they were separated.'

'They all say that, though, don't they?'

Irene rolled her eyes. 'Of course they do. Promise the moon and the stars until they get what they want. Dogs, the lot of them.'

Emer stabbed a fried cheese ball with her fork and popped it into her mouth. Her husband was a lovely man, but Irene's husband, well, ex-husband, lived somewhere down the country with a younger, much younger, model. Her sister was nothing if not bitter about this so it was best not to rile her. 'If you ask me, she's better off this way. No messy shenanigans. Can't argue with being shot.'

'I wish you'd tell her that.' Irene sat back and sighed. 'That child's picker is wrong, first the other lunatic and now this.'

'Is that Kennedy lout still bothering her?'

'Chases her all over social media, makes up fake accounts just so he can follow her, it's a nightmare really.'

'He's not well in the head, that one.'

'I know. I spoke to the guards and they say they can't do anything unless he does something first.'

'What the hell kind of logic is that?'

'You tell me.' Irene pulled a face. 'She's moved back home, you know.'

'Oh.' Emer thought that over for a second. 'She probably doesn't want to stay in the flat, not after what happened.'

'That's all well and good, but I don't have a ton of room either.'

'Ah,' Emer said, always the softer, the kinder of the two. 'It will be nice having her home, though, be good for her too. She must be in bits, God love her.'

Irene reached for the wine. 'I don't know, Emer, I'm not cut out for babies. I've already raised one family.'

'It's different when it's a grandchild,' Emer said firmly. 'You get to enjoy the good bits and then you get to hand them back to their mammies when they start crying.'

'Great,' Irene said, sounding browned off, but secretly feeling quite delighted and excited about Marcy's little passenger. If only Marcy would stop crying long enough to see the upside to freeing herself from the clutches of a lying toad like Arthur Ward.

The sisters finished their meal and were on their way home when Irene's phone buzzed.

'Speak of the devil,' she said, pulling a face. 'Hey, chicken, all right?'

'Mammy.' Marcy's voice was a terrified whisper. In the background, Irene could hear her German shepherd, Ned Stark, barking furiously. 'Mammy, there's someone out back.'

'Are the doors locked?'

'I don't know.' Marcy's voice broke. 'I'm afraid to go downstairs.'

Irene put out her hand and waved furiously for a taxi. 'Stay on the phone, honey, Mammy's coming. Keep Neddy with you … Mammy's on her way.' She turned to Emer. 'Call the guards, tell them to go to my address. Do it now.'

A taxi spotted her and did a U-turn on the street. Irene was pulling the door open before it had even stopped. She shouted her address and shifted over to make room for Emer.

'Stay on the line, Marcy, I'm on my way. Do you hear me? I'm on my way.'

They arrived before the guards and found Marcy hiding up in her room, her arms wrapped around Ned Stark. Emer stayed with Marcy to calm her, while Irene went downstairs, with Ned racing ahead. He stood up and pawed at the back door, keening, until she let him out. She waited in the doorway holding her elbows as he raced around the garden, hackles up, sniffing everywhere.

When she was sure there was no one hiding in the bushes, Irene went outside to check that the side gate was still locked. The security lights were on, and when she saw what was hanging on the inside of the gate she stopped dead in her tracks.

Pinned to the gate was a dark-red lace-trimmed bra with a knife through the left cup. Irene knew without hesitation it belonged to Marcy.

Ned Stark went by her in a flash, stood up on his hind legs, sniffed the bra and growled, as flashing blue lights filled the cul de sac.

18

Murray was working in the garage on the North Circular Road when he heard a car pull in to the yard. He dried his hands on a filthy towel, turned the radio down and walked outside in time to see a dark blue Hyundai bounce over the potholes.

Cops.

He tried to remember if there was anything scattered around the yard that might be of 'interest'. Too late now if there was. Rally had cleaned the van after the last delivery and the Scania was still holed up at the farmhouse.

He relaxed a little, enough to keep what he hoped was a genuine expression of plain old hostility on his face.

Two men got out, one tall, the other shorter. The taller one looked around as he approached. 'Mr Murray?'

'Yeah.'

'Charlie Murray?'

'Still yeah.'

'Good afternoon, my name is Detective Inspector Maken, this is my colleague Detective Sergeant Flood.'

'Right.'

'We're here about the death of your cousin, Arthur Ward, and the shooting of Francis McCabe.'

'Right.'

'You were close to Arthur, am I correct?'

'He was my cousin.'

'And Francis McCabe?'

'He's a mate.'

'Arthur's brother-in-law, am I correct?'

'If you know this already, why are you asking me?'

'You worked for Arthur, yes?'

'I work for myself.'

'You're a haulier.'

'I drive. I drive trucks, vans, cars. If it has an engine I drive it, if it's broke I fix it.'

'A renaissance man,' Maken said, grinning at Flood. He took a notebook from his pocket and flipped it open. 'Your nephew works for you, am I correct? John Paul Ward?'

'That's right.'

'Goes by Rally, right?'

'To his friends.'

Maken smiled. 'Keep it all in the family, eh?'

Murray didn't reply, he was growing tired of Maken's smirk.

'Where were you the night Arthur died?'

'Why?'

'We're just trying to get a feel for timeline.'

'I was at home, asleep.'

'Can anyone vouch for you?'

'No, but that's where I was.'

'You get along with Arthur?'

'You asked me that already, and I told you, he was my cousin, of course I did.'

'How about Francis?'

'Fine.'

'Not as close, eh?' Maken said, which irritated Murray because it was true.

'I said we get on fine.'

'How about Declan, Arthur's brother? How do you get along with him?'

Murray thought of Duchy's face in the doorway of his house, the way his voice changed when he talked to his wife, the English woman he had brought over from Birmingham. What was that about, what was she doing here? Who was she?

'Fine.'

'Duchy and Arthur, they had a good relationship, did they?'

He thought of Mariposa's asking, 'Do you?' to Duchy. The look on Duchy's face. What had it been? Fear? Anger? Guilt?

'You're barking up the wrong tree, inspector. Arthur was one of our own – we didn't want to see him hurt.'

'Well, somebody did.' Maken closed the notebook and put it back in his pocket. 'Someone wanted him dead and somebody carried it out.'

'Like I said, you're barking up the wrong tree. Why don't you go talk to Liam Kennedy?'

'Who?'

'Liam Kennedy. I heard himself and Arthur were in a dust-up the night he died. Plenty of witnesses heard him threaten Arthur. Maybe you should be looking into him.'

'Do you have an address for him?'

Murray looked affronted. 'Want me to hold your cock while you piss too? Get the hell out of here, I've got work to do.'

He went back inside and turned the radio up full.

19

Irene Dunne was hanging out the washing when she heard Ned Stark barking from inside the house. She spat the pegs out of her mouth, put the basket down, went inside and made her way to the front door.

She shushed Neddy, made sure the chain lock was securely fastened and peered through the spyhole. A man and a woman stood on the steps. She didn't recognise either of them, but thought they looked like undertakers.

'Can I help you?'

'Mrs Dunne?' The man spoke, leaning forward, his hands clasped before him.

'Yeah.'

'Might I have a word?'

'What's this about?'

The man looked directly at the peephole. 'It's about your daughter, Mrs Dunne. It's about Marcy.'

Irene got a jolt, hearing her daughter's name on this man's mouth. Her nerves were still jangling from the bra on the gate incident.

As though sensing her uncertainty, the man said, 'Mrs Dunne, I'm not here to cause further upset, quite the opposite. I just want a few moments of your time and I'll be on my way.'

Irene put Neddy in the sitting room, unlocked the door and stood with her arms folded. 'All right, you've got one minute.'

The man smiled. His teeth were yellow and crooked. 'My name is Declan Ward, and this is my friend and colleague, Corrine.'

'Ward?'

'Arthur was my brother.'

'Oh.' Irene looked past him to the street to see if any of her neighbours were watching. She couldn't see any, but that meant nothing. 'I see. Sorry for your loss and that.'

'Appreciated. Actually, I came to see how young Marcy was doing. She wasn't at the funeral.'

'I wouldn't let her go.'

'Probably for the best. I can imagine this has all been a terrible shock for her.'

'It has, actually,' Irene snapped. 'She's been very upset.'

'I can imagine,' Duchy repeated. 'And upsetting for you too, no doubt.'

'Yes, yes it has.' Irene narrowed her eyes, suffering from an acute bout of mixed feelings: fear, and a desire to give out stink. 'Look, she didn't know he was still married, okay? He told her he was separated.'

'I understand. My brother was an unscrupulous cad, if the truth be told.'

'That's one way of putting it,' Irene said, with plenty of feeling. 'I know others.'

'I should imagine you do,' Duchy said, laying on the empathy with a trowel. 'Much deserved.'

'Whatever your brother was into, and I'm sorry for, you know, how he died and that, but it's got nothing to do with Marcy, all right? She's a good girl, she has nothing to do with … any of this.'

Duchy inclined his head. 'I hope not.'

Irene straightened up. 'What do you mean by that?'

'I hope it's got nothing to do with her.'

'It hasn't!'

'It's just, my information is that my brother was with your daughter the night he was killed—'

'So what? He was with her most nights this last while. They were practically living together.' Her face flushed dark red. 'You listen to me. My daughter is broken up about what happened. Broken. She's doesn't sleep, hasn't stopped crying, she's lost weight, she's terrified.'

'Maybe she has guilt.' Corrine spoke for the first time.

Irene made to slap her and found herself facing the opposite direction with her slapping arm twisted up behind her back. 'Here,' she yelled. Inside the living room Ned's barking racketed up a notch. 'Let go of me!'

'There's no need for any of this unpleasantness,' Duchy said. 'Corrine?'

Corrine released her.

Irene spun around, her arm throbbing in pain, tears in her eyes. She should have been terrified, but fear for her daughter had turned to fury. 'Who do you think you are coming around here making accusations like that. Guilty? The only thing that child is guilty of is picking the wrong fuckers to love. You leave her alone, the lot of you.'

She went to slam the door but found she couldn't because Duchy's foot was in it.

'About that,' Duchy said. 'What *can* you tell me about Liam Kennedy?'

20

Two days after the funeral, while Stefan was restocking the lounge bar, he had the strangest sensation he was being watched. He stood up slowly and turned around.

A woman was standing on the other side of the bar, a woman he had never seen before. She was taller than him, though that was hardly unusual, with white-blonde hair and the palest eyes he had ever seen on another living being; she was dressed head to toe in black.

Run away, his brain tried to warn him, but he over-rode it. 'You startled me,' he said. 'How did you get in here?'

'Through back door,' she said. 'You are Stefan, yes?'

Stefan twitched. Lakeside was a private members' club and, much like Vegas, what happened in Lakeside stayed in Lakeside. Okay, admittedly there had been the occasional blip here and there over the last few years, like when suspicious wives checked bank accounts and found discrepancies that didn't always add up, but trouble rarely darkened their door and, if it did, it didn't sidle up on silent feet.

Stefan kicked a crate under the bar, put on his jacket, smoothed the strands of his toupee back into position and tugged the ends of his waistcoat down smartly over his ample belly. When it came to trouble he preferred to be in full battle gear.

'That's right. Who might you be?'

'I am Corrine.'

'Corrine? Just Corrine?' He made a stab at humour. 'Like Cher or Beyoncé?'

'You did not attend the funeral of your employer, Stefan.'

Years of hanging around Arthur and Mariposa had given Stefan a certain ability to recognise danger. He was a pilot fish swimming with sharks, this he knew and accepted, but he also understood there were other predators in the deep blue and this was definitely one of them.

'What business is that of yours?'

She smiled, or at least her mouth moved. He tried not to stare, but her eyes were so disconcertingly pale. He could detect nothing in them: no warmth, no curiosity, nothing. It was like looking at clouded glass.

She leaned her forearms on the bar.

Stefan blinked.

Corrine didn't. 'You are in charge here, yes?'

'In charge? No. I mean, I manage the business for Mariposa, so … I mean, you could say—'

'You know Mariposa long time, yes?'

'We go back aways.'

'Aways?'

'A time. I mean we go back a long time.'

'You are friend?'

'I like to think so.'

'You are friend also with Arthur?'

'Why are you asking all of this? Who are you?'

'I am … consultant.'

'A consultant for what? For who?'

'For Mr Ward.'

'Arthur?'

'No, his brother.'

'Oh … oh, okay.' Stefan felt a momentary bubble of relief. 'You work for Duchy.'

She tilted her head. He realised she was still waiting for an answer to her question.

'Well, Arthur and I were … you know, we had a very … um, we had a … on a professional level, you see, we had … rapport!'

'Rapport?'

'Yes, on a professional level, we had it.'

'What is rapport?'

'It's … um, a … an understanding, a relationship of understanding … in a professional capacity.'

Corrine stared at him. Stefan felt himself wilt. When he was a child, his father used to look at him like this from time to time, like he was a broken gift with a 'no return' policy.

'Mariposa is here?'

'Yes, she's upstairs. I can call her if—'

Corrine rapped the bar with her knuckles. 'I go.'

'I really don't think—'

'I go,' she repeated, and walked away, her movements light, balletic almost. No wonder he hadn't heard her come in.

Corrine found Mariposa smoking by a long window in her office overlooking the lake. Her hair was loose and hanging over one shoulder and she was not dressed. It was not yet eleven a.m. but already she had a drink in her hand. She glanced round when she heard Corrine enter. There could be no mistaking the surprise, then immediate animosity, on her face.

'I know you. I saw you at the funeral.'

'Yes.'

'One of his dolly birds, were you?'

'What is this expression?'

'One of Arthur's bits on the side. Don't see it myself. If you don't mind my saying, you're a bit long in the tooth for his taste.'

'You talk much.'

'What do you want?'

'Duchy sends me.'

'Duchy?' Mariposa turned all the way around. 'For what?'

'There is meeting with family. You will come.'

Mariposa gaped. 'What meeting? What are you talking about?'

Corrine lifted her shoulders a fraction. 'I bring message. Tomorrow, one p.m., at house in Castleknock.'

Mariposa laughed. 'No offence, love, but I don't know you from a shit on the street. If Duchy wants to talk to me, he can come here and talk to me face to face.'

Corrine pointed to the phone on the desk. 'Call him, he will explain. I am certain.'

'My arse,' Mariposa said. 'I'm going to no meeting with him or anyone else. Not without my brother, who, I'm sure you know, is still in the bloody hospital.'

'The family will meet,' Corrine said. 'One p.m.'

'I said what I said.' Mariposa drained the last of her drink, stubbed her cigarette into an already overflowing ashtray and stalked out of the room.

Corrine waited for her footsteps to fade away before she looked around. Compared to the opulence of downstairs the office was plain, even a little grubby. Two large corduroy sofas; a television bolted onto a wall; squat coffee table covered in fashion magazines; cushions, clothes, make-up, hairdryers; ashtrays that needed to be emptied.

Corrine picked up one of the magazines and read the cover: '*Is Your Va-Ja-Ja Spring-Ready?*'

Corrine put the magazine back and rubbed the tips of her fingers with her thumb, grimacing.

What a time to be alive.

21

Liam Kennedy lived in a small townhouse in a private estate off Stocking Lane in Rathfarnham. It was late afternoon and he was playing video games with his best friend Baz when someone knocked loudly on his front door.

Baz bolted out of his seat, moving with a speed he hadn't in many months. 'Cop knock!'

He snatched up the bag of grass on the coffee table and stuffed it up the chimney where Liam had a secret shelf for contraband.

Liam got to his feet. Barefoot, but too stoned to care, he wandered out to the door and opened it with a sneer already in place. 'What?'

'Aren't you going to invite me in?' Pat asked.

'I'm busy.'

'That's a first,' Pat said, and walked in anyway. He glanced into the living room to where Baz was spraying the air with a can of deodorant from his gym bag.

'Relax,' Liam told him. 'It's Pat.'

'Hey, Pat!' Baz said, his voice overloud because Pat always made him nervous. 'How's it hanging?'

'You should open a window.'

'What do you want, Pat?' Liam asked. 'We're in the middle of a game.'

'Leo's home, he's staying in Aunt Gina's old place.'

'You came all the way here to tell me that?'

'The fight at the hotel, you didn't mention it was with Arthur Ward.'

'Yeah, so?' Two points of colour immediately rose on Liam's cheeks.

'I've been making some enquiries—'

'Ah, here we go.' Liam turned and walked down the hall to the kitchen. Pat followed, trying not to notice how untidy the house was, determined to stick to the script.

It wouldn't be easy. Even now he could feel the gas being lit under his temper. Liam drove him mad. He'd had every opportunity life could give – money, an education, a roof over his head, bought and paid for by Kennedy Construction – and how did he repay this largesse? By dragging their name through the mud every chance he got. By trying to undo everything Frank, and then Pat, had tried to do.

'Why do you do this?' Pat opened his overcoat but did not sit down. 'Turn everything into a fight? I'm trying to help you.'

'I don't need your help.'

'I beg to differ.'

'You can't help yourself, can you, Pat? You can't keep that big beak of yours out of my business.'

'You *are* my business. You're my brother.'

'I don't tell you how to live your life, do I?'

'Why,' Pat raised an eyebrow, 'what would you have me do differently?'

'Take the stick out of your arse for a start.' Liam leaned back against a sink full of plates and takeaway cartons. It made Pat feel sticky even looking at it. 'You're thirty-four. Maybe get a life?'

'A life?'

'You're always going around as if your shit doesn't smell. I mean, look at the get-up you're in.'

Pat looked down, puzzled. He was wearing a slim-fitting charcoal grey suit and a cashmere overcoat from Reiss. 'My clothes offend you?'

'Everything about you offends me: the get-up, the way you talk, the way you think you're better than everybody else—'

'I don't think—'

'I don't need you pulling strings. I don't need you turning up here like a fucking stink to give me a hard time. I don't need you watching every step I take.'

'You could come in with me, take a position in the company, work the—'

'Ah, here we go,' Liam snorted. 'Here's the speech, right on time.'

'Liam—'

'Save it. I've heard it all before. I've heard if off Da, I've heard it off you. And you know what? I'm sick of it. I could puke the words up at this stage.'

Pat's temper went from lukewarm to bubbly. 'You think it's easy, what I do? You think I don't have days where I want to doss around like an ungrateful arsehole?'

'Oh, is that what—?'

Someone else knocked on the door.

Liam swore under his breath and went back down the hall. He flung the door open a second time.

'Liam Kennedy?'

Pat leaned backwards to have a look. Two men were standing on the front step. Cops, he could tell by the cut of them.

'Yeah?' Liam asked.

'May we have a word?'

'About what?'

'It would be better if we could talk inside.'

'It would be better if you told me what the fuck you want.'

Pat moved. 'Is something the matter?'

'Who are you?'

'I'm Pat Kennedy, Liam's my brother. Who are you?'

'Detective Inspector Maken. This is Detective Sergeant Flood.'

Neither man looked friendly. Pat was acutely aware of the stench of grass and Lynx drifting from the living room. He put his hand behind him and pulled the living-room door shut.

'What do they want?' Liam asked Pat, his tone belligerent.

Maken looked at him. 'Mr Kennedy, what can you tell me about Arthur Ward?'

'Why do you want to know about him?' Pat asked. 'He's dead, isn't he?'

'That's right, Mr Ward was killed the same night he got into a public fight with young Liam here.'

'So?' Pat glanced at Liam, who scowled. 'My brother had nothing to do with his death – why would you be looking at him?'

'We'll ask the questions, if you don't mind.'

'But I do mind. My brother was assaulted by Arthur Ward at a party and in the ensuing row was arrested and placed in custody, where he remained until he was released the following day, several hours after Arthur Ward was shot.'

'Is that so?'

'Check with Harcourt Street, they will confirm this to be the case.'

Maken smiled. 'That's very neat.'

'Those are the facts.'

'What was the fight about?'

'Climate change.'

'Excuse me?'

'Climate change. It got heated.'

Maken grinned, Flood scowled.

'I still think he should come down to the station, have a chat.'

'I don't think so,' Pat said. He reached into his overcoat and took out his phone. 'My solicitor's name is Sandra Breen. I'll get her number for you right now. If you have any other questions for my brother you can arrange it through her office.'

'Here, what's this about? Who told you I was—?'

'Liam, will you stop talking.' Pat put his hand on the door. 'Her number is as follows.' He read out Sandra's number and noticed it was taken down in both notebooks.

'I'm closing this door now, good afternoon.'

He shut the door in their faces and turned to his brother. 'Liam, promise me you had nothing to do with that man's murder.'

'Fuck you, Pat. Get out of my house.'

'Liam—'

Liam reached past him and opened the front door. The cops were still outside, standing by their car, watching the house.

Pat didn't want to make a scene. 'You need help,' he said quietly, trying one more time. 'Let me help you.'

Liam's expression was anything but brotherly. 'No,' he said, and shut the door in his face.

22

Eddie stood on the damp concrete outside the Aungier Street building with her hands in her pockets. She stamped her feet to keep them warm. 'A restaurant? Really?'

'Nothing fancy. Eight tables, serving local produce. Compact and bijou.'

'You're stone mad.'

'Why?'

'I can think of several reasons, if you must know. Chief among them, this place is a wreck.'

Leo bent to the lock, opened it, grabbed the shutter and managed to haul it two-thirds of the way to the top before it creaked to a stop, revealing a wood and glass door that had several advertisements stuck to it, none of them, Eddie noticed, dated after 1992.

'Think about it, Eddie,' Leo said slapping the sprinkles of rust from his hands. He unlocked the inner door. 'The location is perfect: it's fairly central, and there's lots of foot traffic.'

'That is why there's a ton of restaurants on this street already.'

'Just get in, will you?'

Eddie ducked under the shutter, pushed open the door and stepped into a room that reminded her of an old airport lounge – lots of low tables and battered chairs arranged around a fake log fireplace. It had a grubby carpeted floor and some truly god-awful wallpaper to boot. The air smelled musty.

'Seriously, would you not be better off selling it?'

'And do what?'

'I don't know … travel, see the world, buy a flat?'

Leo yanked a curtain to one side, sending a cloud of dust into the air. Several spiders scuttled up the walls towards the ceiling.

'I don't have a job, Eddie, and I don't have a place to live. This covers both. There's a kitchen back there, it's functional, though it's going to need a bit of updating.'

'Where?'

'Come on, I'll show you.'

She followed him, albeit reluctantly. The deeper they went into the building, the more the smell of decay intensified.

Leo backed through a swing door and groped for a light switch. 'Voilà.' An overhead bulb flashed and popped. Leo crossed the room and drew back another curtain to reveal a window covered in metal bars; it barely let in enough light to see with.

Enough though to see what a total dump it was, Eddie thought, looking around, aghast. There was an ancient gas cooker against one wall, a sink, shelves and cupboards against the other and a tiny alcove to the rear, filled with black plastic bags – no doubt the source of the smell. Some of the ceiling tiles had fallen out and everything that wasn't covered in dust and cobwebs was covered in a film of grime and grease.

'What do you think?'

Eddie put her hands in her pockets, opened her mouth to say something sarcastic, caught the look of hope on Leo's face and swallowed her words. 'What did you say it was before?'

'A guesthouse. Gina used to take in lodgers, but she packed it in and moved to Sligo when her husband died.'

'It's going to take work,' Eddie said. 'A lot of work. And money, a whole lot of money. Do you have a whole lot of money?'

'No,' Leo said. 'But think about it, think about the potential.' He spread his hands wide. 'There's two floors upstairs. I bet they'll prove useful down the line.'

'As what?'

'I can rent some of the rooms out.'

'You? A landlord?' She snorted. 'Are they in the same condition as down here?'

'They're … a bit outdated.'

'Define "outdated".'

'Nothing a lick of paint and some new carpet can't fix. Come on, I'll show you. There's a bathroom in there, by the way. I wouldn't go in, though.'

She followed him back through the double rooms. She was trying hard not to be negative, she really was. But this place? It was a money pit. A big, dirty, stinking money pit.

Leo unlocked a second door, one she hadn't even noticed in the gloom, and stepped into a hallway. What little light there was came from a broken fanlight over the un-openable street door. There was a mound of mouldering junk mail stacked up behind it.

Some of the mail had distinct tattered edges that suggested it had been spirited away for nests. Eddie's heart found deeper levels to sink to.

Rats. Of course there were rats.

'I think you should stay with me a while longer, think this over some more.'

'It's all good, Eddie. The electricity is on and there's a plumber coming tomorrow. Honestly, I'll be up and running in no time.'

He wasn't quite as optimistic as he was trying to sound. In truth he might have taken Eddie up on her offer, but over the weekend Dom had made it crystal clear that she'd reached the limit of sharing space with a man she considered bad news. She hadn't said anything to him directly, but he'd overheard one or two hissed conversations and knew it was time to go. The last thing he wanted was to cause Eddie any problems.

'This way.'

Eddie followed him down the hall, stepping carefully as she went. At some point someone had gained access to the building and used it to sleep rough. Needles and empty cans littered the floor, along with other, less savoury, evidence of habitation.

At the end of the hall Leo took a sharp right and here Eddie stopped dead in her tracks. 'You have got to be kidding me.'

Leo looked at her sheepishly. 'It's not ideal, I know, but—'

'It's a ladder!'

'Right, yes, I know—'

'Where are the rest of the stairs?'

'Not sure, exactly,' Leo said, looking up at the remaining steps several feet above his head. 'The agent said there was an issue with woodworm and … well, he thinks someone might have used it for firewood.'

'Woodworm,' Eddie said flatly. 'Firewood.'

'It's perfectly safe,' Leo said. He grabbed the ladder and gave it a good shake. 'Like you said, the place needs a bit of work.'

'Did you fall and hit your head?' Eddie threw her hands up. 'This place needs demolition.'

Leo started to climb. 'Are you coming up?'

Eddie sighed and started up after him. 'What are you going to call this restaurant of yours?'

'Bocht.'

'Booked?'

Leo looked down and grinned. 'Bocht. It's Irish for "poor".'

'Fitting,' Eddie said, and began to climb after him. 'Because that's what you will be before you get this place up and running.'

23

Stonewall McCabe woke up. It was several seconds before he could make sense of his surroundings. He turned his head a fraction towards the window. It was still dark outside. He wondered what day of the week it was.

He must have fallen asleep again, because when he woke it was light and there was a strange man sitting in the chair to his right, reading a newspaper.

'Who are you?' Stonewall asked.

The man lowered the paper, folded it and put it down, out of sight.

'Detective Inspector David Maken.'

'What do you want?'

'I came to see how you are. I read the statement you gave my colleague Detective Sergeant Flood. I was hoping you might have remembered a few more details.'

'Nope.'

Maken smiled. 'It must run in the family, this stoicism.'

Stonewall stared at the ceiling. Cops. Was there anything worse than waking to find a cop in your room? There probably was, but he couldn't think of anything off the top of his head: thinking hadn't been his strong point since that night.

'I'm told you're making a good recovery. Walking again.'

Stonewall counted the ceiling tiles. Fourteen long, eight across.

'It's a shame you missed Arthur's funeral,' Maken said. 'It was a fancy affair too, no expense spared.'

Stonewall swallowed. If he closed his eyes he could still see Arthur's face, see the terror in his eyes, see the blood streaming from his head. Hear the dull thunk of bullets striking metal. The memory hit him hardest when he least expected it, during the twilight hours when the old pain medication was wearing off and his new medication had yet to kick in.

Maken was still talking. He heard him mention a name, Marcy Dunne. Arthur's skirt. Pretty … yes, she was pretty. Big eyes, he could see them now if he had a mind to.

The door opened, and Corinne came in. She looked at Maken, then Stonewall, one eyebrow raised.

'He's not staying,' Stonewall said.

'Hello,' Maken said, but she ignored him, so he turned back to Stonewall. 'I'm curious how that works. The relationship, I mean. I've met Mrs Ward, of course, charming lady. She must be very understanding.'

For the first time, Stonewall turned his head. 'Watch what you say about my sister.'

'Open relationship, was it?'

'What business is that of yours?'

'Arthur was at a party the night he was shot, at a hotel in Blanchardstown. There was a fight.'

Stonewall went back to staring at the ceiling. This time he counted the dots on the ceiling tiles.

'He didn't mention anything to you about what happened?'

Stonewall shifted his weight up in the bed and winced.

'Don't you want to find who shot you? Don't you want to know who killed your friend?'

'That's your job.'

'Yes, it is, Mr McCabe,' Maken said, suddenly serious. He glanced at the blonde, who stared back with no expression on her blank face. 'I want you to remember that.'

'We done?'

Maken stood up. 'For now,' he said, and left the room.

Stonewall exhaled sharply, conscious of the sweat running down his back, of his need to use the toilet. Gingerly he folded the covers back and eased his legs onto the floor one at a time. Getting up took concentration, balance. It was not an act for an audience.

'What?' he said to Corrine. 'What do you want?'

'Description.'

'Of what?'

Corrine left the room and returned a moment later carrying a pen and paper. She put them on the bed. 'What you remember.'

Despite the pain, Stonewall laughed. But his humour was short-lived.

'Wait, are you serious? You want me to draw the men who shot me?

'Description,' she repeated, and Stonewall understood it was not a request.

'I don't remember much. The one with the gun … he was thin, he wore black.' He scrunched his eyes up. Recalled the thunk of bullets on metal. 'He had tattoos, on his neck.'

'Draw,' Corrine said.

Stonewall drew.

24

Mariposa was livid.

'Who the hell does he think he is? He's a jumped-up ex-con, that's what he is, he had no right to demand I do anything.'

Stefan put the hairbrush down and took the pins from his mouth so he could speak. 'Then why are you going?'

'Because I want to know what he's up to.'

'Twist or lift?' he asked, holding a hank of her dreadful hair aloft.

But Mariposa was not listening. It was early. Well, eleven in the morning, which was the middle of the night for the occupants of Lakeside. And far too early to be dealing with the likes of Duchy Ward.

'Twist, I think.' Stefan rolled the hair tight and twisted it close to the back of her head, pinning it securely into place. He brushed out the end strands, wrapped a band around them, tucked them under so that they were not visible and added more pins and sprayed it with half a can of hairspray. Now, he patted the mound carefully; nothing short of a skydive would loosen it.

'She'll be there, of course,' Mariposa snarled, batting her face with a huge powder puff.

'Who?'

'Sylvia, who else?'

Stefan glided across the room and disappeared into Mariposa's walk-in wardrobe. He looked at the lines of clothes, tapping his forefinger against his lip. To the untrained eye, most of the outfits looked vaguely similar, lots of black, leopard print, leather, velvet and lace, but to Stefan the outfits represented a window into Mariposa's charred soul. Like her hair, her outfit would reveal a lot about her emotional state. This meeting was already about entering enemy territory, but the presence of Sylvia made it positively hostile.

He pulled a dress from a hanger, eyed it critically, tossed it aside and reached for another. Ah, yes, a dark magenta number with a laced bodice and full-length sleeves. If he added a leather waistcoat, fishnets, the boots with the silver heel, a butterfly belt …

*

Cally opened the door and smiled.

'Mariposa! How lovely to see you. Please, come in, come in.'

Mariposa stepped into the hall and looked around with an imperious tilt to her head. She was pleased to see the house was slightly shabby.

'Can I take your coat? Oh, that's a fabulous dress. I wish I had your figure, everything suits you so wonderfully.'

'Thank you,' she said stiffly.

'They're down in the study, come this way. Can I get you anything? Tea, coffee?'

God almighty, Mariposa thought, the study. Notions. 'No … thank you.'

They were all there, waiting. The atmosphere was tense, even prickly, and she guessed harsh words had been spoken before her arrival.

Duchy, seated behind a large mahogany desk, looked her way, a supercilious smile on his face. 'Thank you for coming, Mariposa,' he said, 'I appreciate you taking the time out of your busy schedule.'

At this, Sylvia issued a little sarcastic snort.

Mariposa put another black mark on the long list she had against her sister-in-law. She looked around the room. Corrine stood behind Duchy's left shoulder; Sylvia, looking like an overly stuffed sausage in a crumpled linen two-piece, sat in an armchair facing the desk; and Murray and Rally shared an uncomfortable-looking leather two-seater sofa that wouldn't have looked out of place in the window of a charity shop. In fact, Mariposa thought, the entire room, with its floor-to-ceiling bookcases filled with dark spines, dreary carpet and dusty window slats, looked like it had been lifted lock, stock and hideous barrel from the mid-eighties.

'Well?' She glared at Duchy. 'You got your audience. What's this about?'

'Sit down, Mariposa.'

'I prefer to stand.'

'Suit yourself.' Duchy leaned forward. 'No point in beating around the bush. I called this meeting because I felt it was time we all had ourselves a little chat … about the business.'

'Shouldn't Francis be here?'

'Your brother is in no fit shape to join us.'

'Then you should have waited until he was.'

'Matters are pressing,' Duchy said. 'I've noticed, since I came home, that things are not what they once were. Now, I'm not one to speak ill of the dead, I loved my brother, but he was weak—'

He held up his hand to silence Mariposa who had begun to speak again.

'That's not a criticism, it's a fact. So here we are, with what remains. And I've had to ask myself, what do I do?' He glanced at Sylvia, gave her a little smile.

'So we've decided it's time to streamline the business.'

'We?' Mariposa asked, icily.

'Sylvia and me.'

'And what does that mean?' Mariposa asked. 'Exactly.'

'It means rebuilding, rebranding in some cases. It means taking back control of some of our previous enterprises and shedding others.' He looked around the room. 'There is a sea of money in this country and we're piddling around with small fish.'

Mariposa did not like the sudden smirk on Sylvia's face. 'When you say shedding ...'

'Lakeside will have to go.'

Mariposa was stunned. It felt like all the air had evaporated out of the room.

'Go? Go where? What are you talking about?'

'From here on,' Duchy said, ignoring her, 'all business will be run by family and only by family.'

'I *am* family,' Mariposa said.

Sylvia turned in her chair to look at her. 'This isn't personal, Mariposa.'

'Not personal? Not personal? How much more personal can it get? You're trying to destroy me.'

'Oh, get off the cross,' Sylvia said. 'Everything is always about you, isn't it?'

'Shut the hell up.'

'Lakeside,' Duchy went on, 'will be sold. We will use the profit to pay for a stake in some real business.'

Mariposa stood very still. 'No,' she said. 'I don't give a shit what you do, what any of you do, but Lakeside is mine.'

'Lakeside is owned by Spruce Holdings,' Duchy said, referring to the company Arthur had set up to 'clean' some of their less than clean money years before when Duchy was incarcerated.

'Arthur nominated his shares to me in the event of his death.'

'That gives you a third stake.'

Mariposa felt a raw blast of fear when she saw the look of triumph on Sylvia's face. 'I built that business from the ground up with my bare hands.'

'Well, you can buy us out, or we can buy you out … or we sell it, taking our percentage, and leave it at that.'

'It's my home.'

'I told you,' Duchy said. 'From now on family make the decisions, blood.'

'My brother isn't blood,' Mariposa's voice was hard as flint. 'He bled for your lot though. Are you *shedding* him as well, Duchy?'

'Of course not, there'll always be a place for Stonewall in the organisation, if he wants it.'

'But just not making any decisions.'

Duchy spread his hands. 'Simpler this way.'

Mariposa looked around, at Rally, at Murray, who at least had the good grace to look uncomfortable. 'You should be ashamed. Arthur would spin in his grave if he could see—'

'My God,' Sylvia said. 'Just stop. Nobody's buying your act – everyone knows you and Arthur were separated in all but name.'

Mariposa felt the heat rise to her face. 'I will leave Lakeside feet first.' She turned and walked towards the door, her head high.

'That can always be arranged, Mariposa,' Duchy said. 'Don't push me.'

25

Many miles south of Dublin, Yulia's sister Celestine was staring at a postcard pinned to a corkboard in a chilly disused office overlooking a factory floor.

The postcard had a picture of a donkey wearing a straw hat. The donkey was leaning its head over a low stone wall and in the background a field of grass led to a choppy sea. There was writing too, scrawled diagonally across the card in big white curly letters. Celestine had no idea what the letters said, but she liked the cheery expression on the donkey's face, so she took the card down, folded it carefully and put it in the back pocket of her jeans.

She sat down on the edge of her sleeping pallet and absentmindedly picked at the tray of takeaway food the man had brought earlier that day. It was a strange dish, bright orange in colour. There was some chicken in it – she was sure it was chicken. It had tasted okay when it was hot, but now the sauce was cold and congealed, and although her stomach grumbled with hunger, she could not bring herself to eat anything other than a few forkfuls of rice that came with it in a separate box. She thought about the man. He was unfriendly and did not seem to like her, but that was okay, she did not like him either. He was gruff and sometimes shouted, but he did not hit her, and she was glad about that.

After a while Celestine left the office and walked over to the metal railings and leaned on them. She looked down at the rows and rows of plants, stinking, fleshy, thirsty things that grew thick and vibrant under hydroponic lights. Most of them were flowering now and the man seemed happy about this. At least, she thought he was happy; it was very hard to understand his language. She had figured out a few words, and knew 'water', 'light' and 'food'. The rest of his words blended together, and it gave her a headache trying to separate them.

She watched the plants until she grew bored and went back to the office. She thought about the donkey some more. Why had it been wearing a hat? Why would a donkey need a hat? Did donkeys like wearing hats? She had never considered this before.

She dozed.

A few hours later, the digital watch the man had strapped to her wrist made a beeping sound. Celestine stretched, went down the metal stairs to the factory floor and began to work. She checked the water pumps first, the plastic lines, making sure none of them had become tangled and that each individual root system was being fed directly. After that she checked each plant for any sign of rot or insect infestation. The man had shown her what to do on the first night and she was confident in her abilities. If she did her job properly and stayed out of trouble, he might take her to see Yulia. She missed her sister so badly it hurt. She tried not to think about her. Thinking about her made her sad. And lonely. Angry too.

When she was finished her chores, Celestine adjusted the light levels and climbed the stairs back to the mezzanine. Upstairs the office felt chilly compared to the factory floor, and Celestine shivered at the sudden change in temperature. There was an electric heater, but it didn't work, and no one had thought to replace it. She switched on the tiny television and twiddled with the antenna until the static lessened. It could pick up three channels but one of them was in a language so incomprehensible it might as well have been from another planet.

A sudden squall of hail hammered the corrugated roof, startling her. It was so loud it drowned out all other sounds and the television lost its signal completely. Celestine switched it off and sat down on the wooden pallet, tucking her sleeping bag in tightly around her legs. She leaned her shoulders against the wall and tried to think about happy things. She thought about the day at the lake, months before they fled home. It had been hot because it was summertime and Yulia was wearing her yellow bikini, the one that showed off her tan. Strands of her golden hair, soaked from the lake, curled around her upper arms and chest in tendrils. She had never looked more beautiful. Like an angel.

Celestine had been wearing denim shorts and a cotton T-shirt with a cartoon mouse on it. She liked it because the T-shirt was soft and loose enough to cover her stomach.

She wondered where the T-shirt was now and wished she still had it.

Thinking of Yulia brought tears but she blinked them away because Yulia had made her promise not to cry and she always kept her promises. She would keep her head down and not attract attention to herself. It was very important not to attract attention. She would be good, and she would see Yulia again.

Be good, see Yulia. Simple.

Celestine closed her eyes. If she concentrated really hard she could pretend she was somewhere else, somewhere with Yulia, somewhere warm and sunny, like that day at the lake, somewhere safe, somewhere there was chocolate cake and lemonade. Somewhere nobody was angry with her and nobody was cruel. Where nobody hurt her.

And nobody tried to have sex with her.

The hail eased a little and the wind died down. On her wooden pallet in a dusty, cold, abandoned office, Celestine snuggled down under her sleeping bag and thought of happy things until finally she drifted off to sleep.

26

Yulia lay perfectly still until her client flopped over onto his back and started snoring like a buzzsaw.

Slowly she slid off the bed and felt around on the floor for his trousers, removed a wallet from his back pocket and tiptoed to the bathroom.

She turned on the light, sat on the toilet and opened the wallet. There were several cards inside and a large wad of cash.

She selected a fifty-euro note, folded it into a tiny square no bigger than a stamp and slid it up into her ponytail. She couldn't risk taking more. The clients were stupid, but even stupid people got suspicious.

She counted to ten, flushed the loo and returned to the bedroom. The client was still snoring, so she put the wallet back where she found it, crept around to the other side of the bed and checked his watch (girls at Lakeside were not allowed wear watches; their time, as Mariposa frequently said, was not their own). It was twenty to two, twenty minutes left before Doug, the mansion bouncer, did the rounds and set the alarms for the night.

She put on a silk robe, tied it tight and left the bedroom. On the landing she paused, listening. She could hear the music from downstairs and guessed there were stragglers in the lounge. She made her way to the balcony overlooking the main hall, hoping to get a look at who was down there, without being seen. If the doors were unlocked, maybe she could slip out and climb into the back of one of the cars, and be miles away from here before her client woke up and Mariposa checked and realised she was not on the premises.

She leaned over the balcony, then darted backwards into the shadows as Stefan exited the lounge and fetched a coat from the cloakroom under the stairs.

Too risky, her head said, as she listened to him wish someone goodnight. Not the front. Maybe if she took the back stairs?

She was still standing there thinking when a huge figure lumbered towards her out of the shadows. Her heart sank.

Doug.

'What are you doing out here? I thought you had a visitor?'

She smiled and made the universal sign, indicating she wanted a drink.

'You know better than that,' Doug said. 'If you want anything you're supposed to call me or Stefan, them's the rules.'

She stepped closer, rose onto her tiptoes and kissed his cheek. 'Sorry.'

Doug sighed. 'Okay, this one time I'll let it go. Don't let me catch you out here again, though.'

'Thank you,' she said, pronouncing the words carefully. She slipped by him and walked – 'don't run' – back down the hall to the bedrooms.

'Hey.'

She stopped and turned around.

'What drink did you want?'

'Coke, please.'

'You know, if you want I can bring you more of them magazines tomorrow.' Doug looked sheepish, awkward even. Six foot six inches of blush. 'To help with your English, you know?'

'Yes, Doug.'

'Right, okay. I'll leave it outside the door. Night-night then.'

'Night.' She fled.

Doug watched her go, turned and carried on downstairs to the lounge.

Poor kid, he thought sadly. He had overheard Mariposa talking to Stefan about her earlier that evening; he heard her say she thought Jewel – Mariposa never referred to the girls by their real names – was more trouble than she was worth. That usually meant only one thing: Yulia was to be sold on.

Doug didn't like to think about what happened when the girls were sold on. He wasn't a bad man, at least he tried not to think he was.

He was just doing his job.

Yeah, just following orders.

27

The skies over Howth were cloudless, filled with screeching gulls that soared over the rooftops, waiting for an unsuspecting tourist to buy an ice cream and foolishly believe they could eat it out in the open.

Leo mooched from one shop to the next, eyeing up the produce. It was good, but it was expensive; the margins, once he got started, would be tight. In the end he bought a squid, several scallops, some whelks and some very robust Dublin Bay prawns and drove back across the city to cook them.

'I don't understand it,' he complained later that day to Eddie, who was standing on a ladder, grumpily slapping white paint onto the ceiling of the front room, or the 'parlour', as she had christened it. She was beginning to regret her foolish offer to 'lend a hand'.

'Understand what exactly?'

'I put a sign in the window earlier for staff and no one has called. In London, if you put up a sign like that you'd be inundated with enquiries.'

'Yeah, in case you haven't noticed, half the cafés and restaurants in the city centre have "help wanted" signs,' Eddie said. 'You're hardly unique, Bosco. Besides, what do you need staff for? You don't even have a restaurant for them to work in.'

'Yes, thank you, Captain Obvious.'

'So why do you—?'

'You don't hire staff the day you open, Eddie, you prepare in advance.'

'What are you going to pay them with, cobwebs?' She glared at a splatter on her sleeve. 'Did I ever tell you how much I hate painting?'

'You paint for a living.'

'I create! This is … this is manual labour.'

'I manual laboured you a lunch.'

She snorted. After half an hour she climbed down and stretched, hearing her muscles pop. If she was being honest, she was quietly impressed with what Leo had managed to achieve in such a short period of time. The heinous wallpaper and carpets were gone, replaced with soft grey paint and a scrubbed and waxed original-wood floor. Fitted wall lights provided a welcoming glow, and a stack of prints lay against one wall, ready to be hung. It wasn't fancy, but it was serviceable.

All he needed now were some flesh and blood customers.

Please, she asked the universe, please don't let this blow up in his face.

'When do you think you'll be ready to open?'

'I'm aiming for the week after next.'

'Wow, that soon?'

'I'm down to my last shillings; if I don't bring in some money soon I'm going to have to start catching and sautéing the street pigeons.'

Eddie fetched a beer from the new kitchen fridge and drank it standing by the service hatch. Her mobile phone bleeped. She read the message and grinned. 'Remember that journalist I told you about? Susan? She's available tomorrow if you are.'

Leo looked around him in a sudden panic. 'I'm not ready!'

'If you want customers, you're going to need some publicity in advance.'

Leo righted a table and started putting the next one together straight away. 'I don't know, Eddie.'

'You don't know what?'

'It's … it's …' He put the screwdriver down and looked at her. What was it, what was it really? How did he tell Eddie he was having second thoughts; how did he tell her that he wasn't sure he could pull this off, that deep down he knew he was a screw-up and that this was just another project doomed to failure?

In the end he didn't have to say anything because she could read him like a book.

'You're scared.'

'I'm not scared, I'm terrified. What if I don't have what it takes?'

'Then you sell this pile and do something else.'

'That's it? That's your solution?'

'Aw wah wah, Leo.' Eddie put the bottle down. 'Seriously, what the hell? You're a thirty-two-year-old able-bodied man with no kids, no mortgage, a sweet car and talent. Seriously, if you could grow a bigger arse you'd have everything.'

'Er …'

'What I'm saying is stop second-guessing yourself. If you're so worried about failure, test it out first. Set up a tasting day. You'll find out soon enough what works and what doesn't. Here, give me your phone.'

He handed it over.

'What's the pass code?'

'1988.'

'You used your birthday?'

'It's easy to remember.'

Eddie shook her head, logged in and started typing.

'What are you doing?'

'Shh.'

She typed some more. 'Voilà.'

'What did you do?'

'I made Bocht a Twitter page. Now you can drum up publicity for yourself too. But first let's use my contact.'

'I don't like journalists,' he said, plumbing for a pathetic cop-out. 'They twist shit, Eddie, you know they do. Put words in your mouth.'

'In or out, Leo? I need to let her know.'

Leo bit his lip. 'Okay, in. But she's coming to talk food, right? Nothing more.'

'I'll make sure of it,' Eddie said firmly. She kissed Leo on the cheek. 'I got to go, I'm meeting Dom for a film at the IFI.'

'Tell her I said—'

'Yeah, sure.' Eddie left.

Leo finished the last table and was hanging art deco prints of various Dublin landmarks when someone knocked hard on the street door. Thinking it was a delivery, he opened it and found a shorter, broader, slightly more ginger version of himself standing outside, only this version was decked out in a loud check suit and a flat cap, the whole ensemble finished off with a carefully sculpted beard.

'You mad bastard!' the leprechaun said.

'Hello, Liam.'

'Don't "hello" me, you daft prick.' Liam grabbed him and lifted him off the ground in a hug. 'Pat said you were back. Why the hell didn't you call me?'

'I did call you. I called you twice and left several messages.'

'Didn't get them. Whoa, will you look at this place.' Liam bounced past him into the middle of the room. Leo closed the door and watched him warily. Liam was the youngest of them, a late lamb, their mother used to call him, fondly. But there was nothing lamb-like about Liam. Certainly not these days.

He was still a kid when Leo left Ireland for London vowing never to return. Of course, they'd kept tabs on each other via WhatsApp and Instagram, like everybody did these days. Caught up on birthdays and the like, made small talk, dribs and drabs. But apart from blood, they didn't have a lot in common. It had been Eddie who broke the news of Liam's arrest the year before, Eddie who told him about the drugs and the brawl outside a nightclub that left another man on life support for the best part of five weeks, the hush-hush rehab in a very salubrious 'treatment facility'. None of which surprised Leo, not really. The briefest glance at Liam's social media accounts showed a lifestyle that did not lend itself to a nine-to-five existence, and the blood covered the rest. Even as a kid, Liam had a hair-trigger temper; now he had the muscle to back it up.

'Jaysus.' Liam looked around in admiration. 'So, you're turning Gina's old place into a restaurant? That's mad.'

'You think?'

'Does Dad know?'

'I have no idea. I assume so.'

'What are you going to do with the rest of the place?'

'Not sure.'

'You could turn it into a hotel.'

'I'd need a set of stairs first.'

Liam cocked his head to one side. He reminded Leo of a little flushed-faced bearded robin. For the first time Leo noticed his brother's condition. Sweaty, shiny, black pupils fully dilated, jaw tight as a drum.

Off his head, and it not even six o'clock on a Friday evening.

'Are you wasted?'

'Me?' Liam threw back his head and laughed. 'Nah, man, I'm grand. What's the story with the stairs?'

'I don't have any to the first floor.'

'No shit.' Liam laughed again. 'Can't you, like, get someone to build some? Pat knows a shitload of chippies. I can ask him if you like.'

'I could, if I hadn't spent the last of my money on a dishwasher yesterday.'

'If you're stuck for money …' Liam reached inside his jacket.

'I'm not.'

'You just said—'

'It's fine. So, how are things with you? Are you working?'

'Doing a bit of this and that.'

'Oh?'

'You know yourself.'

'Not really.'

Liam put his hands in his trouser pockets and leaned back on his heels. Leo felt a jolt of recognition so sharp he caught his breath. It was like looking at his father, right to a T.

'What kind of food are you planning to dish up?'

'Traditional Irish fare with a modern twist.'

'Steak and chips, that kind of thing?'

'Not really. Slightly more esoteric.'

'Aw yeah?' Liam sniffed. 'Good on ya, we need more esoters, that's what I say. What's through here?'

He wandered off through the swing door and into the kitchen. Leo heard him clattering around.

This and that, the Kennedy trade.

Suddenly Leo felt very tired, like toddler tired. In the distance he heard Liam's phone ring and heard him answer it. He hoped he'd leave.

Someone else knocked on the door. He opened it to find a big red-faced man glaring at him from under an impressive set of eyebrows.

'I see sign.' He pointed at the window.

Leo had worked with a number of Russians in London and recognised the accent immediately. He opened the door a little wider. 'Oh, you're here about a job.'

The man looked at Leo like he was an idiot. 'I see sign,' he said again. 'What is work?'

'Right. It's a chef's position,' Leo said. 'But it's not for right now, you see. It might be a week from now, maybe two.'

'What?'

'Tell you what, if you'd like to leave your name and a CV, someone will get back to you—'

'Oleg Taktarov.' The big man leaned closer. 'Like Bear. You know him?'

'Do I know … bear?'

'Fighter, very good, very strong. Like Oleg.' He tapped his chest for emphasis as Liam came sauntering back into the room.

'Here, sorry, bro, but I got to make a run—' He stopped when he saw Oleg. 'Who's the cowboy?'

He was eating the peach Leo had been saving for a snack; the juice was dribbling over his beard. The edges of his nostrils were red-rimmed and lined with white crystals.

'This is Oleg Taktarov,' Leo said. 'Like the bear.'

'Oleg? All right, comrade!' For some reason Liam performed a weird straight-arm salute.

'What are you doing?' Leo asked. 'Put your arm down.'

Oleg peered at him. 'I don't work with junkie fuck.'

The atmosphere curdled.

'What did he say?' Liam said, glaring, squaring up like a little rooster.

Leo groaned inwardly. Here it came, the rest of the Kennedy traits.

'What did you call me, comrade?'

'He doesn't work for me,' Leo said. 'He's my brother and he's leaving.'

'You better watch that mouth, pal.' Liam jabbed a finger towards Oleg, who snorted. Even his snorts had a Russian accent.

'Liam—'

'He called me a junkie. To my face.'

'Well, you are acting a little …' Leo waved his hands.

'What?'

'Wired.'

'Wired? The fuck you mean … wired?' And now Liam was squaring up to *him*. Jaw clenched, red nostrils flaring. It would be hilarious if it wasn't so sad and pathetic.

'What do you want me to say?' Leo spread his hands. 'I can see the bloody coke on your nose.'

Liam pinched his nostrils, grunted and threw the peach at Oleg, who caught it with one hand and took a bite. It was a pretty neat move: Leo was impressed by the speed of his reflexes.

'Liam, will you—?'

Liam slammed Oleg's shoulder as he stormed past.

It didn't seem to trouble the big man a whole lot. He looked at Leo with his eyebrows raised. 'Brother?'

'Yes.'

'Humpf. I have brother.' He chewed for a moment.

Leo waited, but this was all he had to say on the subject, though Leo sensed they had made a connection.

'Why don't you come inside, Oleg Taktarov, like bear, and let's talk food.'

Oleg finished the last of the peach, carefully wrapped the stone in a tissue and pocketed it. 'Okay, we talk food.'

All things considered, Leo thought as he showed him around, things were starting to look up.

28

'Booked?'

The journalist, Susan, raised her eyebrow, fingers poised over the keys of her laptop. She was sitting at a table in the restaurant, while a tall, rangy photographer named Ollie snapped photos of the dishes Leo had served for tasting.

'Bocht. It's the Irish word for "poor".'

'Ah.'

Leo smiled, aiming for charming and hoping he hit it. It was twenty-five past twelve and he had been up since … well, truth be told he'd been up since the day before, running on coffee, fingernails and nerves.

'When we think of peasant food we usually think of Italian or French cuisine, forgetting we have our own tradition of peasant food. I want to concentrate on recreating some of our more traditional dishes, but with a modern, fresh twist.'

'Interesting.'

Oh God, he thought. It was the third 'interesting' of the interview; the first when she saw the restaurant, the second when she read the menu, and now this.

He felt like he was dying.

'Take coddle, for example, it's a maligned dish, I think.'

She pulled a face. 'With good reason.'

'Well, no, not really,' Leo said, warming to his theme. 'Traditionally coddle is made from scraps of whatever people had left over in the kitchen by the end of the week, usually bacon, potatoes, sausages. Purists would blow a gasket if you fried the sausage and the bacon first before you cook it, but I'm no purist.'

Susan was typing furiously.

'Have you ever eaten coddle?' Leo asked.

'No, I can't say I have. No offence, but I think it sort of looks like willies floating in a bowl.'

Leo blinked. 'Er … the original dish doesn't look very appetising, I agree. But when I cook it I fry the meat in a little oil first before I add pearl barley to—' He stopped. 'You know what, it's actually easier if you sample some of the dishes.'

He galloped into the kitchen, where Oleg was singing along to Journey. 'We good to go?'

'Tasting menu. Yes, yes, good to go.'

He started with a single rock oyster, with a splash of porter. Next up was Leo's personal favourite, rock shandy ceviche, followed by a portion of liver and onion pâté on soda bread (that Susan declared delicious). That was followed by poached whelks with lemon butter, and lastly the famous coddle in a baked bread bowl. It was washed down with several glasses of chilled white wine. For a slip of a thing Susan could pack it away, Leo thought, trying not to add up how much he was spending on this free publicity. Hollow legs.

When she finished eating, Susan accepted another glass of wine and settled back in her seat. 'I think you're going to do really well; your food is super scrummy.' She leaned towards him.

'Thank you.'

'How do you know Eddie?'

Leo stiffened slightly. Relax, he reminded himself. Eddie had warned him there might be some minor personal questions to frame the article, but it was nothing he couldn't handle.

'Oh, we grew up on the same street.'

'Where's that, now?'

'Sheriff Street.'

'So, you're a local boy.'

'The localist,' he replied, and instantly regretted sounding like such a tool, but Susan didn't seem to notice. If anything, she seemed amused by his attempt at humour.

'What made you decide to come back to Ireland?'

'I lived in London for twelve years, twelve really great years, but I felt it was time for a change and when I inherited this place, well, it was a no-brainer, really.'

'You inherited this?' She looked around. 'The entire building?'

'Yes, my great-aunt left it to me.'

'That's incredibly generous.' She put the glass down and started typing. 'Your great-aunt?'

'Gina. Gina Marsh.'

'Was she, like, on your mother or your father's side?'

Leo's smile was becoming very strained. 'She was my father's aunt. Did I show you the drinks menu? It's small, but again I'm very keen on sourcing Irish—'

'What does your dad think of your enterprise?'

Leo stared at her, all thoughts of food instantly gone. 'My father … is … I can't imagine what he thinks of this.'

'Did he have any input into the business?'

'Input? No, no, there was no … input.'

'But I bet he's really proud of what you're doing. What's his favourite dish? It's the coddle, right?'

Leo could not think of a response, so he said nothing.

'He's quite a character, your dad. I met him at the Galway Races a few years ago. I tried to interview him, but he wouldn't talk to me.' She laughed. 'Instead he put money on a horse in my name and it won. Quite a lot of money, as it turned out.'

That sounded like Frank all right. Leo could picture the scene perfectly, the paternalistic bonhomie, the refusal of an interview, followed by the charm assault. Oh yes, textbook Frank.

She tilted her head. 'You look like him, you know. Similar bone structure.'

'To be expected.'

'Do you have any brothers or sisters?'

It felt like he had put his foot in a snare. 'Brothers.'

'Younger or older?'

'Both.' Leo got to his feet. 'You know, I really don't want to discuss my family.'

'It can be off-record if you like.'

'On- or off-record. I appreciate you taking the time to come today, Susan, I really do, but I've got to crack on. Lots to do still.'

She drank the rest of her wine in two mouthfuls and stood up. She was, he realised, a little tipsy. She dug a card from her bag and pressed it to his chest. 'You know, if you ever take a night off, I know a great little cocktail bar.'

He took the card and waved it. 'I will certainly keep that in mind.'

When she left, he went through the kitchen. Oleg was sitting on a stool drinking a glass of red wine.

'She like food?'

'Scrummy.'

'Good, she eats like badger.'

Leo emptied the bin and carried it out to the skip in the concrete yard at the back of the building. God, he wished he still smoked; at that moment he would have quite cheerfully parted with a lesser organ for a single Rothmans.

It took several seconds for his heart rate to come down, several more for the anger to abate. Stupid. This was Ireland, not London; of course people were going to be curious and ask questions. Frank Kennedy was a prize prick, but he was an enigmatic one. The bad boy turned good, the poster boy for Road to Damascus conversions. People lapped that kind of shit right up.

He looked at her card and dumped it in the skip with the binbag.

On Saturday he got up early, went out and bought the newspaper. It was a bright winter's morning and he felt in surprisingly fine fettle as he carried it back to Bocht under his arm. He went inside, made a pot of coffee and a slice of toast and sat down. He ditched the main paper and snagged the magazine. Susan's article was about two-thirds in. It was short and didn't take a lot of time to digest.

When he was finished reading he drank his coffee, ignored the toast and called Eddie.

'I know,' she said. 'I'm reading it now.'

'It would be a *crime* to pass up on this menu?' Leo read aloud. '*Criminally* good small plates and the prices are a *steal*?'

'Yeah.'

'No *porridge* here for Leo Kennedy, son of the legendary Frank Kennedy, one-time gangster turned successful businessman.'

'I'm sensing she had a theme.'

'This is a pile of shit.'

'This is free publicity.'

'For who? Me or Frank?'

'Tomato tomay-to. Look, the photos are great and she loved the food, that's the main thing, right? Honestly, the glass is half full … shit, now I sound like her. Right, I've got to head, Dom is insisting we go to IKEA. Talk later, okay?'

Leo hung up and read the article again.

When he was done, it and the rest of the newspaper went into the bin.

29

Frank Kennedy threw another log on the fire and settled back in his leather recliner to read the article once more, chuckling softly to himself.

'Prices a steal?'

Jackie, his wife, snorted.

'They're so obvious, aren't they? I mean, they think they're being clever, but really.'

'Food looks good.'

'I thought so. I must say, I like the sound of rock shandy ceviche. Wouldn't be mad for whelks … or eels.'

Jackie put down the novel she was reading and curled her legs to one side. 'Why don't we pop in and have lunch when he's a little more settled in?'

Now it was Frank's turn to snort. 'What?'

Jackie arched an eyebrow. 'For goodness sake, Frank. It's been five years. Besides, he has a very good reason to be grateful to you; if it wasn't for you, Gina would have given that building to a cats' charity or something equally ludicrous.'

'If he knew I was behind it, he wouldn't have taken it.'

'You don't know that.'

'I do. He's stubborn, that one, always was.'

'Well,' Jackie smiled, 'he didn't lick that off a bush, darling.'

Frank glanced at her over the top of the paper. Even now, after so many years together, the sight of her warmed him, pleased him in a fundamental way. She was an elegant woman, sophisticated and far too good for the likes of him. But it was him she chose, despite everyone telling her to run in the opposite direction, and he thanked the universe for her every single day of his life.

Especially now.

'Are you calling me stubborn?'

She held her finger and her thumb up and pinched them together so that only the tiniest sliver of space remained between them.

'I'll think about it,' Frank said, knowing she wouldn't quit until she got the answer she wanted. It seemed stubbornness was contagious.

'What about my birthday?'

'What about it?'

Jackie gave him the 'look'. 'I know you're planning a surprise party.'

'Just a little something. Friends and family.'

'Well, isn't Leo family?'

'You think he'd come?'

'I think it would be rude not to ask.'

'All right, woman, all right.'

Jackie beamed at him. 'How about some tea?'

'Lovely.'

She put her book down and got up, but before she left the room, she walked over to his chair and kissed the top of his head.

'What's that for?'

'For trying, Frank, for trying.' She left the room.

Carefully Frank lowered his legs to the ground and slid his feet into his slippers. It took a lot of effort to get up, more than it should have done, and this both frightened and infuriated him. He was not a man used to weakness.

He shuffled to the French doors and stood looking over the

rolling lawns surrounding the great house. It was far from The Elms he had been reared, and no matter how many years he lived there, the view from this window cheered him. He looked to the Wicklow Mountains in the distance, their peaks shrouded by mist and cloud, and wondered how much longer he would get to enjoy this view.

When he was a younger man, death was not something he feared. He had grown up in the tenements where death was simply a fact of life. Moved from there to a life fraught with danger, learned a deeper understanding of himself and his capacity for violence.

It was only after he married Jude and had the boys that things changed. The bloodlust left him a little, retreated to a place he didn't know he possessed. When Jude got sick she needed him, so he did what he had to do to make her happy and tried to be strong for the boys.

For a while there had been a kind of peace. For a while he thought they'd won, then the cancer came galloping back and death finally carved a nick on his soul.

When Jackie entered his life he'd been falling. Jackie, with her cut-glass vowels and her tinkly laugh, her knowledge of fine wines and bawdy sense of humour. He'd never met anyone like her, he hadn't known people like her existed.

He shouldn't have been so complacent; he should have known there was always a price to be paid for happiness.

Now he was old and sick, and probably dying, if the truth be told. It was time to mend the fences, time to try put right what he had broken.

He hoped there was time to tell his children he was sorry.

He hoped there was time for them to forgive him.

30

A week passed since the terrible meeting in Duchy's office, a week when Mariposa hardly slept a wink and lost close to half a stone in weight. She lay in bed day after day, on her laptop, reading about Frank Kennedy, his sons, his business, his successful marriage.

No wonder Duchy didn't want the boy harmed. What a bargaining chip he was, what a perfectly moveable pawn in the greater game.

Her mood was black. When she wasn't screaming at the girls or snarling at the clients she drank incessantly and nobody, not even Stefan, could get a good word out of her. Stefan was worried, and wondered if she might be suffering a delayed reaction to Arthur's death.

The only ray of light in this otherwise bleak period was Francis leaving the hospital. Though he was weak and still in some discomfort, it made Mariposa feel a million times safer to have her brother back on his feet again, though his reaction to Duchy's new decision-making was strangely muted so far.

On the morning of the sixth day, her mood broke. She rose from sleep and stared out across the lake with something approaching serene calmness.

She showered, dressed in her best velvet and brocade and went downstairs to get her Mercedes from the garage.

Mariposa heard barking as she drove across the cattle grid. She parked in front of the old stone cottage that had been in the

McCabe family for over a hundred years, shut off the engine and sat listening. From the echo, the dogs were loose in the courtyard behind the house. She lowered her head to the steering wheel and took a deep breath, mentally preparing herself for the next step.

When she and Francis were children, their father had insisted they spend entire summers at this farmhouse to get, as he put it back then, 'a feel for the land'. What they got were hours of intensive, back-breaking labour at the behest of their paternal grandfather, Chester, a foul, stubborn husk of a man, who was prone to melancholy and known to be 'bad with his nerves', though bad nerves didn't stop him from taking a gnarled hawthorn stick to his grandchildren whenever the mood struck him. Mariposa and Francis endured copious beatings until her brother hit puberty and over a single wet, cold summer grew too broad to trifle with. That didn't stop the old bastard from tormenting Mariposa every chance he got, and even now, thirty years later, she could not hear his name mentioned without the desire to spit on the ground.

Mariposa remembered little about their grandmother except that she was a dour woman with iron-grey hair and a face full of wrinkles, old before her time and hastened to an early grave by bad blood and a morbid distrust of doctors. By the time the real reason for her various physical symptoms was uncovered, the cancer had already spread to her brain. She shrank to nothing, becoming so wizened she resembled one of those strange dried-out bodies scientists discovered preserved in peatbogs. Her death was a release, so everybody said. God had called her home. When Chester was found swinging from the aged oak rafters at the gable end of the cottage a week later, the same people blessed themselves and said he wanted to join her in paradise.

Mariposa, who had never witnessed a single act of affection between her grandparents, thought it laughable that such a narrative was accepted without a flicker of dissent. On the day of Chester's funeral, she and Francis wore black and stood next to their whiskey-soaked father, accepting condolences and listening to all manner of pious nonsense. In reality, they were keeping an eye out for discord among the sharper relatives. Nobody, apart from Chester's sister Belle, who had been born with a mistrusting soul, guessed the truth of it. Suicide was frowned upon by their people, so the death of Chester McCabe went down as the final act of a broken man, a man soured by bad nerves and grief, and not, as Mariposa knew it to be, the brute strength of Francis, who still bore the bruises of Chester's death struggle beneath his mourning attire.

One week later, Malachy Ward, Duchy's father, offered Francis a place on his crew, and Mariposa, terrified of being abandoned, set her sights on Malachy's youngest son, Arthur, who, despite having a girlfriend, found Mariposa's wiles irresistible.

It was to Mariposa's arms he fled for comfort when his poor little sap of a nurse girlfriend came to a tragic end, falling to her death under the wheels of a 15B heading out of town towards Rathmines.

A tragedy, everyone agreed.

A terrible, awful tragedy.

Oh, there were questions; the girl's distraught parents found it hard to accept the verdict of accidental death. They put out an advert, asking for eyewitnesses to the incident. It had happened in the evening, when there were plenty of people about.

Someone must have seen something.

One woman answered: she said she was sure she had seen a dark-haired girl in conversation with the deceased minutes before the accident, talking. Was that it? Had something been missed?

The gardaí canvassed the area again and came away empty-handed.

Besides, two girls talking, it was hardly a crime.

Mariposa missed those days, back when she and Francis were of one mind and one desire. Maybe Duchy was right, maybe Arthur had weakened them. The McCabe family were of ancient stock, proud people who had long lived outside the cultural norms, not beholden to law or what society decreed.

Mariposa grabbed her handbag and got out of the car.

She unlocked the front door of the cottage, entered a tiny vestibule with a crooked flagstone floor and proceeded into the narrow hall that separated one half of the house from the other. She eyed the sliver of light under the kitchen door to the rear and took a moment to compose herself before she entered.

Her brother was in an armchair by an empty fireplace, wearing his coat. There was mud on his boots so he had clearly been outside. She removed her own coat and sat down at the vast oak table Chester had made with his own hands from a storm-damaged tree. 'How are you?'

He did not look at her.

She linked her fingers and studied him. Even wearing the coat, she could see he had lost a lot of weight. Francis had always been a big man, like their father back in his pomp, even had the same McCabe black hair worn longer than was considered fashionable. The beard was new. It suited him.

'Francis, I—'

'I've been thinking about what you said, about Lakeside. If they sell it, you can stay here.'

She stared at him in disbelief. 'Here?'

'That's right.'

'No offence, Francis, but I don't want to live here. This is your home, not mine.'

'It's your home too, Mariposa, Chester left it to both of us.'

She scowled at Chester's name but stayed on track. 'Duchy has betrayed us, Francis. He's sullied Arthur's memory. I can't forgive that, I won't.'

He looked at her. 'What do you mean?'

'All this talk, all this nonsense about how he wants to rebrand, rebuild. But what about us, what about our sacrifice?' She sat forward, her right hand to her left breast. 'He's trying to shut us out.'

'He told me he offered to buy you out.'

'I don't want to sell.'

'Yeah, but without Arthur—'

'That's another thing. I'm not stupid, Francis, I know there were other women. There were always other women. But I loved Arthur and he loved me, and I will not sit idly by as his killer walks free, no matter how convenient it is for Duchy Ward.'

'You want to start a war, is that it?'

'I want the man who murdered my husband and almost murdered my brother to pay for what he did.'

'Mariposa—'

'I told you, I'm not a fool. I've heard about that girl he was seeing. I've heard she was involved with another man, a jealous man. Arthur should have known better, but …' She paused to regain her composure, looked away. 'I know Liam Kennedy was behind it; for God's sake, the dogs on the street know.' She lifted her head. 'So why do you think he's out there walking around?'

Stonewall rubbed his thigh. 'I don't know.'

'You do know. It's because it suits Duchy Ward. Because he has some other plan up his sleeve.'

'You think I don't know that.'

'Are you going to let him away with it?'

'Me?' He stared at her. 'Christ, Mariposa, what are you saying?'

She stared back. 'I'm saying, Francis, we need to protect ourselves. We need to ensure we don't lose everything we worked for.'

She got to her feet and crossed the room to the window overlooking the courtyard. The dogs were still out there, waiting patiently for the master to join them. She stared at them, controlling her breathing. The seeds had been sown, time to—

'I see him, you know.'

Mariposa turned back around in surprise. 'Who?'

'Chester.' Stonewall glanced towards the shadows at the other end of the room. 'I think he's trying to reach me in my dreams.'

Mariposa's throat tightened. Goose bumps rose on her arm. 'He's dead, Francis.'

'He'd like you to think that, all right.'

'He's dead, Francis,' she repeated. 'He can't hurt us anymore.'

'Sometimes I think it's karma, what happened.'

'What do you mean?'

'My leg, my head. It's karma for what I did, for what I took. Our own flesh, our own blood.'

'Nonsense.' Mariposa frowned. 'You don't … discuss what happened to Chester with anyone, do you?'

'What is there to discuss?' he said slowly. 'Whatever price that needed to be paid, I paid it. Chester paid it.'

'Why are you talking like this? Why are you talking about price? Chester was an abusive pervert and he got what he deserved. This is not karma: what happened to you was down to that scumbag Liam Kennedy, and somebody needs to pay for this, for all of it.'

'You use so many words, Mariposa, like a bird twittering on a branch, singing a pretty song.' Stonewall hauled himself from his chair and stood a little unsteadily, but so tall the crown of his head almost brushed against the exposed beams.

'Francis, sit down. Let me make you something to eat and we can—'

'No. I've listened to enough birdsong for one morning. I need to feed the dogs.'

He limped across the floor, kissed her forehead, turned his collar up against the cold and went outside to where the dogs, huge and overjoyed to see him, leaped to their feet. Mariposa watched him scratch their ears and talk to them, marvelling at how puppy-like they acted around him. She had called in every day when he was in hospital to feed them and they had never treated her with anything other than polite disinterest.

She watched him and thought about Duchy's threat, the brass neck talking to her like that in front of Murray and the others.

She would bow to no man; she would allow no man to treat her like a second-class citizen.

Not her husband, and not his brother.

No, certainly not the likes of Duchy Ward.

31

The morning was bright and cold under a clear sky and leafless trees. Pat was on-site talking to the building foreman about parking spaces when a dark blue Volvo drove in and parked opposite the Portakabins.

He glanced over as a man and a woman exited and spoke to a passing builder, who looked around and pointed towards Pat.

'All right, Jerry,' Pat told the foreman, 'I'll look these over later.'

The two visitors approached.

'Mr Kennedy?' the man said, offering a thin smile on a pasty face.

'Guilty as charged,' Pat said.

'My name is Declan Ward. This is my associate, Corrine.'

He had an Irish accent with a trace of English, midlands if Pat was a guessing man. Pat knew who he was immediately.

'What can I do for you, Mr Ward?'

Duchy's smile increased and he looked about as if he was expecting a tour. 'This is a prime bit of land, I must say. Very nice.'

'Thank you.'

'All yours?'

'Yes.'

'That's lovely. I always say a man must be king of his own domain. What are you building here, then? Townhouses? Flats?'

'A blend of homes.'

'What you call a boutique collection, yes? Am I using the lingo correctly?'

'Like a native,' Pat said. 'Are you in the market for a new home, Mr Ward?'

'Could be, could be. In the market for business opportunities, that's for sure.' He winked.

Pat glanced at Corrine, who was wiping mud from her boot on a tiny patch of weeds. She wore a sharp-fitted blazer over a black shirt and as she leaned to check the sole of her boot he saw the outline of a holster.

'Why don't we head up to my office and talk,' Pat said, over the sound of a nearby JCB. 'It's a little less noisy.'

'Lead on,' Duchy said, all Mr Magnanimous.

Upstairs, Pat removed his hat and took a seat behind his desk. Duchy sat down in the chair opposite, but Corrine stood close to the door, next to the window overlooking the yard.

'You can sit down, you're perfectly safe here,' Pat said.

'She likes to stand,' Duchy replied.

'All right.' Pat opened his jacket. 'My condolences on your loss, Mr Ward.'

Duchy's smarmy bonhomie slithered off his face in an instant. 'Yeah, well, it can be a difficult world out there for men like us, Mr Kennedy.'

'Call me Pat.'

'Pat. Did you know my brother?'

'I never had the pleasure.'

Duchy grinned and waggled his finger. 'You're a slick little tomato. I like that.'

Pat inclined his head. He had been called worse by better.

'Do you know why I'm here, Pat?'

'I could hazard a guess.'

'Nasty thing, rumour. Spreads like a weed, pops up everywhere.'

'If left untreated, yes.'

'Keen horticulturalist, are you?'

'Not really, but I know enough to tend to my own garden.'

Duchy did the smile again. It was starting to grate on Pat's nerves.

'My brother is a hot-head, Mr Ward, of that there is no question. But he's not an assassin.'

'Love does strange things to a man. I imagine he's not a peeping Tom either.'

'Excuse me?'

Duchy waved a hand. 'More rumour.'

'What do you want, Mr Ward?'

'Ah, the crux of the matter. I like directness, very underrated in this modern era. I suppose, young man, what I want is legitimacy.'

Pat raised an eyebrow.

'See, I've spent time in the big house, nearly spent my life there in the end. I survived, kept my trap shut. Come home and suddenly I find myself looking around me thinking, "Is this it?" Now, my wife is a simple woman, she was raised in a council flat in Putney and doesn't ask for much, but I promised her, see? I gave her my word that if I survived I'd make a proper go of it.'

'A proper go of what?'

'Of living above board, on the level, straight up and down.'

Pat sensed Duchy might have a slew of metaphors and sayings waiting in the wings and decided he'd rather floss with razor wire than hear them. 'Mr Ward, I'll say it again. What is it you want?'

'A piece of the action. Not charity, mind. I'm not looking for charity, rather a way to … earn a slice of the pie, if you will.'

'And?'

'And in return I'll put the word out that it wasn't your boy that killed Arthur.'

'Liam did not kill your brother.'

'Well,' Duchy inclined his head, 'whether he did, or he didn't, it's perception what counts, don't you agree?'

Pat did agree, in theory at least, but he'd never admit such a thing to a wart like Duchy Ward. 'And how would I deliver your … slice of pie?'

'Your old man used to rob banks now he's on the boards of charities and the like, rocks up in pages of who's who going to this and that.'

'My father has paid his debt to society.'

'Has he indeed?' Duchy suddenly looked crafty. 'I do wonder if he's been called to account for everything he's done.'

'More rumours?'

'There's always talk.'

Pat was mildly bemused. This was an old-fashioned shakedown, no doubt about it, daring, even.

What to do? Shoot them both here and now and cry self-defence, or play along and see how it pans out?

'I see, and what happens if I choose to keep the pie for myself?'

Duchy raised his hand, palm up, and Corrine dropped a mobile phone into it. Duchy took a pair of reading glasses from his pocket and popped them on before he made a call.

'It's me. Yeah.'

He slid the phone across the table to Pat, who turned it around. On screen Liam and his mates were lifting weights and messing about in a gym. Whoever was shooting the video did so with a steady hand and could not have been more than five feet away. Pat could even hear Baz, Liam's best friend, making a stupid joke over the background noise.

The call ended.

Duchy reached for the phone and handed it to Corrine. He got to his feet and stuck his hand out.

Pat ignored it.

Duchy grinned. 'Well, I can't say I blame you. Think over my offer, Mr Kennedy, but don't think on it too long. Time and tide wait for no man.'

He winked.

He and Corrine left.

32

While Pat was watching Duchy Ward's Volvo pull in to the site, Liam Kennedy and two of his mates were in the free weights section of Gary's Gym, watching a young man perform a front squat, openly critiquing his form.

The gym was busy that morning. Metallica's 'Saint Anger' blared over the speakers and several teenagers waited their turn to spar, hanging on the ropes of the boxing ring.

'Watch your knees,' Baz said, shaking his head. 'Keep 'em turned out.'

'Keep the weight over your ankles,' Spud agreed. 'Keep your chin up, eyes forward.'

'Elbows up,' Liam said. 'Right, now lift!'

The squatter, whose name was Cian, weighed about seventy-five kilos and he was lifting eight kilos. Chords stuck out in his neck and a vein throbbed wildly in the middle of his forehead.

'Come on, you pussy! Stand up!'

With agonising slowness, Cian started to rise from his squat.

'Come on, you got this! Keep going!'

Face beet red, Cian bared his teeth.'

'Lift!' Spud and Liam yelled in unison.

With a yell, Cian flung the bar away and fell backwards onto the mat.

'Bad luck, kid,' Baz said, lifting the bar back onto the rack with an insulting amount of ease.

'I thought I had it,' Cian gasped.

'Next time.'

'You get that protein powder like I told you?' Spud asked. He offered Cian his hand and helped him to his feet.

'Yeah, yeah, I bought some last week.'

'It's good stuff, get you up to speed in no time.'

'Gary says I'm a hardgainer.'

All four heads glanced up to the office, where Gary, the gym owner, was ensconced, most likely making bets online.

'Gary talks a lot of shit,' Liam said darkly. 'Don't mind him. Drink two shakes a day, eat well, train hard. You'll be jacked and pulling the hot birds in no time.'

'Thanks, Liam.' Cian beamed at him, face pink with pleasure. He was seventeen; the idea of pulling anyone with a pulse seemed too good to be true.

'Go on, hit the showers. We'll see you tomorrow, yeah?'

'Will do.'

They watched him walk towards the changing room, bouncing along like an eager puppy.

Spud chuckled. 'Remember when we were like that?'

'We were never like that,' Baz said, loading more weight onto the bar. 'A stiff wind would blow him away.'

'Give over,' Spud said. 'You were like a stick when you were a kid.'

'Better a stick than a vegetable,' Baz said, and winked. He laughed and ducked out of the way as Spud made a grab for him.

'Shurrup, you bleedin' thick.'

The two men wrestled and jostled, shrieking and laughing as they tried to trip each other onto the floor.

'Here!' The bellow came from above. 'Knock it off!'

Baz and Spud sprang apart.

'Sorry, Gary, we're only messing!'

'You will be sorry if I have to come down there,' Gary said, but nobody took him seriously.

As they were leaving, they met Cian in the foyer buying an energy drink from a machine. He was scrubbed clean, his hair carefully gelled into place.

'All right, fancy Dan,' Baz laughed, hooking his arm around the kid's neck. 'Where are you off to, then? Got a hot date already, have ya?'

'Heh, no, I wish. I have to go to work.'

'Where's that, then?'

'Lidl. I've got a part-time job there.'

'Oh yeah? Do they give you a discount on grub at all? The steaks are good, aren't they, Spud.'

'Yeah, they're not bad now.'

They walked outside together. Liam looked up at the sky; it was a fine bright morning, the kind of day that made you think winter would soon be over. He glanced at Cian; the kid was grinning – a young knucklehead with the whole world ahead of him. Liam wanted to drag him to one side and give him a stern talk. Warn him that life wasn't always this simple.

'Protein, that's where it's at, Kemosabe,' Baz was saying. 'The more protein you get, the more muscle—'

Liam heard his phone ringing in his gym bag. When he took it out, he saw he had nine missed calls from Pat. He shook his head and tossed the phone back into the bag angrily. Some people just didn't know when to stop.

33

Eddie was right. (Leo was beginning to consider the possibility that Eddie was always right.) There was no such thing as bad publicity, and on the morning of the tasting day, he had a full reservation sheet.

All he had to do now was cook and not make an absolute hames of things.

Oleg arrived early and he wasn't alone. 'This is Nadia, she is very good waitress.' He stomped past and straight into the kitchen. Moments later Leo heard him change the radio station.

Nadia was small, with short dark hair, brown eyes and dimples when she smiled. Leo shook her hand. 'Hello.'

'Hello.'

'I appreciate you coming. Um … I … it's a sort of experimental menu today, Irish products for the most part—'

'Oleg say.'

'Oh, did he? Good, good. Well … good.'

Why was he so nervous?

'Let me show you the menu.' He grabbed one of the little blackboards off a table. Nadia took it and read it carefully. 'Eggs à la Aungier?' She tilted her chin. 'What is this?'

'Lightly fried in brown butter with chopped chives, served with boxty.'

'Boxty?'

'Fried potato.'

'Like hash brown?'

'Yeah. No. Sort of. Yes, like hash browns.'

'Okay. And this? Shirred eggs?'

'Oh, eggs and cream, baked in individual ramekins with a grated hard cheese on top.'

'Ah, many eggs.'

For a moment, Leo looked doubtful. 'Do you think there's too many eggs on the menu?'

Nadia shrugged. 'People like eggs.'

'They're versatile. Good for lunch, slow release.'

She laughed when she saw his anxious face and rested a hand on his shoulder. 'People like things that are …' she searched for a word … 'com-fort-able.'

'Comfortable.'

'Like socks.'

'You think my food is like … socks?'

She nodded. 'Yes, socks are good. Warm for the feet, com-fort-able. Better to have socks than not have socks.'

'Could you fill the water jugs, please, and set out the napkins?'

'Sure.'

Leo hung a larger board outside and returned to the kitchen to continue his prep work. Though he had been up since six, he still felt he was chasing his tail a little, so he made coffee and tried to ignore the volume on the radio. Oleg was red-eyed and sullen, smelling vaguely of stale cigarettes and alcohol. He drank several cups of strong black coffee and guzzled a can of Monster Energy, which perked him up. At half eleven he belched and clapped his hands twice. 'Ready to rock and roll?'

Leo nodded. He felt sick, and it had started to lash rain. He was convinced this was a bad omen.

Thankfully, the rain did nothing to hamper the lunchtime crowd.

When the last customer left at ten after four, Leo felt like he had run a marathon and climbed a mountain at the same time. Giddy with exhaustion, he helped Nadia empty the dishwasher and prepare the room for the evening crowd.

When they were finished, he poured a glass of red wine for Nadia and Oleg and a glass of sparkling water for himself.

'Cheers,' he said, raising the glass in salute. 'To socks!'

'What?' Oleg asked.

'Socks.' Leo winked at Nadia, who smiled. 'Long may we have comfortable socks.'

Oleg shrugged and tossed his wine down in one mouthful. 'Right, I see you tonight, boss.' He grabbed his things and left.

'That man,' Leo said, 'he's a machine. How do you know him?'

Nadia took a sip of her wine. 'Through his wife.'

'Oh. Is she a chef too?'

'No.'

He waited, but there was no more information forthcoming.

'What about you, Nadia? Do you have family here?'

'No.'

'Back home?'

'Yes.'

'Right, right … very good.'

Nadia was clearly not com-fort-able talking about herself or her background. Leo understood. Families … what was there to say about them really? You were born into them, with little or no say in the matter. What more did he need to know about her other than she was twenty-six and she lived in shared accommodation with five other girls in a house in Crumlin and she liked going to the cinema, she really liked trashy action movies, she was punctual, and she was a hard worker.

And she had a wonderful smile.

'Right,' he said again and stood up. 'Well, I'd better get going, things to do and all that.'

She finished her wine, gathered her things and put on her coat.

Leo walked her to the door. The rain was still hammering down. 'Do you have an umbrella?'

She shook her head.

'I can give you a lift, if you like.'

'No, it's okay. There is bus.'

'Honestly, it's no trouble.'

'You are sure?'

'Sure I'm sure. Give me a second.'

He ran around, closing doors and turning off lights. He grabbed his jacket and a golf umbrella he'd found in one of the bedrooms. Together they splashed up the street to the flats where Leo paid fifty quid a week to use a car-parking space. By the time they reached the car, the umbrella had turned inside out. Leo stuffed it into a bin and used his coat to protect them from the worst. Nadia slipped her arm around his waist.

The weight felt good there. Com-fort-able.

'This is mine.'

Nadia looked at the Ford with genuine delight.

'I inherited it.'

He opened the door for her and she got in. Leo ran around and got behind the wheel.

She pushed her wet fringe back from her eyes and looked at the dashboard. 'I never see car like this. What is called?'

'Bellisa.'

Nadia looked confused.

'Oh, you mean the model? Shit, sorry. It's a Ford Capri. Sorry, my girlfriend Eddie said I should name her.'

She looked at him. 'Your girlfriend?'

'My friend who is a girl.' Leo cursed his idiocy; why was he acting this way? 'Don't worry, Eddie bats for the other team.'

Nadia looked even more confused.

'I mean, she's not ... *She* has a girlfriend.'

'Ah!' Nadia leaned back in her seat. 'Bats for team?'

'It's a stupid expression. I don't know why I said it.'

'You have many strange words.' She glanced at him and smiled. 'I like your words.'

'Yeah?' Leo turned the key. The engine rumbled into life immediately and for a split second he forgot about everything except how lovely it was to be smiled at by a good-looking woman with dimples.

34

The main lounge of the Lakeside mansion was unusually busy for midweek, the air thick with cigar smoke and cologne. Tucked away in one corner, a glamour-puss with honey tones sang Nat King Cole songs accompanied by a smiling pianist in a white jacket. That night the singer wore feathers in her hair and millions of sequins that shimmied and sparkled with every wiggle. The duo was ridiculously expensive, but Mariposa only hired them once a month on poker night; she reckoned it added a touch of class to the joint.

She watched the performance for a while, then set off through the tables, stopping here and there to say hello and make polite but impersonal conversation. She did not like to socialise with her patrons; indeed, for the most part she preferred to avoid them as much as possible. She was happy to take their money, but she did not pretend to enjoy their company.

When she finished her rounds and checked each girl was where she should be, she went to the bar and signalled to Stefan, who immediately mixed her a gin and lime juice and deposited it before her.

'On the house, m'lady.'

Mariposa lifted it in a salute and forced a smile. 'Did you see who came in with Toby?'

'I saw.' Stefan waggled his eyebrows. 'Didn't think the old *dear* had it in him.'

'I thought Evan Stag married that actress, what's her name.' Mariposa frowned. 'Chanelle?'

Stefan rolled his eyes. 'Total beard.'

'What?'

'She's a beard. Arranged marriage for both of them.'

Stefan glanced towards the young man they were discussing. Evan Stag was deep in conversation with an older man in a sharp suit, a well-known mover and shaker in the music industry and no stranger to Lakeside or indeed any of the private clubs around town. Toby Dillon was sitting behind them at a little table, alone and scowling, pretending to be interested in the cocktail menu though Mariposa knew he never drank anything other than champagne.

Mariposa sipped her drink, one eye on the singer, one on the crowd. On any other night she'd probe further, but right now she was in no mood for gossip.

She finished her drink and left the lounge, tripping along a luxurious hallway, kitten heels sinking into the thick carpet. Behind a plaster-cast statue of the Venus de Milo, she pressed a panel and slipped through a mirrored door into a narrower, unadorned hall leading to the control room, the heart of the Lakeland mansion.

'Who's in?' she said, lighting a cigarette with a slender onyx lighter, a gift from Arthur and one of the few things he'd ever given her that she valued.

Vincent, the controller, a sweaty, rotund man in his mid-twenties, tapped a number of buttons and zoomed in on one of the screens before him, revealing six men seated around a poker table, jackets off, sleeves rolled to their elbows.

Mariposa smoked her cigarette and studied the players. She focused on one man in particular, a regular at the Lakeside poker night: Ivan Dolan. Minister Ivan Dolan. 'How's the minister playing?'

'He's doing that thing he does with his lower lip,' Vincent said. 'He's bluffing.'

The dealer dealt, and one by one the players folded until only Dolan and a cigar-smoker remained. The dealer queried the play.

Dolan threw his cards across the table in disgust. The cigar smoker reached two stubby hands for the stack of chips and dragged them towards him like a drowning man reaching for a lifebuoy. Dolan's face was a picture.

'He's always unlucky.'

'But he'll stay in the game,' Vincent said. 'Try to win it back.'

'God bless his eternal optimism,' Mariposa said. 'Why don't we send in a round of complimentary drinks with … let me see,' she scanned the other screens and pointed with the tip of her cigarette, 'Topaz.'

Vincent spoke over his coms and the message was relayed immediately to Stefan, who set to work readying the order. Mariposa finished her cigarette and immediately lit another while Topaz, one of the prettiest of the girls, fetched the drinks and entered the card room, all shy smiles and coquettish eye flutters.

'Quite the actress, isn't she?' Mariposa said.

Vincent shrugged, his interest in the women who worked at the club on a par with a cat's interest in chess.

On screen, Topaz set Dolan's drink down and laid a hand on his shoulder. He barely noticed her, which was not unusual. Dolan, Mariposa knew, did not canoodle with the help. The dealer dealt the cards and the hand was underway.

Mariposa watched Dolan's face as he turned the cards over. The skin around his lips tightened, whitened. Disappointment.

Wonderful.

Vincent's com crackled. He listened, then glanced over his shoulder. 'There's a problem upstairs.'

Mariposa was on her feet before he'd finished speaking. 'Get Stefan to meet me there and tell him to bring Doug.'

She dropped the remains of her cigarette into one of the empty cola cans on Vincent's desk and left.

35

Mariposa ran up the main staircase, pushed through the fire doors and almost collided with Jade and Ruby standing in the hall. They were bawling and clutching each other like children, speaking so fast she couldn't make any sense of what they were saying.

'Slow down, slow down.' Mariposa grabbed Jade her by the shoulders and shook her. 'What's going on?'

'It's Jewel,' Jade cried, pointing towards a closed door. 'She was screaming and then she stopped.'

Stefan appeared, with Doug lumbering behind him. Doug was panting slightly, unused to travelling at speed, a little like a manatee out of water.

'What's happened?' Stefan asked.

'Trouble,' Mariposa said grimly. She shoved Jade into Ruby's arms. 'You two stay here; and stop making such a racket. Doug, get in there … and be careful.'

Doug took a heavy-duty sap from a pouch on his belt and used it to tap on the door.

'Management, open the door, please?'

They waited, but there was nothing, no response.

'Try the handle.'

Doug tried the handle; it was locked.

Mariposa rapped the door with her knuckles. 'Hello, in there. This is Mariposa. Can you open this door?' She waited five seconds and knocked again. Nothing. 'Okay, I'm coming in.'

She fished in her pockets for the master key and unlocked the door. She motioned to Doug, who pushed it open and entered. Mariposa followed. Stefan brought up the rear, keeping well back in case there was any actual danger.

'There's nobody in here,' Doug said.

Mariposa shoved him aside. This was the Emerald suite, a mid-range room for guests who liked a little privacy. The four-poster bed was a mess of tangled sheets, and a bottle of champagne and two empty glasses sat on a tray on an oval table.

Doug walked towards the bed. 'Look at this.' He pointed to a thin pearl-handled knife in the middle of the sheets. There was blood on the blade.

'Mariposa,' Stefan said quietly. He pointed to droplets of blood on the carpet leading towards the bathroom, the door of which was closed.

'I'm sorry.'

Mariposa whipped around.

The voice came from the man sitting on the blind side of the freestanding wardrobe. He was naked, his knees pulled up to his chest. Forties, thin, reedy-looking, with pale, thinning hair and a pockmarked face. There were cuts and scratches on his shoulders and face and his lower lip was bleeding. Mariposa recognised him. He was Ivan Dolan's younger brother, Noel.

'What happened?' Mariposa asked. 'What are you sorry for?'

He rubbed his hands over his head and started snivelling. 'I didn't mean to … okay, I didn't mean for this to … I wasn't going to really hurt her … it was a game, a fantasy! I didn't mean anything, it was just role play.'

'Stefan,' Mariposa said.

Stefan hammered on the bathroom door. 'Jewel, honey? It's Stefan. Honey? You okay in there?' He pressed his cheek against the wood for a moment. 'I don't hear anything.'

'Move out of the way.' Mariposa tried the door handle; it was not locked. She pushed it open.

There was blood everywhere: on the tiles, on the ceiling, on the rim of the bath. A towel-rail had been ripped from the wall. It was on the floor by the sink, one end bare, the other bloody with strands of hair on it.

Jewel was on the floor, covered in blood.

'My God.' Stefan put his hands to his head. 'My God.'

Mariposa ran in, almost slipping on the slick tiles. She knelt down and pressed her fingers to the side of Jewel's neck.

'Is she dead?' Stefan asked. 'Oh my God, look at her arm. Is that … is it dislocated?'

'Call …' Mariposa removed her hand and tried to think. Call who? They couldn't call an ambulance and they couldn't bring her to a hospital, not like this; there would be too many questions, reports filed; the guards would be notified. No, it was out of the question, it would create more problems than she could fix.

'Mariposa,' Stefan hissed. 'We've got to do something.'

'Go to my office and call Murray. Don't explain anything over the phone, but make sure he understands that I need him here immediately.'

'Murray?' Stefan was confused. 'We need to call an ambulance!'

'Don't be so stupid, we can't take her to a hospital.'

'But she—'

She shot him a look of such unbridled malice he fell silent.

'Doug.'

'The bouncer stood stricken in the doorway.

'Doug!'

He dragged his eyes away from Jewel.

'Put those two girls into a room and stay with them; don't let them talk to anyone. Are we clear? Don't stand there gawking at me like that. Go!'

'Is she going to die?'

'Will you do as I say, please?'

Doug left.

'It's not right,' Stefan said. 'This is not right, Mariposa. She needs medical care.'

'Do you want to explain to the cops where she came from? Do you want to explain to the cops what she was doing here?' She took her phone from her pocket and started snapping photos of the room, the girl, the blood, taking them from as many angles as she could.

'What are you doing?' Stefan asked.

'Covering our arses.' She backed out into the bedroom, driving Stefan out behind her. 'When you've called Murray, get some plastic bags.' She closed the door. 'I want the knife and the towel-rail bagged, and make sure you use gloves.'

'Mariposa—'

'Not now.'

She stepped past Stefan and located some discarded clothes on the floor. She kicked them towards the weeping man. 'I think you should get dressed and come with me.'

Dolan looked up, wretched, his eyes brimming with tears. 'I didn't mean to hurt her.'

'Of course you didn't. So why don't you come down to the office and we'll discuss it.' She glanced at Stefan. 'When you're finished bagging, go to the card room and find Ivan Dolan – don't make a fuss or a scene. Bring him straight to my office.'

Stefan left the room and went downstairs. He was breathing heavily and close to tears, for despite his role in running the day-to-day business at Lakeside he liked to think he wasn't a bad man. He liked to think he at least had the girls' best interests at heart.

The lie helped him sleep at night.

36

Corrine was standing on a busy cobbled street in Temple Bar wearing a black baseball cap and wire-rimmed glasses watching a shop belonging to a man who went by several names, but the most prominent one was 'Pork Chop'.

It was late, and most of the other businesses were closed or in the process of closing, but Pork Chop was a busy man. A steady stream of young men and women wearing black clothes and copious amounts of eyeliner had drifted in and out of the shop for close to an hour. Some of the girls were very young and one of them, a pretty blonde with a nose piercing, looked a little worse for wear as she left the shop, waving and blowing kisses through the window as she staggered up the street laughing with a friend.

The shop stood empty after ten. Corrine stepped neatly across the street and slipped in through the door.

'Sorry, love.' Pork Chop had his back to her, stacking tins on a shelf behind the counter. 'I'm closing up.'

Corrine closed the door, turned the lock. 'Mr Pork Chop?'

Pork Chop turned around. He was a singularly unattractive man, with dull eyes and long hair, which he wore in a bun on top of his head to cover how thin it was. His earlobes had been stretched to such a degree Corrine could see the shelves behind him by looking through the holes. Corrine wondered what the girls saw in him; to her Pork Chop looked like every other low-level creep with the IQ of a wasp.

'Mr Pork Chop? That's a new one on me, love, real formal.'

'I like formality,' Corrine said. 'I am told, Mr Pork Chop, that you have very good connections.'

'Connections?'

'Yes, to drug dealer.'

'Sorry, love, you must have me mixed up with someone else. I don't know what you're talking about.'

'Oh, you have bad memory?'

'My memory is fine.' He stopped talking and looked at her properly for the first time. Like a snake sensing a vibration, he suddenly felt the first twinge of danger. 'You need to leave.'

Corrine walked around the room, looking at the many photos on the walls. Most were of Pork Chop wearing gloves, working on men and women. There was a back room, the entrance way covered by a curtain of coloured beads. Corrine parted them with both hands and stepped through.

'Hey, hey, you can't go back there.'

Two large reclining chairs, a sterilising cabinet, posters of Judge Dredd, one of AC/DC, more photos. Corrine studied them carefully. Only one interested her. She reached up and ripped it off the wall.

Pork Chop came into the room behind her. 'Put that back.'

She held it directly in front of his face. 'Who?'

'No one. A client.'

'You make this tattoo?'

Despite his desire for her to leave, this rankled him. 'I don't *make* 'em, love, I create 'em. It's a recognised art, you know.'

'Art.' Corrine smiled. 'You are artist.'

'Exactly.'

'Who?' she asked again, tapping the photo with her index finger.

'I told you. I don't know.' He threw his hands up. 'Someone is fucking with you, I don't know why, but your intel is wack, you know?' He stepped to one side, indicating she should leave.

She walked back into the front room and Pork Chop darted behind the counter.

Corrine put the photograph down, reached inside her jacket and took a sketch page from it. She opened it and laid it next to the photo. 'Do you recognise your art?'

Pork Chop looked down. Corrine saw he had a barcode tattooed on the base of his neck and wondered briefly why anyone, let alone an adult, would do such a thing.

'This is just a drawing,' Pork Chop said.

Corrine tapped it with her index finger. 'Look.'

'Could be mine, could be anyone's.'

'Who wears this tattoo?'

'Yeah, well, that's not my business, is it? I do art, not snitching.'

'Who did you *art* with this?'

'Fuck this. I've been polite.' Pork Chop's hand drifted under the counter.

It did not take a bright spark to guess he had some kind of weapon under there. Corrine reckoned it was a baseball bat, or something flashy like a machete or a sword. He looked the type.

To save time and effort, she reached across the counter, caught his manbun and slammed his head straight down.

'Ugh,' was all he said, as his legs folded under him.

Corrine walked around to his side of the counter and had a quick look underneath. Machete.

She shook her head. 'Mr Pork Chop.' She turned towards him. He was trying to sit up, so she kicked him under the chin and removed a stiletto blade from a leather holder beneath her jacket.

He groaned as her face loomed over his.

'I am also artist,' she said, slicking through the thin material of his T-shirt. 'I will show you my art.'

37

Murray was incensed. 'Are you serious, Mariposa? You called me here for this?'

'Well, I can hardly call Stonewall, can I? He's still . . . incapacitated.'

'Is she dead?'

'No. Unconscious.'

'Then take her to a hospital.'

'Now who's being stupid? You need to get her out of here.'

'And do what?'

'Take her to Winston, see if he can patch her up.'

Murray put his hands on his head and tried to keep calm. But this wasn't just bad, this was final-frontier bad. 'What the hell happened to her anyway?'

Mariposa shrugged. She was standing in the doorway of the bathroom, with her scrawny arms folded across her chest. Murray had not seen her since the funeral and he thought, if anything, she looked crazier than ever.

'No idea. The girls found her like this.'

'Don't you have cameras?'

'Not on this floor. They'd spook the horses.'

He looked at her disbelievingly.

'I'm serious. Arthur was adamant there were to be no cameras up here.' She turned her head and yelled over her shoulder. 'Doug!' No answer. 'Where the hell has he gone now?'

She left. A few minutes later the bouncer appeared in her place, filling the doorway with his massive presence. His wide face was blotchy in places and it looked to Murray like he had been crying.

'Doug.'

'Hey, Murray.' Doug looked at the injured girl and looked away again. He had wrapped her in a blanket: some of the blood had already soaked through. 'Did she say anything?'

'Not since I got here.'

'I think her arm is broken.'

'Yeah, can you carry her?'

Murray followed behind as Doug carried the unconscious girl down the back stairs and outside to the waiting van.

'She's real light,' Doug said, the words choking in his throat. 'Hardly weighs a thing.'

'Yeah.' Murray unlocked the back doors of the van and stepped aside.

Doug looked in and frowned. 'You already got someone in here.'

'That's okay.' Murray said. 'He won't mind the company.'

'Don't seem right. She didn't deserve none of this. He didn't need to hurt her like that.'

Murray cocked his head. 'Do you know who did this to her, Doug? Do you know what really happened?'

Doug grunted. 'I don't know nothing.'

He lowered Yulia down and tucked the blanket in around her with a gentleness that, like his voice, belied his great size. 'You think she'll be okay?'

'I don't know,' Murray said, to save his feelings. 'Maybe.'

'You met her before, didn't you, Murray? She was only a kid, a real sweet kid. I was teaching her English.'

'Don't go over-thinking things, Doug, all right?' Murray had to reach up to pat him on his back. 'Why don't you head on inside, I'll handle it from here.'

Doug left as Mariposa arrived, a velvet brocade coat draped over her shoulders to ward off the cold. Her complicated hairstyle had come loose, and strands of hair stood out from her head as though electrified. For the umpteenth time Murray wondered what the hell Arthur was thinking when he hitched his wagon to this woman the way he had. Love? Unlikely. Who could love a thing like Mariposa?

She glanced through the van doors and arched an overdrawn eyebrow. 'Who's the passenger?'

'Just some gouger.'

She surprised him by leaning over the girl and snatching away the plastic covering. Her eyes narrowed when she saw the terrible wounds on his torso.

She covered him up again and climbed back out. 'Who is he?'

'Talk to Duchy.'

'I am asking you. Was he one of the men who killed Arthur?'

'I don't know. Corrine seemed to think he had information.'

'What's the deal with her and Duchy?'

'I don't know that either. I know Duchy knew her old lad. That's it.'

She looked back up at the brightly lit windows of the mansion and scowled at the noise of drunken revelry. 'Listen to them,' she said. 'They'd make you sick, wouldn't they?'

'Who?'

'Them, our *betters*. Don't they make you sick?' She glanced at him slyly. 'Sometimes I think we're nothing but drones, Murray, drones. Little worker bees, disposable.'

'I don't think about it.' Murray closed the van doors. 'We done?'

'Yes,' she said after a moment. 'See if there's anything he can do for her.'

'And if there isn't?'

She turned her head to look at him, her face half hidden by shadow. 'Then she shouldn't suffer, should she?'

Murray, who didn't shock easily, was shocked. 'You want him to—'

'He'll know what to do.'

Murray got back in the van and took the service lane to the rear of the mansion, driving past disused stables and on to a secondary road. The moon was high and bright, so he drove without headlights until he bounced out onto the road and accelerated away.

Mariposa watched the tail-lights disappear, her arms wrapped tight across her chest.

Just some gouger.

Lies. She had recognised Conor Stanley, or what was left of him. Conor had been an acquaintance of Arthur's around the time Duchy got arrested.

She went back inside the mansion, troubled and deep in thought, the wounded girl forgotten about.

For now.

38

By the time Murray reached Winston's house, less than twenty miles from the mansion, the girl's breathing had grown ragged and laboured. She was as limp as a wet cloth when he dragged her out and hoisted her over his shoulder. A wasted journey, but he had his orders and he would carry them out, for as much as he disliked Mariposa, the mansion was still a Ward asset, at least for the time being.

Winston was waiting for him inside the front door, a small man wearing carpet slippers and a cardigan with more holes than fabric. When Murray staggered past, he thought he smelled alcohol on the older man's breath. In Winston's case it was a necessary precaution to steady his hands.

'Take her in to the room on the right, please,' Winston said, closing the front door. 'I have an examination table set up.'

Murray did as he was directed, glad to put the girl down. She might not weigh a lot, but then neither did he.

Winston followed him in, donned a pair of glasses and fetched a stethoscope. Murray unwrapped the blood-stained blanket and stepped aside.

'Oh dear. What happened to her?'

'One of Mariposa's girls. Apparently a punter wasn't satisfied.'

Winston placed the stethoscope in his ears, the other end on the girl's chest. 'Can you sit her up?'

Murray did so.

Winston listened to her lungs. 'Set her down.'

Murray lowered her. The girl was a dead weight and her arms fell out limply from her body. Murray tucked them back by her side as Winston walked over to a sideboard and opened a black bag that had seen better days. Everything in Winston's home had seen better days, including Winston.

'Let's see …'

He prized open the girl's eyes one at a time and shone a pen-light into each one, moving it this way and that, left to right. 'Hmm,' he said. 'Strange.'

'What is?'

'Please be quiet.' He lifted the girl's bare feet and, using a biro, scraped the soles.

Nothing.

Murray could hardly stand to watch him go through the motions: he looked around the room instead. It was a nice room, he thought, pricing the marble fireplace and the quality furniture with a practised eye. The whole house had been a fine house once; now it reeked of neglect and the passing of time. Dust tickled his nostrils. Murray wondered when was the last time Winston had cracked open a window; he doubted it had been any time in the last decade.

When the examination was finished Winston removed his glasses and tucked them into the neck of his undershirt where he wouldn't lose them. 'Well,' he said. 'I can tell you her shoulder is dislocated.'

'And?'

'It's odd. Her pulse is strong, steady, but her breathing is wrong and … take a look.'

Murray stepped beside him. 'What am I looking at?'

'Her pupils. Do you see? This one is perfectly normal. But this one … well, you can see for yourself, there's no reaction to the light at all. Pupils should contract reflexively, but alas, as you can see, it's blown.'

'Right.' Murray stepped back again. 'That's bad, is it?'

'It suggests neurological damage.' He looked her over again. 'She had lacerations here in her scalp.'

Murray remembered seeing the blood on the floor, the missing towel-rail. 'Yeah,' he said. 'I think she put up a hell of a fight.'

'One she lost, it seems.'

Murray nodded, more to himself than in agreement.

'Is she suffering?'

'Now?' Winston glanced at the girl's blood-stained face. 'No, I shouldn't think so.'

'What's the best course of action here?'

'She needs to be in a hospital.'

'Not going to happen.'

'Well,' Winston put his hands into the pockets of his cardigan, 'if she was a patient of mine—'

'She'd be a cat or a dog.'

'In any event, the diagnosis would be the same.'

'Right.' Murray looked down at the floor. The carpet was like something from the late seventies, early eighties, patterned full of weird swirls and shapes; if he squinted, it looked like thousands of souls were trying to free themselves from the weave.

Doug had been correct – he remembered her from the first night. He remembered her trying to shield a younger girl behind her. Remembered her screams when Stonewall slapped the kid senseless. Remembered how she'd cried and fought when Stonewall carried her outside. She was fine-boned, long-limbed, slight, but with a nice shape. It would not have taken much to subdue her, so why the need for this level of brutality? He looked at her again and felt a blanket of shame settle over him. Poor kid, she looked like she was sleeping.

'Take care of it,' he said to Winston. 'Don't leave her like this.'

'Where are you going?'

'For a smoke. Call me when you're done.' He left the room, went down the hall and outside, closing the front door behind him.

Winston went to the bag again and extracted a small vial and a syringe. He shook the vial, pierced it and filled the syringe with a measure he deemed suitable.

Finding a vein proved a little difficult. Winston scowled, put the syringe down and went to his bag to get a tourniquet.

Outside, Murray smoked his cigarette and watched the clouds chase across the moonlit sky. He was thinking about his sister, his kid sister. The dying girl reminded him of Triona: same slight build, same colouring. Triona hadn't made it to adulthood, leukaemia saw to that.

That's why this business was getting to him more than usual. Yeah, that was it.

Had to be.

He took a last drag, pitched the butt into Winston's flowerbeds and went back inside. 'All right,' he said. 'Give me a hand—'

Winston was lying on the crazy carpet, a needle jutting out of his chest.

'Winston!'

Murray dropped to his knees and yanked the needle out and tossed it aside.

'Winston!' He slapped Winston's face. The older man's mouth was moving, but then, very quietly, his head lolled to one side and he was gone.

'Shit. Shit, shit, shit, shit.' Murray sprang to his feet and wheeled around. The blood-stained blanket was on the ground but there was no sign of the girl. He ran out into the hall, looked one way and then the other. Then he headed towards the back of the house, saw the open door leading into darkness.

He sprinted outside and immediately stopped. The moon had gone behind the clouds and the overgrown garden was pitch black. He had no idea which direction she had taken or – the thought suddenly struck him – if she was hiding somewhere with a weapon.

He backed up the path into the house, pulled the door closed and locked it.

Now what?

He returned to the front room. Winston was still there. Still dead.

He slapped the side of his head. Think!

The old man was something of a recluse, but he had family. People knew him; they would notice after a while if he didn't collect his pension or buy milk. People were bastards, but they were nosey bastards.

If he left him here, he'd be found. There would be questions, links back to Mariposa, to Arthur, to Duchy, to him.

But if he wasn't found … no body, no crime. Right?

Swearing loudly, Murray pocketed the syringe and, with some considerable effort, dragged Winston out of the house by his heels, reversed the van right to the back door and wrestled him inside. Done, he went back inside, collected the blood-stained blanket and backed out of the room, taking care to turn off the lights and close the front door with his sleeves.

Sweating profusely, he tossed the blanket over Winston, slammed the doors, got behind the wheel and set off in the direction of the Toyne quarry, a desolate place with sheer drops into a deep, still lake. The quarry had long been out of business, at least out of legitimate business, but there was more than one body at the bottom of the lake, fastened to concrete blocks and chains, covered by silt several feet deep.

He put on the radio, flicking around until he found a stream of eighties classics. He put his foot down. Toyne was a good sixty miles away, and by the time he'd get two bodies properly weighted it would be—

He rounded a bend on the narrow road, saw the flickering blue lights ahead and slammed on the brakes.

A Garda checkpoint.

'Bollocks!'

Murray threw the van into reverse, pulled a U and tore back the way he came. Seconds later, flashing lights filled his rear-view mirror as two squad cars gave chase.

39

Nobody, not even Rally, who drove like a maniac and was technically barred from having a legal licence, could have outpaced the squad cars indefinitely, and certainly not in the ten-year-old Peugeot Murray was driving.

Foot to the floor, he shot over humpback bridges and took corners on two wheels, going up and down the gears like a madman, and still they were gaining on him. Bonnie Tyler was screaming about holding out for a hero when it dawned on Murray that the cops would have radioed ahead for backup, or a stinger to blow his wheels, and if *that* happened, it was all over.

How exactly would he explain not one but two bodies in the back?

Funny story, officer.

Shit.

Teeth clenched, he swung around a bend and hung a hard right into a narrow laneway and killed the headlights. The squads raced past six seconds later.

Too close.

Way too close.

Murray reversed out and drove off in the opposite direction. He knew they'd figure out his trick in no time, but for now he had a slight bit of breathing space. The quarry was too far away. Time for Plan B.

He called Rally.

'I need you to come get me. The cops are on my heels. I need to ditch the van.'

'Where?'

'Drogheda. I'll call you when I know exactly where.'

Murray hung up, tossed the phone onto the passenger seat and sped on, heading north-east. From memory he knew several places he could dump the bodies if time was on his side. But time was not on his side. The river was his best – no, his only – shot.

He screeched to a stop two miles below the Boyne viaduct and reversed the van as far as he dared onto the riverbank. The cursed moon was back. He jumped out, ran around the back and flung open the doors. He hauled Winston out and, staggering slightly in the mud, dragged him down the bank and into water up to his knees. Recent heavy rains had swollen the river, and a few feet out the current was strong and fast. Winston bobbed for a moment before he was sucked away.

The second man was heavier. Much heavier than Murray had anticipated, and awkward to move too. By the time Murray had hauled him out of the van and dragged him down the bank by his heels he was sweating hard, gasping for breath and ready to collapse.

He clawed back up to the van, got in and started the engine. For a horrible few seconds the wheels spun uselessly before they caught. Murray gave a triumphant whoop as he shot back onto the road and drove away, the van veering wildly until he got it under control again.

Half a mile south of Drogheda he parked behind a derelict house and climbed out. From here he could travel across the fields to the outskirts of town and have Rally collect him from a petrol station. He made the call and then took anything that might identify him from the van. He removed his jacket and shirt and T-shirt, then put the jacket and shirt back on. He wadded the T-shirt up tightly, inserted a third of it into the petrol tank and lit the other end. He was halfway across the first field when the van exploded.

By the time he reached the petrol station he was covered in mud and cowshit, his face and hands cut all over from briars and barbed wire.

'Jesus,' Rally said when he arrived. 'What happened?'

Murray got in and turned up the heat. Now that the adrenaline had dropped off he was cold and tired and feeling extremely sorry for himself, and very angry. What happened? Mariposa happened, that's what.

He gave an incredulous Rally a very terse summation of his night.

'Duchy's going to go spare,' Rally said when he was finished. 'Spare.'

He dropped to third and shaved a hedge taking a sharp bend. 'Were they at least weighted?'

'I didn't have time, all right? The bloody cops were right up me hole.' He picked a piece of dung from his eyebrow. 'None of this is my fault.'

'Not me you need to be telling.'

'Just drive, will you?' Murray found his phone and called Duchy. It went straight through to his answering service. 'Call me when you get this, we have a problem.'

He hung up. 'None of this would have happened if it wasn't for Mariposa,' he said after a while. 'She's a liability.'

'She needs to be taken in hand,' Rally agreed. 'She's lost the run of herself since Arthur died. I told you, didn't I? I said she was trouble.'

'Off you go then,' Murray said nastily, because he knew Rally was afraid of Mariposa. 'Go take her in hand.'

'I'm only saying.'

*

They turned left, drove for a mile until they reached a roundabout and took a slip road onto the motorway heading south. A squad car passed them going in the opposite direction, blue lights flashing. No siren. Neither man looked at it.

No need.

They knew where it was going.

40

Yulia climbed over a rotting fence, dropped into a field of wet grass and ran until she made it to the other side of it. Sides heaving, she crawled under a hedge to listen for sounds she was being followed.

She lay for a long time, shivering from shock and cold. Her left arm was completely numb, but her shoulder burned.

The moon went behind clouds, but by then her eyes had grown used to the dark. She got to her feet and made her way down a long muddy access lane between fields and kept going until she saw lights in the distance.

A farmhouse.

She hesitated. Friend or foe, it didn't matter. They'd call the authorities and she'd be taken away, arrested. Celestine was out there somewhere. She had to find her, she had to help her.

She staggered on, gritting her teeth against the pain until she reached a barred gate. It was locked, but she could see now the source of the light, a gable light, over-looking a large square yard beside a two-storey house. The house itself was in darkness, save for a single light in an upper-floor window. There was a lawn to the front of the house, semi-frosted, surrounded on three sides by raised walled flower beds. And strewn across the lawn, from one side to the other, a clothes line, full of clothes.

Yulia shivered, licked her lips. They felt dry and chapped. The cold was slowing her down, making it hard to concentrate, to think.

House. Clothes.

Yes.

But what if there was a dog or the owners had a gun?

Should she die from hypothermia instead?

Decision made, she climbed over the gate, lost her grip and fell onto the soft ground on the side. Her shoulder screamed, but she managed to choke the pain down.

Get up.

She could not.

Get up.

Slowly, painfully, she dragged herself to her feet. She needed to do something about the shoulder: this was now the priority. She took a breath.

The gate was supported by two concrete posts on either side. It looked strong. She knew what she had to do. She turned, lifted her useless arm out to the side and gripped the top bar as tight as she could. She took a deep breath, then another, then … dropped to a low squat as hard and fast as she could manage. She felt her joint pop, bit her lips so as not to scream and let go.

There. It was done.

After a moment she used the bars to get to her feet again and set off towards the line, sticking close to the walls and the hedges. No dog barked and no other lights from the house came on.

The owner of the house got up the next morning and went across the yard to let the chickens out. It was only on his return that he noticed some of his washing was missing.

He stood on the lawn, scratching his head in genuine wonder. Socks, jocks, a fleece shirt and a truly ancient pair of Wranglers.

'Well,' he said, after a while, 'if that don't beat the damned.'

41

Without opening his eyes or making it in any way obvious he was awake, Doug grunted, rolled on his side and slid his hand under his pillow, his fingers searching for the steel bar he kept there. He realised it was gone at the exact moment the bedside lamp clicked on.

'If you are looking for weapon, I have it.'

He opened his eyes and rolled back. Corrine was standing over him, holding the bar in her right hand, bouncing it gently up and down on her left.

Doug eyed the bar, wondering how she had known it was there, since he'd never mentioned it to a single soul. He was also wondering how she had been able to reach across him and take it out without him feeling a thing. Wondering what she was doing here, in his bedroom, and if he was about to die.

'You will not need weapon,' she said, 'if you are not stupid.'

'Good to know.'

'May I sit?'

'Sure.'

She walked to the other side of the room, removed some newspapers from an old wooden chair he kept by the dresser and carried it next to the bed. She sat, put the bar down, out of his reach, crossed her legs and linked the fingers of her hands over her knee. Her every movement was precise and deliberate.

Doug craned his neck to see the radio alarm clock on the bedside locker. Twenty past seven. He'd been asleep less than two hours. 'How did you get in?'

'Your door was open.'

That was a lie. Doug had worked as a bouncer for various clubs and 'establishments' for over twenty years. He was conscious of security, particularly his own: he knew he had checked all the downstairs doors and windows before he'd gone to bed.

'Can I get up?'

'I'd prefer if you did not. You can sit up if you like.'

He pushed himself upright, a little sorry he hadn't put on a vest or a T-shirt or something before getting into bed (but then he hadn't been expecting visitors). All his life he had been big: a big kid, a bigger teenager and now, at thirty-eight, he was massive, some of it still muscle, though not enough. Faced with this woman, scarcely a third his size, he felt alarmingly vulnerable.

'I am not here to hurt you,' Corrine said, as though reading his thoughts. 'There was incident tonight, a girl was hurt. Who hurt her?'

'Don't know. Some of the other girls found her—'

'Don't do that,' Corrine said. 'It is stupid, and it will serve to annoy me.'

Doug had tried to smile but found he couldn't pull it off with her staring at him. 'Sorry, force of habit.'

'The girl is gone.'

'Oh.' Doug looked at the wall. 'I didn't know that, nobody said. Nobody told me she died.'

'Not dead. Gone. Escape.'

'Yeah?' Doug was pleased about that, but quietly so.

'How is possible?' Corrine asked. 'This.'

'Mariposa will slice me a new one if she finds out I've been talking to you. She hates your guts.'

Corrine shrugged. She wasn't the type of woman who offered promises or assurances and she couldn't care less about what Mariposa thought of her.

Doug sighed and rubbed his face with his two hands. 'I swear, I don't get paid enough for any of this shit.'

'You can leave, find other job.'

'I got commitments.'

'Then tell me what happen, Doug, omit no detail.'

Doug lowered his hands onto his lap and began to talk.

Corrine sat immobile and made no interruptions. The tale did not take long, and when he was done talking, she leaned back in her chair and closed her eyes. 'She took photos? Evidence in bags? You are sure?'

'Yeah, and I saw Stefan carry the bags down the hall.'

'Stefan? You are certain?'

'I was in the room with the two girls. They were crying and scared so I said I'd go get them a drink, brandy, you know? To calm their nerves and that. I opened the door and saw Stefan, but I don't think he noticed me.'

'Tell about the man.'

'Noel Dolan,' Doug said. 'Weedy little fucker.'

'Weedy? What is this?'

'Thin, small, scrawny build.'

'He is member?'

'No, he comes with his brother as a guest.'

'Who is this, please?'

'Minister Ivan Dolan. Now, he's a gold member.'

Corrine leaned forward a fraction. 'A minister? Of government?'

Doug nodded. 'Yeah. He comes for the poker. Noel comes for the girls.'

'Was he … appraised of situation regarding girl? This minister.'

'You mean did he know?'

'Yes.'

'Yeah, I reckon so. Mariposa brought him up to the office and they left together, him and his brother. He had to know.'

'A fair and accurate assessment.' Corrine held out her hand. After a moment, Doug took it and they shook. Her skin was cool and smelled faintly of peppermint. It was a slightly surreal experience.

'Thank you,' she said. 'I appreciate ... candour.'

'Look, don't tell her it was me that talked. I need that job.'

'Mariposa? I have no intention to talk a single thing.' She looked at him, her pale eyes gleaming in the lamplight. 'My advice is same. Forget conversation, Doug, forget this ...' she looked around her '... moment.'

'No worries on that score.'

She rose in one fluid movement and looked at him with a strange expression on her face.

'What?'

'You liked her, this ... Jewel?'

'Her real name was Yulia. Yeah, she was nice,' Doug said, looking down at his massive hands resting on the duvet. 'That bastard should pay for what he did to her.'

'You would like man to pay? For hurting this Jewel?'

'Yulia. Yeah, he should pay, shouldn't he? I was teaching her how to speak English. She was a quick learner.'

'Why?'

'Why what?'

'Why you help her?'

'I told you. Because she was nice. There's not enough nice people in the world, if you ask me.'

Corrine offered him the tiniest hint of a smile and left.

Doug waited until he heard the front door close before he got out of bed. He went to the window to make sure she was gone. The street was deserted, and there'd been no sound of a car.

Taking the steel bar with him, he crept down the stairs, stopping now and then to listen, heart thumping, his skin prickling from the cold.

Downstairs was quiet, empty: Corrine was gone.

Doug thought, setting the bar down on the kitchen worktop so he could lean both hands against it to steady his nerves, it was as though she had never been there at all.

42

Leo was lying on Gina's old double bed, reading, when his mobile rang. He picked it up from the locker, saw it was from a blocked number and ignored it. Seconds later it rang again.

This time he answered. 'Hello?'

'I'm sorry for the hour. Can you talk?'

Leo sat upright. 'Pat?'

'Yes. I was calling to … well, to say welcome home, obviously.'

'Obviously?' Leo said. 'It's been weeks.'

'Yes … well, I've been meaning to call.'

'Right.'

'I'm also calling to tell you that the old man is having a party tomorrow night.'

'Good for him.'

'The Glenmore Lodge, seven sharp.'

'I hope he has the time of his life. Was that it?'

'Swish gig. I'd wear a suit, assuming you have one.'

'I won't need one. I'm not going.'

'Did I mention the party is for Jackie? Her birthday, her sixtieth.'

That complicated things. Leo had no real beef with his stepmother, only with the man she'd married.

'Why didn't Frank call me himself if he wants me to come?'

'Does it matter who delivers the message?'

'It's been five years, Pat, it wouldn't have killed him to pick up the phone.'

'I imagine he feels the same way about you.'

'He's the one who broke contact.'

'Is that how you remember it?'

'That's how it was.'

'If you say so.'

Pat sounded bored. But then, Leo remembered, Pat always managed to sound bored when he spoke to people. Bored or vaguely nauseated, as though human interaction was a sordid pastime and utterly beneath him.

'Tell Frank I appreciate the invitation, but I can't come. I'm busy.'

'Tell him yourself.'

'You're the one relaying his messages.'

'You know *she'll* be upset.'

'Don't use Jackie as bait.'

'It was her idea to ask you.'

'Hah, I'll bet it was.'

'Listen to yourself. Do you want him to come crawling, cap in hand? You didn't even bother to tell him you were coming home.'

'What difference would it have made if I—?' Leo stopped. He didn't have to justify his actions to Pat, he didn't have to justify his actions to anyone. That ship had long sailed. 'Look—'

'No, you look,' Pat said. 'I don't care if you come or not, Leo, that's up to you, but like I said, it would mean a lot to her.'

'Since when do you care so much about Jackie's feelings?'

'She's family.' Pat's voice slipped from bored to glacial. 'That should mean something, even to you.'

'Uncalled for.'

'If the cap fits.'

Leo pinched the bridge of his nose. He had forgotten how

aggravating it was dealing with his older brother. 'Fine, I'll stick my nose in for half an hour … for Jackie's sake.'

'Good.'

'Should I bring a present?'

'Won't your sparkling personality be present enough?' Pat hung up

'Last-word merchant,' Leo muttered and flung the phone on the bed.

43

Minister Ivan Dolan was not a stupid man. When it came to business, he was driven, hard-working and considered by many to be an utterly ruthless bastard, the sort of man who would stop at nothing in order to make a profit. This ruthlessness translated well into a career in politics. Ivan understood politics, he understood pressure, he understood guile, he understood quid pro quo; he understood how to play the long game.

No, definitely not a stupid man: a bully and a braggart, sure; a philanderer, certainly; a poor poker player, most assuredly.

A coward? Possibly.

But not stupid.

And because he wasn't a stupid man he somehow managed to keep his wits about him when a call came through on his mobile phone that evening, though his heart lurched the moment he heard her voice.

'Timothy!' he said, maintaining a steady and pleasant tone. He rose from the armchair and skirted around the living room where Olive and his two girls were on their various seats glued to some dreadful talent show. On screen a woman with a lisp was bawling crocodile tears to a panel of plastic celebrities with deeply touched faces and dry eyes. 'What a pleasant surprise.'

Olive, wearing a familiar irritated expression, glanced at him.

He smiled, but that only made her frown deepen. When had she stopped returning his smiles?

He pressed the phone to his chest. 'I've got to take this, darling, it's work.'

'It's after six, Ivan. Family time. Can't it wait until the morning?'

He rolled his eyes, pulled a 'you're so right, but what can I do?' face and skedaddled.

'I do apologise for the late hour, minister.' Mariposa's voice oozed down the line with oily insincerity. 'But I couldn't seem to reach you at your office yesterday despite leaving a number of messages with your staff.'

Ivan scuttled across the hall to a downstairs toilet and locked the door behind him. 'Who do you think you are, calling me at my home—'

'Dear me, there's no need to get so defensive, Ivan. You don't mind if I call you Ivan, do you? You're a hard man to reach – what choice did I have?'

'How did you get this number?'

'A friend of a friend. It's Ireland, hardly much of a stretch to locate a phone number now, is it?'

'This is outrageous—'

'Shut up.'

He stopped talking, speechless. Nobody spoke to him this way.

'I think we have an urgent matter to discuss, don't you?'

'Is this about … the incident?'

'Is that what we're calling it now? The incident … how tidy, how practical. I can see why you're a politician.'

Ivan tried to swallow and found his mouth was bone dry. 'What do you want?'

'What does anyone want really?'

'What?'

'Rhetorical question. I want freedom.'

'What?' Ivan repeated.

'Freedom, minister. I couldn't have been clearer.'

'Freedom?'

'That's right.'

'I don't … I don't understand.'

Mariposa chuckled. The sound made his skin crawl. 'No, your sort never does. Shall I pop by on Monday for a chat?'

Ivan stared at his reflection in the oval mirror above the free-floating sink. He looked ghastly, guilty, terrified. Olive would smell the fear on him a mile away.

'Are you trying to blackmail me?'

'Such an ugly word.' Mariposa sounded positively poisonous. 'I suppose it would never cross your mind that I might actually have something to offer.'

'What's that?'

'Forgetfulness.'

'What?'

'God, you're like a broken record.'

'Wha— I mean, I don't understand what you mean by that.'

'Well, let me give you an example. I can forget how much money you've lost at the card table. In fact, I can forget just about anything if I put my mind to it.' A pause. 'I can forget what your brother did to that girl. Unfortunately, she died.'

'She died?'

'Yes,' Mariposa lied. 'Yes, she did.'

Time stopped. Ivan felt his body disconnect from the universe; there was no night and no day; there was only this moment, hearing the words on this creature's lips. He clutched the phone tighter. 'Mariposa—'

'No, not now. Your office, Monday. Say around eleven?'

He froze. Was that the living room door?

Someone rattled the bathroom handle. 'Dad?'

'Occupied!' he said. 'Use the one upstairs.'

He heard muttering, the word 'gross'. He tugged at his collar and realised he was sweating heavily, so heavily his shirt was stuck to his back. He'd have to go upstairs to change before he went back to the living room.

'And try not to worry,' Mariposa said. 'I'm sure we can find a solution that suits us both, an equitable one.'

Ivan closed his eyes; this bitch was playing him like a bloody fiddle. He felt a surge of resentment and found it preferable to terror. 'All right, my office, Monday morning.'

'Good evening, minister. My best to your family.'

44

On Friday evening Leo pulled the only suit he possessed from the back of the wardrobe and hung it from the curtain pole.

'What do you think?' he asked Eddie, who was lying on his bed, flipping through a magazine, her legs crossed at the ankle.

'I told you what I think,' she said, without looking at him. 'I think you're an absolute gobshite.'

'I'm going to pop in for literally half an hour.'

'Whatever.'

'Eddie, it's Jackie's birthday – what was I supposed to say?'

Eddie tossed the magazine aside and got to her feet. 'Well, if you want my opinion—'

'It was more of a rhetorical—'

'In my *opinion*, you should have said "no" because getting involved with any of those people again is the most egregiously stupid and moronic thing you could ever do, and I want no hand in it.'

'They're family.'

'They're poison. Have you forgotten what happened, what he did?'

'Of course not.'

'Your father murdered your uncle – he murdered him in cold blood.'

Leo flinched. Nobody had ever said it aloud, not since Frank had come to see him when he'd had his … little spell five years previously.

'He had his reasons.'

'So, he deserved it then, is that what you're saying?' Eddie looked disgusted. 'No trial, no defence, Frank Kennedy, judge, jury and executioner, order one, get three for the price while stocks last.'

'Eddie—'

'Oh, give it a rest.'

She left the room and went downstairs. Leo let her go because he didn't want to keep arguing with her. Eddie didn't know everything. As far as she was concerned, black was black, white was white and never the twain shall meet.

Judge, jury and executioner.

She wasn't wrong, was she?

The suit was a navy-blue number. Not terrible, but it looked horribly out of date and could, he realised, brushing it hopelessly, have done with being dry-cleaned.

Oh well, there was nothing he could do about that now.

He left the bedroom and went down the landing to the avocado-green bathroom. He showered as best he could under the uneven trickle from the ancient showerhead and tried to shave using a make-up mirror he'd bought in the euro-shop down the street.

Back in the bedroom, he dressed quickly and stood before the wardrobe mirror, trying to picture what his old man would see. His reflection did nothing to bolster his self-confidence. He needed a haircut, and at some point, without his noticing, he'd had lost even more weight, and it wasn't like he'd had much to spare in the first place.

Half an hour to pay his respects to Jackie.

Be the bigger man.

It was fifteen minutes past seven before he reached Glenmore. He parked the Ford, got out and tried to tug smooth the wrinkles in his jacket as he made his way along azalea-lined gravel paths. To take his mind off the suit, he thought about the last time he'd seen his father and tried not to remember some of the things they'd said to each other. He'd been under psychiatric supervision at the time, but that hadn't stopped Frank from winding him up like a clock.

Still, he thought, it had been five years ago. Five years was plenty of time for anger to coagulate into mean indifference.

A ridiculously handsome doorman ushered him into the foyer, offering him a polite smile but cool eyes. Leo guessed the suit was a bit of a giveaway: it screamed 'not a regular'. Nevertheless, he entered a double-height reception area, desperately affecting the air of a man so comfortable in his surroundings he could wear any goddamned suit he pleased.

The hotel was high-end, but not oppressively so. Twin staircases hugged the walls leading to a pointless mezzanine, and logs crackled in an oversized fireplace. To the right of the fire, a beautiful woman in sparkles tinkled the ivories of a baby grand piano. When he approached the reception desk, another strikingly beautiful woman beamed at him. Leo's fake self-confidence wilted. Where had all these beautiful people suddenly come from?

'Good evening, sir, and welcome to the Glenmore Lodge. How can I help you?'

'I'm here for the Kennedy party.'

'Of course.' She glanced down at a flat computer screen built into a marble-topped desk and touched some buttons. 'May I have your name, sir?'

'Leo Kennedy.'

She tapped some more. 'Ah, I see you'll be staying with us this evening, Mr Kennedy.'

'No, no, I won't be staying.'

She tapped the screen again. 'I have you down for a suite.'

'I won't be staying,' he said, a little more firmly. 'Definitely not, no.'

'Very good.'

She gave directions to the Elba Bar; Leo muttered his thanks and followed them, pushing through one set of heavy doors after another until he heard jazz and the sound of people in high spirits. Pat had said to be there for seven, but when he entered the room it was clear many of the attendees had been there a while and were thoroughly enjoying the free lubrication provided.

'Champagne, sir?' A young lad, bearing a tray laden with snipes, tilted towards him.

Leo took a glass to be sociable and set off through the crowd. He thought he recognised a few familiar faces, but nobody approached him or said hello, and nobody returned any of his smiles. As he skirted the room, he felt he was being scrutinised from all angles, picked apart seam by seam. *There's the one who turned his back on his family*, their eyes said, *there's the one who ran away to England like a gutless coward.*

There's the one who tried to kill himself.

Oh yes, Leo thought, his smile beginning to waver, their eyes said plenty.

Pat was standing at the bar talking with his long-time friend and wingman, Tommy. Leo drifted behind a large plant to avoid being noticed, suddenly feeling shy and a little out of his depth.

Tommy had been stitched to Pat's shadow since they were kids, yin to his brother's yang. Leo hadn't seen him in years, but he looked much the same: hair shorn to the point of baldness, round head, round body, pale pink skin, like an anaemic tomato. He was the kind of guy people never took much notice of until it was too late.

Everybody took notice of Pat, though. His brother was thirty-four, tall, lean-built, his dark hair already shot through with grey at the temples. Like Frank, Pat's eyes were brilliant blue, set above a broken nose he wore well. He carried himself with the quiet confidence of a sociopath. Back in the day people used to say Pat and Leo could pass as twins, but looking at his brother now, Leo felt like a cheap copy.

He was seriously beginning to regret coming.

'Jay-sus, will you look at what the cat dragged in.'

A hand the size of a shovel dropped onto his shoulder and another squeezed the back of his neck. He wiggled round to find 'Uncle' Sean – no blood relation – towering over him. Six feet four, moustachioed and made from a collection of boulders, Sean was Frank's oldest friend. He was a tough son of a bitch who'd survived a hit in his misspent youth, taking four bullets from close range. Legend had it he drove himself to the hospital, sloshing blood from the various holes, parked the car and walked to the reception area before collapsing through the sliding doors onto the welcome mat. Everyone felt full sure he would die. He didn't. Everyone should have known better.

'Hello, Sean. It's good to—'

'How long's it been, you little shit?' Sean wrapped his arms around him, lifted him clean off the ground and squeezed.

Leo, with his face pressed against the massive chest, was rendered incapable of reply. Mercifully, Sean set him down before he smothered, though not without a slap on the shoulder so hard he staggered a little.

'Too long, son, too long, that's what. Let me have a look at you!' He gripped Leo's shoulder's and peered at him intently. 'Jaysus, you're a fierce skinny streak of piss.'

'Give over.'

'And you're back a while, I hear?'

'I am.'

'And you haven't come to see me?'

'I've been flat out, in fairness. I'm opening a restaurant.'

'So I hear. In Gina's old place?'

'That's right.'

'And how's it going?'

'Still early days.'

'Now, tell me this and tell me no more: are you still doing a bit of boxing?'

'I don't get much time to go to the gym.'

'Now that's a pity,' Sean said. 'I still have the place down in Ringsend if you ever fancy a training session. By God you used to be a grand little belter. Remember that fight with what's-his-face? The knock-kneed little yoke from Limerick?' Sean raised a fist the size of a Christmas ham and pretended to jab with it.

'Johnny Clark.'

'That's *right*! That was some fight, wasn't it? By Christ, you lifted him out of it, so you did. Lifted him.'

Leo nodded. Yeah, he remembered the fight. He'd broken Johnny Clark, broken him long before the first bell. Johnny's eyes were rattling in his skull by the third, and they'd fought for six. The fight should have been stopped – Leo had known it, so had Johnny's corner, but Johnny's old man was another hard-chaw like Frank, the type who would rather let his son suffer than throw in the towel. And suffer he did, the poor kid. Even now Leo remembered the misery and despair on his face as each bell rang and Johnny staggered out from the corner, trying to decide which one of Leo to aim a fist towards.

Pat sidled up, with Tommy one step behind him. His brother wore a well-cut charcoal suit and a matt silver shirt Leo immediately coveted. Tommy, dressed more casually in black jeans and a black polo shirt, boasted a number of shaving nicks. They didn't improve him any.

'Boys, look who I found hiding in the weeds,' Sean said.

'Patrick.' Leo inclined his head.

'Leopold.' Pat stirred his bloody mary with a swizzle stick. 'Shall I go tell the kitchen to prepare the fattened calf?'

'I'll survive without it. How's it going, Tommy? Long time no see. How are the fam—?'

Tommy turned on his heel and walked away.

Leo grinned, unoffended by the snub. The human tomato was letting him know in no uncertain terms that the only place he'd bury the hatchet was right between Leo's eyes, given half the chance. That was the thing with Tommy: at least you always knew where you stood with the ginger shite.

'The fizz not to your liking?' Pat said, eyeing the champagne glass, the contents of which Leo hadn't touched.

'It's fine. Where's the birthday girl?'

'No doubt timing her grand entrance.'

'Is Liam here? I didn't see him.'

'Not yet.' Pat took a sip of his drink. 'Sean, how was your golf trip?'

'Miserable. It rained five days out of seven, would you believe it?'

The three men stood chatting about an array of safe subjects – weather, sports, roads, work, back to weather – carefully avoiding anything too personal, laughing in all the right places like seasoned actors. Despite the charade, Leo was almost relaxed by the time he heard a sprinkling of applause and caught sight of his father and Jackie winding their way through the crowd.

Leo got a shock. Frank had changed: he looked older, diminished, somehow. The last time Leo had seen him he had looked as he always did: tall and trim, with a head full of silver hair. Leo had once heard him described as the Irish Blake Carrington, a description that had fit him to perfection. But now he was a shadow of his former self.

Leo watched him pause to talk to a fat man in an ill-fitting suit. Frank clapped the man on the shoulder, laughing, smiling, making a great show of pressing the flesh: still Mr Smooth, Mr Charisma, a blue-eyed barracuda with a master's degree in bluff; everyone's friend, everyone's go-to guy. It wouldn't have surprised Leo one iota if someone had suddenly whipped out a baby for him to kiss. That was the thing: everyone loved his father, this self-made man from the streets, beloved graduate of the school of hard knocks. Except nobody really knew Frank Kennedy, least of all those who thought they did.

But Leo knew him. He'd seen behind the façade a long time ago. The real Frank Kennedy was a stone-cold killer.

45

Jackie, eagle-eyed as ever, spotted Leo first and held up a finger to let him know she was aware of his presence and would be right over. He watched her hug a woman in a blue dress and accept a kiss on the cheek from a toupee-wearer, wondering, as he had often done, what the hell a woman like her ever saw in a man like Frank.

That evening Jackie wore a coral silk blouse and cream linen pants that hung as though draped by a courtier moments before she'd stepped into the room. Her ash-blonde hair was twisted into a French knot worn low at the nape of her neck, and pearls dangled from her earlobes. If he hadn't known she was sixty, he would never have guessed she was a day over forty-five, though he suspected she had a little subtle outside help to keep it that way.

She approached the group, her hands extended at waist level. 'Leo!' Her voice was warm and harmonious, welcoming.

'Hey, Jackie. Happy birthday.'

'Thank you. I'm so glad you came.'

'I'm so glad I was asked.'

Her eyes twinkled; Leo smiled to soften the sting and stepped forward to meet her. They exchanged kisses, one on each cheek.

'You look—' she began.

'Malnourished?'

'I was about to say very handsome. The longer hairstyle suits you.'

'In that case I should have let you finish.'

She raised a hand and placed it flat against his cheek. Leo tried not to laugh. It was a practised move, he thought, a little uncharitably, a gesture worthy of a diplomat. See, she told the room with that gentle touch of her skin, the black sheep has been welcomed back to the fold. So behave.

'It *is* good to see you.'

'And you. You look fantastic. Nice party. Pat wasn't kidding, it's very swish.'

'Swish?'

Pat took a sip of his drink. 'Well, it is, isn't it?'

'Now, don't blame me, blame your father. I wanted something simple, just family, a few friends—'

'A couple of pints down the local, some cocktail sausages in baskets,' Pat said.

Jackie ignored him. 'Sean, how lovely to see you. How was Marbella – did you play well?'

Leo watched her and Sean exchange pleasantries, only half listening. He was finding the sudden immersion into the family strange, but not unpleasant.

His feelings about Jackie were complicated. Cancer had taken his mother when he was fourteen, and her passing left Frank a broken, angry man who drank too much, smoked too much, ate the wrong foods and rarely slept a full night. Jude had been dead two years when Frank met Jackie at the Galway Races, already a widow and wealthy in her own right. She had thrown Frank a lifeline and he had grabbed it with both hands.

It wasn't that Leo begrudged them their happiness. It wasn't that their happiness dishonoured the memory of his mother. But Jackie's arrival had coincided with a lot of his own … unravelling, and as much as he did not hold her personally responsible for what had gone down, neither did he absolve her entirely.

'Is Liam here?' Jackie asked, looking around. 'I don't see him anywhere.'

'Not yet,' Pat replied. 'I'll give him a shout.'

She smiled, but still glanced at her watch pointedly. 'Please do, your father would like to make a toast at eight.'

Pat stepped away to make the call.

Jackie turned her full attention to Leo. 'Tell me, how are things going with the business? I read that charming piece in the paper. Bocht … am I pronouncing the name correctly?'

'You are.' Leo grinned again, enjoying her enormously. She'd been keeping tabs and wanted him to know it, but politely, in true Jackie fashion.

'I must say I'm intrigued by your menu.'

'I'm aiming for old school with a modern twist: shirred eggs, coddle, liver, tongue, mutton, tripe, kippers, whelks, that kind of thing.'

'Sounds offal.'

She squeezed his arm and he laughed at her terrible joke.

'I'm hoping people will get a kick out of it.'

'I'm sure they will. I'd like to come sample it myself some time.'

'*You'd* always be welcome,' he replied, glancing over her shoulder towards Frank, who had yet to acknowledge his presence.

'No answer,' Pat said, on return. 'I'll try him again in a minute.'

'I hope he won't be too late.' Jackie tilted her head, her eyes travelling towards her husband, who was shaking the hand of a man Leo thought he recognised from the television.

'He'll be here.'

There was an edge to Pat's voice. Leo heard it clear as a bell. He glanced at him quizzically, but Pat was watching the crowd.

'Oh, here's your father now,' Jackie said, flitting away from the group to meet him.

'What's wrong?' Leo asked Pat, who pretended he didn't hear the question.

'Bloody hell.' Frank shot the cuffs of his shirt from beneath his jacket and smoothed back the wings of his hair. 'That gobshite would talk paint off a wall with a few drinks on him.'

'Frank,' Jackie said, taking him by the arm. 'Leo is here.'

Frank appraised Leo with the same type of look he might give the taxman. 'Where did they put the rest of you?'

'Excuse me?'

'I've seen fatter whippets.'

'It's good to see you too,' Leo said, beginning to feel self-conscious and defensive about his weight. Had he really lost that much?

'Good turnout,' Pat said.

'Not bad, not bad. How'ya, Sean.' Frank nabbed a passing waiter. 'Get us a drink there, would you, son? Jameson, one cube of ice, that fizzy shit gives me heartburn.' He looked around, scowling. 'Where's Liam? Give him a shout, find out what's holding him up. Bloody pup, I told him to be here on time.'

Rather than argue, Pat got out his phone again.

Jackie kept Frank distracted until his drink arrived. Frank took the glass and raised it. 'To Jackie.'

'To Jackie,' they replied in unison, lifting glasses in response.

Frank emptied half of his in one gulp and noticed Leo still hadn't touched the champagne. 'If you don't want that muck, go get yourself a proper drink at the bar – there's an open tab.'

'It's fine. I'm driving anyway.'

'Have a proper drink, for God's sake. You don't need to drive – I have rooms booked.'

'I won't be staying.'

Frank absorbed this for a moment. Jackie fiddled with one of her earrings, her smile a little strained.

'Suit yourself,' Frank said after a moment. He drained the rest of his drink, put the empty glass down on a passing tray, slipped his hands into his pockets and rocked back on his heels. Leo recognised the signs of an approaching gale and mentally brought the shutters down.

Incoming.

'So, you opened a restaurant in Gina's old place.'

'That's right.'

'Surprised you didn't put it on the market.'

'Me too.'

'All going according to plan?'

'For the most part.'

'I read that bit you had in the paper. Queer sort of food you're serving, if you ask me.'

Leo smiled thinly. The strain of being polite was already starting to chafe. But everyone seemed to be interested in the exchange – even Tommy, who had materialised again like a bad penny behind Pat's shoulder.

'I'd hardly call it queer.'

'Wouldn't be mad for eels and all that guff.'

'That's a small part of the menu; the aim is to provide something different.'

'And tripe? Sure who in their right mind would eat that?'

'You'd be surprised.'

'I would that.' Frank guffawed. 'Wouldn't feed it to a dog.'

'It's not for everyone.'

'Eels?' Sean looked a little queasy. 'Tripe?'

'I think it's quite daring,' Jackie said. 'People get so bored eating the same thing all the time – it's nice to have a variety.'

'Nothing wrong with steak and chips,' Frank said. 'What are you calling it again? Booked?'

'Bocht.' Leo felt the first twinge of a headache. 'You see, the menu is … well, what I'm aiming to do is recreate predominately traditional Irish recipes served with a modern twist and—'

'All sounds a bit gimmicky to me.' Frank rocked back on his heels again and winked at Sean. 'Eels. Did you ever hear the like in all your born days?'

'You know, I think I will get that drink. Excuse me.' Leo left them and made his way to the bar, fuming.

Gimmicky. From a man who drank instant coffee and liked three teaspoons of sugar on his cornflakes.

Gimmicky.

The exchange unleashed a flood of unpleasant memories. Like the time Frank took a mad notion to parent and decided to attend one of Leo's football matches to lend his 'support', then stood on the sideline roaring and shouting abuse at the referee, making a holy show of Leo, who was mortified. On the way home he'd driven like a maniac and lectured Leo on all the mistakes he had made during the game; cribbing and going on and on about tactics until Leo grew sick to the teeth of listening to him and vowed there and then he'd quit the team. The next day he told the coach he was done playing, and to his dismay it seemed like the coach was relieved to hear it.

Oh yes, good times.

He ordered a sparkling water with a splash of lime and was glowering at it when Pat set his bloody mary down on the bar beside him. 'You all right?'

'Peachy.'

Pat turned and leaned both elbows on the bar to watch the room, an old habit Leo had forgotten about. 'You know what your problem is, Leo?'

'That I think people who use parsley as a garnish should be shot into the sun?'

'You're too quick to take offence. Too thin-skinned.'

'I didn't lick that off a bush.'

'You know he's winding you up.'

'I'm not a bloody clock, Pat.' He sipped some of his water. 'Look, about the suite—'

'Like Frank said, the rooms are booked. Someone will make use of it if you won't.'

Leo glanced at his brother's profile and felt a rare quiver of fraternal affection. 'So, how are things with you?'

'Same old, same old.'

'Are you seeing anyone?'

'No.' Pat took out his phone, glanced at the screen and put it away.

'How's business?' Leo asked.

'Ticking along.'

The fraternal affection quivered to a halt. Leo watched the bubbles in his drink fizz and plink while he tried to think of something else to talk about and came up empty.

Pat's phone chirped. He glanced at the screen and frowned. 'Excuse me.'

He abandoned his drink and walked off. The next time Leo saw him, he was talking to Frank, his head angled in such a way it was all but impossible to read his lips. The conversation was short. Frank patted Pat on the cheek and then Pat was cutting through the crowd on his way towards the doors with Tommy on his heels.

Sensing trouble, Leo hurried to catch up to him. 'What is it? What's going on?'

'Nothing for you to worry about, enjoy the party.' He pushed through the door and was gone.

Across the crowded room Frank climbed up onto the small sound stage and waved the band into silence. He took the microphone from the lead singer and tapped it a few times until everyone was quiet. With little preamble he thanked them all for coming, said he hoped they were having a great evening and asked that they join him in wishing Jackie a wonderful celebration. The whole thing took less than a minute and he was gone before the quartet finished playing a jaunty version of 'Happy Birthday'.

Leo walked back to Jackie, but it was clear from her expression of complete bewilderment she was none the wiser. 'What is going on?' she asked. 'Where did Pat go?'

'I have no idea,' Leo replied.

Not a word of it a lie.

46

Emmet Quinn didn't see the person on the side of the road until the last possible second. He swerved, clipped them with his wing mirror, braked hard and came to a stop several hundred feet further on, gripping the steering wheel as hard as he could.

'Holy Mary, mother of God.'

He switched off the engine, got out of the van on shaky legs and jogged back up the road. It was empty.

He found a girl lying on her back in a tangle of briars, half in, half out of the ditch. 'Oh mother of God, mother of God. What were you doing standing in the middle of the road? Oh mother of God.'

The girl blinked and looked at him. Her face was covered in blood.

'Don't move, I'll call an ambulance.'

'No.'

'What?'

She raised a tiny, pale hand towards him. 'Help me.'

'You shouldn't move, you might be hurt worse than you think.'

'Help me', she said again.

Emmet looked around, but this stretch of road was quiet with little traffic. Convinced he was making a mistake, he reached down and caught her hand with two of his and hauled her to her feet. It was then he realised the blood was not fresh, she had no shoes on and her clothes were several sizes too big for her.

'What happened to you?' He looked around again. 'What are you doing out here in the middle of nowhere? Where are your shoes?'

'Dublin,' she said. 'Dublin.'

'You're from Dublin? Is that it?'

She began to sway, her eyes rolled up. She would have fallen if he hadn't caught her.

'Hold on there, hold on there now.'

He held her carefully and tried to think. Something wasn't right, he could feel it. He looked at the girl again; she was only a slip of a thing, about the same age as his youngest daughter. And she needed help. 'All right,' he said. 'Come on.'

He walked her down the road and assisted her into the van, where she sat with her head back against the seat, her eyes shut. Emmet hesitated, then grabbed the seatbelt. When he drew it over her body, she opened her eyes and put her hand on top of his.

'Thank you.'

He nodded, clipped the seatbelt into the lock and went around to the driver's side and started the engine. Before he pulled out, he looked in the rear-view mirror, his heart still beating uncomfortably fast in his chest. As he drove away, he touched the religious medal around his neck and offered up a silent prayer. Another inch and he would have killed her, of that he was certain. God had been watching over him, guiding the wheel, protecting him. He would not let the Lord down.

'There's a flask of tea and a chicken fillet roll in a bag behind you there,' he said. 'If you're hungry.'

She shook her head.

'Are you hurt?'

'Yes.'

'If you don't mind my asking, what happened to you at all? Were you attacked? Is that it?'

'Yes.'

'Do you want to go to the guards, the police?'

'No.'

She closed her eyes. Emmet saw she was trembling and turned the heat up. All wrong, this was all wrong.

'Whereabout in Dublin do you need to go?'

'Dublin,' she said again.

'Dublin's a big place, love, Can you narrow it down a little bit for me?'

'Trinity.'

'The college, is it? You're a student there?'

'Trinity,' she repeated, and fell asleep.

47

Back at the Glenmore Lodge, the mood had turned sombre, so, shortly after, Leo decided to call it a night and hit the road. He couldn't find Frank or Sean anywhere to say he was leaving, but Jackie said she would pass on his goodbyes. She looked positively miserable, and Leo felt sorry for her that her birthday should have come to this.

The second he hit the M50 he put his foot to the floor, testing the powerful engine to maximum capacity and hoping he wouldn't get caught in a speed trap. He wasn't entirely sure where he was going or what he was doing, but he was certain something was wrong, something that involved his younger brother.

He swung the Ford onto the slip road heading towards the Tallaght turn-off, turned right over the bridge and throttled towards Rathfarnham, where Liam lived in a two-bedroom townhouse in an estate off Stocking Lane. He'd been there once several years before, but he found it easily enough, especially since there was an ambulance with flashing lights parked on the street directly outside.

'What the—'

Pat's Jeep was parked haphazardly behind Liam's Honda CR-V, the driver's door hanging open.

Fear and dread rising in his throat, Leo got out, raced across the street, up the drive and into the house. He glanced left and saw

Tommy standing in the living room with a younger man he didn't recognise. He was sitting on the sofa with his head in his hands.

'Where is he?'

'Upstairs.'

Leo took the stairs three at a time and raced down the landing. Liam's room was at the back of the house. Pat was standing in the doorway with his back to him, blocking the view.

'Pat?'

Pat turned. Until his dying day Leo would never forget the look on his face.

'Pat?'

'Wait, Leo, don't go—'

Leo shoved him aside.

Liam was on the floor, between his bed and the en-suite bathroom, with two paramedics on their knees beside him. One of the men was pumping air into Liam's mouth with a balloon; the other man was attaching an IV drip to Liam's right arm.

'What happened?'

'He overdosed,' Pat said quietly. 'He tried to fucking kill himself.'

Leo backed out of the room and leaned forward with his hands on his knees, his eyes shut tight.

Breathe, breathe.

He felt Pat's hand on his back. 'It's okay, it's okay. He's going to be okay.'

Leo snapped upright, roiling with fury. Without even being aware of what he was doing, he punched Pat as hard as he could, knocking him backwards against the bannister. Pat shook his head, blinked and tried to get up, but his legs would not support him.

'Don't you touch me,' Leo said, his voice shaking. 'You could have stopped this – you could have done something.'

He went downstairs, meeting Tommy – who had heard Pat fall and was coming up to see what was going on – halfway. Seeing Pat on the ground, Tommy grabbed Leo by the throat and slammed him against the wall. 'You stupid prick—'

'Tommy!' Pat caught the top railing and used it to drag himself upright. 'Stop it. Leave him go.'

Tommy's eyes were murderous, but his fingers dropped away. Leo ran down the stairs and kept going until he reached his car.

Later he would remember nothing about the drive back to Aungier Street or how he parked his car. Or the trip to the off-licence or the walk back to Gina's. He remembered the taste of the first glass, the warm, familiar burn in his chest as he poured his second. The voice started on his third, so he put on some music to drown it out. His fourth was good, his fifth better. Nick Cave chased the voice from his head, kicking its arse with splendid accuracy. Leo lay on Gina's bed and watched lights from the traffic below dance across the wall in time to the beat, and he drank until his mind waved the white flag and gave in.

48

At age nine, Robbie Fox was a year younger than his cousin Jimmy, but the boys were the same height and build and could have easily passed for twins.

Early on Saturday morning, Robbie called to Jimmy's house for a planned excursion. They endured a short lecture about the rules of the road from Jimmy's mam before they left the house and cycled down to the river, seeking the bend where Jimmy's dad said he had spotted an otter the previous week. Neither boy had ever seen an otter in real life and they were very excited at the prospect of seeing one and capturing it, though neither of them was sure an otter would make a good pet, assuming they were allowed keep it.

Which, they both agreed, was unlikely.

The river was a mile and a half from Jimmy's house, and by the time they'd reached it, the weather had turned cold and it was drizzling slightly. Robbie didn't mind the cold, but the rain got on his nerves and he was sorry he hadn't listened to *his* mam and worn a better jacket.

They cycled down a path and turned in to an overgrown picnic area, where they hopped off their bikes and left them hidden in the long grass.

'Come on!' Jimmy said, racing ahead, forcing Robbie to sprint if he wanted to catch up. Jimmy did this a lot, take off without warning, and Robbie, who was naturally quick, had figured out he did it to make sure he was always first.

The grass gave way to the riverbank, made muddy by the rain.

'There's the sad tree.' Jimmy pointed to a large willow on the opposite bank. 'That's where daddy said he saw him. He said he was as big as a dog.'

'What kind of dog?'

'How should I know?' Jimmy said, as if this was the stupidest question he had ever heard.

Annoyed, Robbie walked down the waterline, searching for tracks. He had looked up otter footprints on his dad's computer and wanted to be the first one to identify them.

He walked around for a little while, bending here and there to closer inspect some marks; most were dog tracks and some were from birds. He noticed several that *might* be otter tracks, though looking at them now he was unsure (they were much more defined on the computer). Then on a sharp slope next to a bed of rushes he found a distinct trail leading to the water.

'Jimmy, look!'

He looked up, but his cousin had vanished.

'Jimmy?'

He made his way down to the shoreline and stood looking left and then right. He caught a flash of movement and ran that way, feet slipping and sliding over the wet, slippery stones.

Jimmy was standing with his back to him, ankle-deep in freezing water. This section of the river was narrow, and a recent storm had washed some of the bank away, causing several trees to topple into the water. The current was running fast and hard and Robbie was alarmed when he saw Jimmy begin to wade out a little further, the water rising dramatically around his jeans until it was almost to his waist and tugging him hard.

'Jimmy, stop! What are you doing?'

Jimmy turned towards him and Robbie suddenly felt very scared. Jimmy's face looked weird; he didn't seem like himself at all.

'Jimmy?'

'There's a man in the water,' Jimmy said, and his voice sounded so strange all the hairs on the back of Robbie's neck stood straight up. 'He's floating, Robbie, he's floating.'

49

It was still dark when Celestine woke. She lay on the wooden pallet for a while, listening to the wind whip around the building, rattling the rooftop.

She had been very good and kept her head down. It was time to do things her way.

She tossed the sleeping bag off, stood up and immediately needed to pee. There were two toilets in the building, but only one of them worked, and that meant going downstairs.

The lamps hummed as she passed beneath them, the smell of the plants overpowering. More had bloomed overnight, but they were not nice flowers like roses or daffodils; Celestine thought they were very ugly and could not understand why the man wanted so many of them.

When she was done, she washed her hands and drank some water from the sink, wrinkling her nose at the taste. After a moment she splashed her face, wiping the sleep from her eyes with wet fingers. There was a mirror, but it was old and speckled and only one of the bathroom bulbs worked, so she couldn't get a good look at her reflection. Still, she tried to comb her hair as best she could with her fingers. Celestine did not really care about her hair or her looks, but Yulia was very strict about being clean and tidy; she said hygiene was important.

When the watch beeped, she checked that all the bulbs were

working in the lamps and turned up the heat by five degrees. She found she could hardly concentrate and burned her fingers twice. A blister rose on her index finger. She looked at it in fascination.

When she was small, a man had thrown a cup of coffee over her. The liquid scalded her and hurt so badly she fainted. Yulia did not discover what had happened until she returned home, and by this stage Celestine's skin was already blistered and weeping. Celestine did not remember if she saw a doctor or not, but Yulia put creams and lotions on her skin every day until the pain went away.

Some skin had grown back, but never quite the same as it had been before.

The morning passed. Celestine checked the watch too often and grew irritated and upset at how long each minute seemed to take. She was hungry too, more than hungry. Her jeans, she'd noticed, were no longer tight and they sagged around the knees and waist.

She was upstairs in the office watching a black and white film about cowboys when she heard the sound of a vehicle pull up outside. The factory's metal door began to rise. Quickly Celestine rolled up her sleeping bag, grabbed her things and went downstairs.

The man drove the van inside, got out and waited until the doors were all the way down again. He nodded to her and began to inspect the plants, talking on a mobile phone as he moved up and down the rows. Celestine watched his lips carefully; was he happy with the plants? With her? How could she tell? His face was as unfriendly as ever.

When he was done with the call, he put the phone back in his pocket and snipped a flower from a nearby plant. Celestine watched him crush it in his hand and smell it.

He looked at her and said words. She stared at him blankly, even when he gave her a thumbs-up.

He tossed the flower back into a plant and walked back to the van. He opened the passenger door, removed a white plastic bag with blue writing on the side from the floor and tried to thrust it into her hands. Celestine looked at the bag but made no effort to take it, so he dropped it on the ground next to her feet.

He said words and waved his hands around a bit. Celestine pointed at the metal door.

The man shook his head.

Celestine tapped her chest and pointed at the door again. She had been good. She had kept her 'head down' and done her job.

She wanted to see Yulia.

The man shook his head and began to walk around to the other side of the van. Celestine followed. She made a sound to get his attention, tapped her chest and pointed to the door.

The man caught her by her shoulders and moved her physically to one side. Celestine grabbed the front of his jacket, grunting. A backhand blow caught her high across the cheek, hard and unexpected. It knocked her off her feet. Bright lights bloomed, sounds hissed.

The man was pointing a finger in her face, spittle flying, so angry his face went dark red. Celestine's ears were ringing. She shook her head to clear them but somehow that only made them worse.

Abruptly, the man stopped yelling and reached out a hand to her. Celestine flinched and turned her head away. There was blood in her mouth, copper-tasting like the old coins she used to fish out of the fountain in the village square, people pointing and laughing at her until Yulia yelled at them to leave her alone.

The man gave up. He got into the van, opened the door and reversed out.

Celestine crawled over to the wall and pressed her body against the cold concrete. Beyond the door, she glimpsed several buildings; they were white, single-storey, some with cars parked outside.

People.

The door came down and the automatic lock clicked. She heard the van accelerate away.

In the sudden silence, she pulled her legs up to her chin and rocked herself from side to side, her eyes squeezed shut.

After a while, she got to her feet, spat the blood from her mouth and picked up the bag the man had left. It contained a loaf of white bread and a variety of cooked meats in plastic packets and a plastic packet of pre-sliced red cheese.

At the bottom of the bag she found a six-pack of cola and a packet of popcorn. At the sight of them Celestine started to cry.

She cried so hard her stomach hurt and her nose got completely blocked. But try as she might, she could not stop crying, not even when there were no more tears left to fall.

50

Leo woke up with a groan.

He was, he discovered when gingerly he sat up, still wearing his suit. Now it really looked as though he had slept in it.

Events from the previous day surfaced through his groggy subconscious as he leaned down and picked his phone off the floor, where it had slipped off the bed at some stage. He saw the empty bottle of Jim Beam and tried very hard indeed not to vomit.

His phone had zero battery left. Very slowly he got up and plugged it into the single remaining working power source on the other side of the room, with one hand raised over his face for protection.

The electricity gods were smiling on him that morning: nothing sparked, fizzed or exploded.

He left it charging and staggered down the hall to the bathroom. On the way back, he heard it ringing and snatched it up. It was Eddie.

'Well? How did the reunion go? Was there bloodshed?'

He told her what happened.

'Jesus Christ, Leo. I warned you, didn't I? What the hell is it with you? Are you trying to mess this chance up too?'

'Eddie wait, I—'

She'd already hung up.

Leo grimaced. He thought about calling her back but what was there to say: she was right. He called Pat instead.

'What?'

'Well?'

'Well what?'

'I was calling to see if you knew the price of llama wool in Tibet. Don't be such a dick all your life. How is he?'

'Awake, angry, in denial. I tried to convince him to go back to the treatment facility.'

'That's great.'

'He told me to go fuck myself.'

'So where is he now?'

'Your guess is as good as mine. He wouldn't stay in the hospital, got one of his mates to come pick him up.'

'Idiot.' Leo caught sight of himself in the mirror over the dresser and looked away again. The pot calling the kettle black was too much to bear. 'I'm sorry I hit you.'

'I'm sorry you hit me too. I've meetings all next week and a jaw the size of a brick.'

'Did he mean to do it, Pat?'

'What?'

'Did he mean to overdose?'

'How should I know?' Pat exhaled. 'He's been killing himself slowly for years; maybe he decided to speed things up.'

'It's not his fault,' Leo said.

'No,' Pat said quietly. 'Apparently it's mine.'

Pat hung up. Leo looked at the phone for a long time, feeling sick to his stomach. Despite their differences, Pat was still his brother. The same brother he'd built cushion forts with on rainy days; the brother who'd punched Mickey Mullins in the eye for stamping on Leo's lunch bag; the brother who had taken him by the hand and brought him for a long walk around the grounds of

St Luke's on the morning their mother breathed her last and held him as he wept.

Leo phoned Liam; it went straight to voicemail: 'Yo, don't bother leaving a message, I won't listen.'

Leo hung up and tossed the phone on the bed.

I won't listen.

Yep, Leo thought, It should be the Kennedy motto.

51

Mariposa arrived at Ivan Dolan's outer office shortly before eleven a.m., in a cloud of Shalimar, her crazy hair piled on top of her head like a crow's nest and sprayed into submission with industrial strength hairspray. Ivan watched her look around the room the moment Martha showed her in, saw the open disdain in her expression and wondered what the hell she had been expecting.

He rose to greet her, smiling, because Martha was looking at Mariposa like she was some kind of exotic creature recently escaped from a private collection. They didn't get much peacock feathers around their way.

'Come in,' he said, waving her towards a chair. 'What will you have? Tea? Coffee?'

'Never touch the stuff,' Mariposa said, settling herself primly on the proffered seat, placing a handbag the size of a small car battery onto her knees. Her bony legs were encased in fishnets; her shoes were leopard print. No wonder Martha was staring.

'Water?'

'Got anything stronger?'

'No.'

'Then let's not waste time with formalities.' She gave Ivan a sly smile that made his own falter slightly.

'That will be all, Martha, thank you.'

Martha retreated.

Mariposa unbuttoned her coat and looked around her again. 'This is not what I was expecting, thought it would be … classier.'

'It's a working office.'

'Been here long, have you?'

'Three years.'

'Could do with a plant or two, jazz the place up a little.'

'If you've no time for formalities, let's not bother with small talk.' Ivan looked at his watch pointedly. 'You wanted this meeting.'

'Oh now,' she said, waving one heavily bangled wrist. 'Nothing wrong with taking a polite interest.'

'Polite interest?' Under different circumstances Ivan might have admired her scrawny brass neck, but these were not different circumstances. 'There's nothing polite about any of this. What do you want?'

'You've spoken to your brother, I take it?'

'Yes, and he categorically states the girl attacked him and he was defending himself. What happened was a terrible tragedy and a truly awful … inci— accident. He's broken up about it.'

'Well, he would be now, wouldn't he?' She sat back again and regarded him. 'You're a gambling man, aren't you? Like a flutter?'

He glared.

She opened the handbag, took out a phone, turned it on and put it on the table between them.

'What am I supposed to do with that?'

'Look at it.'

He glanced quickly and looked away again.

'That,' she said, tapping the phone with her index finger, 'is the *incident*. Take a good long look for yourself and tell me how you think this particular card would play out in the court of public opinion.'

Reluctantly Ivan reached for the phone. Using his thumb, he flicked through the photos, trying to keep his expression under control, but beneath his pale blue shirt his heart raced and thudded madly.

'Terrible, isn't it?' Mariposa said. 'Young girl like her.'

Ivan put the phone on the desk and slid it back to her, unable to conceal his distaste. 'You can't prove Noel did this.'

'Prove? Dearie me, I don't need to prove a thing. You must think I came down in the last shower, minister. I can assure you I didn't. That girl,' she picked the phone up and put it back in her bag, 'she fought back, plenty of DNA evidence. You say it was an accident, he didn't mean to do it. Well, if you say so, I believe you.' She shrugged. 'Mind you, there's plenty who wouldn't.'

'You'll be done for running a prostitution ring. You'll be finished.'

'Slap on the wrist. A fine, maybe.' She gave him the smile again. 'What could the neighbours say about me that hasn't already been said about me and mine since the dawn of time? But you, on the other hand, you might be something of a surprise.'

'All right, all right, I get the picture.' Ivan ran his hand over his chin. 'You keep threatening me, but what is it that you want?'

'I want half a million euros.'

Despite the circumstances, Ivan actually threw back his head and laughed. 'Only half? Why not a million! Why not two?

'I'm not greedy.'

'You're insane.'

'I don't think I am,' Mariposa said mildly. 'I think I'm being perfectly and utterly reasonable.'

'I don't have that kind of money, and even if I did—'

'I dare say you know how to find it.' She smiled, leaned forward and picked up the framed photo from his desk. 'Lovely-looking family, by the way; what age is this one?' She turned the photo back towards him, one dark red talon tapping the glass over Sophie's smiling face. 'Not much younger than the girl your brother brutally killed, I'd say.'

Ivan felt a surge of hatred so powerful his hands began to shake. More than anything in the world he wanted to get up, put those hands around Mariposa's chicken neck and squeeze until she was dead. The desire was so intense it frightened him. He'd never felt an emotion like it in all his born days. 'Put that down.'

Mariposa put the photo back where she found it.

'How do you expect me to—?'

'A half a million is a good price for freedom, yours and mine. You're a smooth-talker, Ivan. I'm sure you'll find a way.'

Ivan felt the noose drop around his neck.

One clean break, that's all he had ever wanted, one clean break.

Now he was deeper in the hole than ever.

'I will have freedom, minister,' Mariposa said. 'One way or the other, someone will pay for what happened to that girl. Your choice, of course, but if I were you, I'd think long and hard about what you have to protect, what you have to lose.'

Ivan looked down at his desk, breathing hard. If he agreed to this, she would have a hold on him for the rest of his life. A better man would throw her out of the office and call the guards. Let the chips fall where they may.

A better man wouldn't be in this situation in the first place.

God damn you, Noel.

'How will you play your hand, minister?' Mariposa was watching him like a hawk.

He glanced at the photo on his desk. Olive had taken it over the summer at one of her brother's barbecues. His daughters were sitting at a picnic table with their cousins, all of them haring into a bowl of spicy chicken wings. Polly's face was smeared in hot sauce. Sophie was smiling broadly, squinting a little in the bright summer sun.

His girls.

'You're an evil bitch.'

Mariposa smiled. There was lipstick on her teeth. 'It's a man's world, Mr Dolan. I'm only making my way in it.'

52

Agatha Tulic was pushing the cleaning cart into the lift when she heard someone call her name.

She stopped and looked behind her and tried not to let her irritation show on her face when she saw Rubin, the assistant manager, walking towards her, his heels clicking on the foyer floor.

'Agatha, how many times do I have to tell you, this lift is for paying guests. How do you think it looks, people having to share space with this.' He flapped a hand at her little cart with as much disdain as his fingers could muster.

Agatha frowned. The lift was empty, the foyer was empty, there was no one around to notice what lift she used.

'I am sorry, Mr Tolle, but work lift is not work.'

'What?'

'Work lift, is not …' She took a breath; English was not her first language, it wasn't even her second, but she struggled on. 'Is stop on floor eleven.'

'Stopped?'

'Yes.'

'Well, then you go up to floor eleven and you unstop it.' He grabbed her cart, yanked it backwards and turned it around.

Agatha nodded and stepped into the lift.

'No, put this away first – you can't leave it here. My God, Agatha, what goes on in that head of yours?'

When she got out he poked her forehead with his index finger. Agatha wanted to grab his finger and snap it in half.

'Put this away first. Honestly, woman, this is not a Travelodge.'

Thin-lipped with fury, Agatha caught the cart handles, pushed it out of the foyer and stored it in the little room under the stairs. Why did he always do that, talk to her like she was a simpleton? The other assistant and the actual manager never treated her with anything other than polite indifference, but Rubin seemed to delight in embarrassing and belittling her at every opportunity.

Unwilling to suffer another encounter with him, she took the stairs and climbed the eleven floors, reaching the service elevator slightly winded.

Someone had left the security cage door open. She got in and closed it and pressed G.

When she got out on the ground floor, she was dismayed to find Rubin there waiting for her with a face of thunder.

'Agatha, this is not a drop-in centre.'

She blinked. There were so many things the hotel was not, it was hard to keep up sometimes.

'Mr Tolle?'

'Personal business is not to be conducted during business hours.' He peered down his nose at her, but Agatha hadn't a notion what he meant, until he rolled his eyes and stalked off, beckoning her to follow, but not waiting to see if she did or not.

53

Murray heard the crunch of tyres on gravel. He stood up and walked through the garage, stepping into the darkening day as two men got out of a blue Hyundai. It was the same cops as before, Maken and Flood. He lit a cigarette to calm his nerves, even though he had been expecting them.

'You found it, then?'

'Found?' Maken asked. 'Found what?'

'One of the vans was stolen out of this yard on Wednesday. I thought that's why you were here, to tell me you'd recovered it. Didn't need to come down, mind, a call would have done the job.' Murray blew a smoke ring. It drifted through the air towards Flood, who batted it away.

'What was the make and model?'

Murray told him.

'How serendipitous,' Maken said. 'That's exactly the van we located. Unfortunately, I have some terrible news for you: whoever stole your van used it in the process of a crime and then burned it out.'

'Yeah? Insurance won't be happy, but that's their problem, I suppose.'

'You haven't asked what the crime was,' Flood said. 'Most people would want to know.'

'I'm not most people.'

'When did you see it last?' Maken asked.

'I came to work the day before yesterday and it was gone.'

'Did you make a report?'

'Course I did. Yesterday.'

'You waited a whole day to report it stolen?'

'I wasn't sure it was stolen until then. I thought maybe the nephew had borrowed it.'

'Does he normally borrow things without letting you know?'

'Sometimes.'

Maken looked around; the yard was crammed full of old cars and bits of old cars; a proper old-school scrapyard of a kind that were as rare as hen's teeth.

'I see you have security.' He nodded towards the camera pointing directly at them. 'Did it manage to capture the theft?'

'The van wasn't in the yard, it was parked on the street outside.'

'You said it was stolen from the yard.' Flood spoke for the first time.

'I meant the general vicinity.'

'That's unfortunate. I'd like the see the footage from yesterday all the same, if you wouldn't mind.'

'Got a court order?'

'I can get one.'

'You should do that.'

Maken took a step closer. 'Does the name Conor Stanley mean anything to you?'

Murray tilted his head, as though he was trying to think. 'I knew a Billy Stanley, used to play football with him years ago.'

'We found Stanley's body along with that of a second, as yet unidentified, man in a river not far from where your stolen van was burned out.'

Murray smoked the last of his fag and pitched it into a puddle.

'You don't find that curious?'

'Find what curious?'

'About the bodies.'

'Not really, the way the world's gone.' Murray shook his head. 'Nothing surprises me anymore.'

'It appears Stanley had been tortured.'

'Nasty business.' Murray looked Maken right in the eye. 'Maybe he got in with a bad crowd.'

'Is that what you think happened?'

Murray shrugged. 'Detecting's your line of work. I get paid to fix cars. Speaking of which, I'd better crack on.' He shifted upright. 'I'll need a report, for the insurance, like.'

'I'm surprised you don't remember him,' Maken went on. 'He was a known associate of your cousin Arthur Ward back in the day.'

'Known associate?' Murray grinned.

'They did time together, certainly.'

'Oh well, if everyone Arthur did time with was an associate, half the bleedin' country would be.'

'You still say you don't know him?'

'That's right.'

'I'll need the name of the guard to whom you reported the theft.'

Murray rattled off a name.

'Off the top of your head, just like that,' Maken said, writing it down in his little notebook. 'Impressive.'

'I've a good head for names.'

'Good head for a lot of things, I'd say.'

Murray shrugged again. He was done talking. Maken tipped his index finger to his forehead and he and Flood got back in the Hyundai and reversed slowly out of the yard.

Murray waited until he was certain they were gone and called Duchy. 'It's me,' he said. 'The cops were here … Yeah, they found them … No, not about him, about Stanley. Listen, they're going to be watching me for a while. I think I need to lie low.'

He listened, his face tense.

'Rally? Listen, Duchy, Rally's never … not … She's a kid.' He leaned his hand against the wall, stared at his feet. 'Yeah, yeah, I know she can connect you. Yeah, I know, yeah … I'll tell him.'

He hung up and let his head drop. Murray was not a religious man, nor did he believe in luck or chance, but right at that moment he truly believed in curses.

He looked at the phone and made the call.

'Rally? Yeah, 'member that kid, the one that bit me? Yeah, we need … you need to tidy up that loose string. I know, Duchy said it. I know, yeah, I know. Rally, I know. But it's got to be done. I can't, the cops are all over me.' Murray closed his eyes. 'It is what it is.'

54

'I wonder,' Duchy said, affecting a tone of genteel civility as fake as a three-euro coin, 'if you have given any more thought to my proposal.'

Pat transferred the phone to his left hand, got out of his Jeep and slammed the door. He felt like he hadn't slept in days and his jaw, where Leo had punched him, was huge and throbbing.

'Proposal? Is that what we're calling it?'

'I detect a little note of hostility to your voice, Mr Kennedy. Or can I still call you Pat?'

'You can call me what you like, Ward, but the answer will be the same.'

'What's that, then?'

'Shove your proposal where the sun don't shine.'

'That's a very unfortunate attitude you've taken. I'd reconsider, if I was you. Wouldn't want any harm to come to that little brother of yours, now, would we?'

Pat laughed, genuinely laughed. Some of the workers nearby looked over in surprise. Pat was not known for his jolly nature.

'Harm? Oh, you snaggle-toothed wanker. Oh dear, thanks for that, I needed a good laugh.'

'This is no laughing matter,' Duchy said. 'You and me—'

'There is no you and me, you filthy cockroach. If you come here again I'll cut your head off and bury you in the foundations.'

'You are making a very big mistake.'

'The only mistake I made was not shooting you in the guts when I had the chance.'

'Hard man.' Duchy gave an insincere little snigger. 'We'll see how hard your brother—'

Pat hung up and called Tommy. 'Any trace?'

'No, nobody's seen hide nor hair of him.'

'Did you check with that eejit Baz?'

'First person I called on, said he knew nothing.'

'That I'd well believe.' He climbed the stairs to the office, unlocked the door and went inside. 'Stay on it, he's got to surface at some point.' He hung up again.

Before he sat down, he took several painkillers and drank some water from a plastic bottle, wincing as his tongue sought the tooth the punch had loosened.

He shook his head. There was nothing for it: he'd have to bite the bullet.

What choice did he have?

He reached for his phone and made the call he was hoping he wouldn't have to make. 'Hello, hi, yes,' he said. 'It's Pat Kennedy. Yes.'

He waited, pale, trembling, his eyes shut.

'That's right. I need to make a dental appointment.'

55

Agatha followed Rubin through the same foyer she had so recently been ejected from, her mind in turmoil. Rubin was talking as he walked, but she wasn't paying attention to what he had to say. Someone was looking for her. Immigration? Her paperwork was good, better than good. Had someone made a complaint, sold her out? It was possible, of course it was, but why would anyone single her out? She had made it her business to keep a low profile.

'Not on, Agatha. This is a place of work. I mean, if everyone decided to have people drop by unannounced like this there would be mayhem.'

Rubin stopped at the front door and peered out. 'She refuses to leave until she speaks to you, but Agatha—'

She looked at him.

'I won't hesitate to call the police if she makes any more trouble. And frankly, I feel I need to talk to Jason about your continued employment.' He leaned closer. 'Don't make me the bad guy here, all right?'

He turned on his heel and went off to find someone else to harass.

Agatha pushed through the door and stepped out onto a sun-drenched yet freezing cold Nassau Street. The girl was standing with her body pressed tight against the wall, trying to make herself as small as possible to protect herself against a vicious, biting wind. Her clothes were strange, her hair filthy and she was not wearing any shoes. Agatha felt a burst of relief. A beggar, then. But why had she asked for her by name?

Agatha approached her. 'Hello,' she said. 'You look for me?'

At the sound of her voice the girl turned around. She looked frightened, and exhausted and hurt.

'I found you,' she said in Serbian. 'I found you.'

Hearing the voice, Agatha almost screamed. 'Yulia?'

Yulia fell into her arms, sobbing wildly. Her legs folded under her and she collapsed, taking Agatha down with her.

'Child,' Agatha said, using her mother tongue. 'What have they done to you?' She hugged the girl to her body. 'What have they done to you?'

At that hour of the morning the street was busy, full of people coming and going. Nobody took much notice of the two women, and those that did ignored them and their distress. For this was Dublin on a cold winter's day and people didn't want to get involved, just in case.

56

Pat wasn't expecting the visit, but when he looked up from the ledger he was writing in he didn't appear overly surprised to see Leo enter his office. Leo wondered why that was and decided not being surprised by anything was Pat's default position, that and being unbearably aloof.

'Oh boy,' Leo said when he saw Pat's face. His brother's jaw was swollen, the skin purple and black.

'I should have let Tommy strangle you.'

Leo held up his hands. 'For what it's worth, I'm genuinely sorry.'

'For what it's worth, that means nothing to me. I had to cancel a meeting with a client and you loosened a molar so I'm going to have to go to the bloody dentist and I dislike going to the dentist.'

Leo sat in the visitor's chair Duchy Ward had sat in previously. 'I come in peace.'

'You can go the same way.'

'Pat, please.'

Pat closed the ledger and pinched the bridge of his nose. Aside from the jaw, he looked tired and drawn. Leo felt a sliver of sympathy.

'All right. What?'

'I know where Liam is.'

'How?'

Not where, Leo noticed, how. Wow, he really had a dim view of everyone else.

'I reached out to his friend Baz, the one that was at the house when he, you know—'

'Tried to kill himself.'

'We don't know he was trying to—'

'He injected himself with enough cocaine to stop his heart. Injected, Leo. That's right, right into the vein. Don't sit there and make excuses for him. He knew exactly what he was doing.'

'Okay. Well, like I said, I spoke to Baz and he—'

'How do you know Baz?'

'I don't. I found him from Liam's Instagram page and DMed him.' Leo waited for Pat to say something smart, but he just motioned to Leo to go on talking. 'He said Liam's in Courtown.'

'Courtown? As in County Wexford?'

'Yeah. Apparently his dealer lives there, in a mobile home.'

'You're kidding me.'

'Nope. Says he's crashed there himself once or twice.'

'I've had Tommy looking for him all over the city and the little shit's in Courtown?' Pat scowled. 'Why didn't Baz tell Tommy where he was? He knows we're looking for him.'

'Because he's terrified, scared shitless that if something happens to Liam you're going to have him killed.'

Pat was staring at him with amazement. 'Killed? What the hell does he think I am, some sort of … mob boss?'

'I dunno, but he said he tried to convince Liam to come home, but he wasn't having any of it.'

'Right,' Pat said. He pushed his chair back and got to his feet. 'I've had enough of this.' He took his jacket from a hook on the wall and put it on.

'Where are you going?'

'Courtown.'

'Now?'

'I'm going to stop by Wicklow first.'

Leo raised an eyebrow. 'What for?'

'To get Dad.'

'Why?'

'Because, Leo, this has to stop. I can't keep covering for Liam. All right?'

'I'll come with you.'

Now it was Pat's turn to look surprised.

Leo got to his feet. 'Maybe a united front might make it easier.'

They left the office together and went down the metal stairs.

Pat's scowl deepened. 'Is that Aunt Gina's old car?'

'Yeah.' Leo shrugged a little sheepishly. 'She left it to me in her will.'

'Right,' Pat said, his face a closed book. 'I'll see you at The Elms.'

57

'Hey, wake up.'

Liam opened his eyes.

Pippa was standing over him. She looked angry. A dog was barking close by, rapid barks, punctuated by someone yelling his name.

'There's people outside. They're looking for you.'

'Wha'?'

'I told you. I warned you not to you bring your shit here, bringing trouble to my door. This is my home, man, this is like … some seriously messed-up bullshit.'

Liam could not make head nor tail of what she was talking about. He sat up and instantly regretted it. He wasn't wearing a top and his head felt like it was going to split in two.

'What's going on?'

'Are you deaf? They're outside.' She waved a heavily tattooed arm towards the net-covered windows. 'People. Looking for you.'

'What people?'

'How the hell should I know? Just go out there and get rid of them, will you? Jesus!'

He slid off the bed and stumbled up the narrow hall to the door and opened it outwards. Outside the day was bright and cold. Raffa, Pippa's staffy, was on the raised patio area, tethered to the underside of the mobile home. He was barking furiously at three men standing on the grass next to a Jeep. Liam squinted at them through bloodshot eyes.

'Dad?' He stared at his father and brothers in disbelief. 'What are you doing here?'

'You should be asking yourself the same question,' Frank said. 'Come on, put a shirt on and let's go home.'

'I don't—'

'Get rid of them!' Pippa yelled from inside the mobile.

'Look at the state of you,' Frank said, though his tone was not harsh. 'Come on, son, come on home.'

'No.'

'What are you going to do? Stay here? In this dump?'

'Hey!' Pippa yelled.

Frank started to walk forward, no longer looking at Liam. 'And look at the state of this poor animal,' Frank said, annoyed.

Raffa was straining against the rope, his tail wagging furiously. He was terribly thin, with pressure sores on his ribs. The decking was covered in faeces and stained black from urine. There was no food bowl and only a bucket of disgusting brackish water to drink from.

'That's no way to treat an animal.'

'Dad, don't go near him,' Pat warned. 'He looks vicious.'

'Liam, get rid of those fucking people.'

Frank climbed the steps and approached the barking dog. He leaned forward and let Raffa smell the back of his hand. Raffa's tail was a blur.

'Get away from my dog.' Pippa barged out of the mobile carrying a meat cleaver in her hand. 'Get the hell out of here.'

Frank looked at her, disgusted. He bent down and untied the rope. 'Come on, fella.'

'Hey! That dog is worth five hundred euros,' Pippa yelled. 'If you take him, I'm calling the guards.'

Frank ignored her.

'You're not putting that thing into my Jeep,' Pat said.

Frank walked Raffa down the steps and across the grass and did exactly that. The dog hopped in without hesitation. If anything, he seemed overjoyed by this unusual turn of events.

'I'm calling—'

'Oh, shut up,' Leo said. 'He's taking the dog.'

She glared at him balefully, then turned to Liam. 'You need to leave,' she said, waving the cleaver. 'Pack your shit and get out of here.'

Liam went back inside and came out a few minutes later carrying a pair of runners and a blood-stained T-shirt. 'Pippa, listen—'

She slammed the door in his face. Liam sat down on the damp steps to put his runners down, one of his laces snapped, and without warning he put his head in his hands and started to cry.

'Hey now.' Frank hurried over and put his arms around him. 'It's all right, it's all right. I'm here, we're all here. Everything's going to be all right.'

Liam clung to him, his eyes shut tight. 'I can't do it any more, Dad.'

'Do what, Liam?'

'I can't live with it anymore,' he sobbed. 'It's my fault Niall is dead. I didn't want him to die, I just wanted him to stop.'

Leo stiffened.

'I'm sorry, Dad,' Liam sobbed. 'I didn't—'

'It's all right, it's not your fault.'

Leo remembered seeing Frank drag Uncle Niall's bloody and battered corpse across the patio, his face strained and ghostly in the headlights of the car. Remembered seeing the streaks of blood on the bricks. Remembered the sound of the shovel hitting the frozen earth as Frank dug a hole. Their mother was in Luke's hospital, fading away, one hour, one minute at a time. She died two days later without ever knowing her younger brother had been slaughtered.

'It's all right,' Frank said. He kissed the top of Liam's head. 'We'll get you help; we'll get you straightened out. You don't have to worry.'

'What's he talking about?' Leo asked Pat. 'What's he saying about Niall?'

Pat's mouth was set in a grim line and his jaw looked larger than ever.

'Pat?'

'You weren't the only one.'

'What do you mean?'

'You weren't the only one,' Pat repeated. 'He was a sick, dirty bastard and he got what he deserved.'

Leo felt sick. 'He deserved jail, Pat. He deserved a trial and a jail sentence.' Leo shuddered. 'Frank didn't need to do what he did.'

Pat turned to him. Pat, with his good hair and his neat suits. 'Frank?'

'I saw him, Pat, I saw him dragging Uncle Niall across the yard. I saw what he did to him. I saw him dig the bloody hole.'

'Frank didn't kill Uncle Niall, Leo.'

'I saw the body with my own eyes, Pat. I saw the state of him.'

'You saw Frank take *care* of the body.'

'What?'

'Frank didn't kill Niall, Leo. I did.' He glanced over to where Frank was comforting Liam, talking quietly with his arms around Liam's shoulders.

'Jesus, Pat, why didn't you tell me?'

'That sickness,' Pat said, softly. 'There's only one cure.'

Leo put his hand on Pat's shoulder. 'I'm sorry.'

'Yeah,' Pat said. 'There's a lot of that going around.'

58

They brought Liam to The Elms, where Jackie was waiting. There was a long discussion, more tears, and finally Liam agreed to enter the Children of Lir treatment facility. While Frank made the relevant calls, Leo helped Jackie wash Raffa in the guest bathroom.

'A dog,' she said, lathering the wiggling creature's coat with expensive shampoo. 'What are we supposed to do with a dog?'

'Search me.'

Raffa licked her arm.

'Don't try butter me up,' she said to him. 'I know your sort.'

They rinsed him several times and Leo lifted him out onto a fluffy towel.

'A dog,' Jackie said again, but from the way she carefully dried him Leo suspected the animal was in good hands.

He left Jackie to it and went downstairs. Frank was lighting the fire in the study. Liam was lying on the Chesterfield, asleep, with a grey and blue check blanket over him.

'Where's Pat?'

'Gone,' Frank said. 'He had things to do.' He looked at Leo. 'Did you do that to his jaw?'

Leo nodded.

'Why?'

'I … don't know.' He looked down at Liam. 'Will he be all right, do you think?'

'I don't know,' Frank said. He layered the wood carefully and lit a firelighter. 'I hope so; we'll get that filth out of his body and take it from there.' He got to his feet and slapped his hands together. 'What about you? Will you be all right?'

'I don't know that either,' he said, before heading for home.

Later that day Leo called Eddie and invited her over for what he called an 'apology slap-up'.

'A what?'

'An apology slap-up. I don't know if you are aware of this, but I make the best humble pie in town.'

'I've mentioned this before,' Eddie said, 'but you really are an idiot.'

'How do we feel about pizza and a few cold beers? My treat.'

'Hmm,' Eddie said. 'Pizza sounds more like it.'

'I'll make the call. What do you want on yours?'

'Mushroom, sweetcorn, yellow peppers and pineapple.'

'I'm sorry, but what did you say?'

She repeated it.

'Pineapple … on pizza.'

'Yeah?'

'An abomination.'

'That's rich coming from the guy trying to make coddle hip.'

'Touché.'

Eddie laughed. 'All right, Bosco, I'll be there soon.'

Leo went downstairs, went to the off-licence down the road, ordered the pizza and was sticking four bottles of beer into the freezer to chill them when he heard someone knocking on the restaurant door.

Assuming it was Eddie, he opened it. 'Hey, I was thinking—'

The woman had the palest eyes he had ever seen on a living

human. The strangest sensation of déjà vu hit him; here was the glitch in the matrix. Danger, his tired brain tried to warn him. Danger, you fool. 'I'm sorry, but who—?'

The first punch caught him by surprise, the second split his eyebrow, the third was aimed towards the hinge of his jaw and it was only through the miracle of instinct and muscle memory that Leo managed to get his hands up in time to absorb some of the blow.

He saw the glint of metal on her knuckles as the blonde stepped in close. He dodged a hook and managed to land a clean jab of his own.

She stumbled backwards, touched her hand to her mouth, surprised. Her lip was bleeding.

'Not bad,' she said. 'Fast hands.'

She skipped in and kicked him straight between the legs.

At first there was nothing. No pain, nothing. For a second Leo stood stock still. Then he gasped, his legs collapsed under him, and he fell down. He lay on his side cupping his testicles, trying to breathe, trying desperately to hold still, dreading what was coming next and powerless to do anything to prevent it.

The woman stepped over him. He heard her walk down to the rear of the restaurant and enter the kitchen. She came out and checked the bathroom and the hall.

The first wave of pain hit hard as white fire spread along Leo's stomach to his back. It was so intense he could do nothing but squeeze his eyes shut and try not to vomit or void himself.

The woman came back. She leaned against one of the tables and crossed her legs by her ankles. She had found his mobile phone; she used his face to switch it on and took some photos of him, then a selfie, and pressed send. When she was done she placed the phone on the ground by his head.

'Now we wait, yes?'

Even if he'd wanted to answer her, Leo had neither the capacity for speech nor the will.

'Look at me.'

Slivers of pain travelled up along his guts.

'Don't try be stupid. You have pain,' she said. 'I can make worse.'

She smiled. Her teeth were stained with blood. Leo had never seen a more terrifying sight. In agony, he rolled onto his stomach and tried to crawl towards the front door. He hadn't made it five inches when she brought her foot down on the small of his back, digging her heel into his spine.

'I'd prefer you stay.'

Leo gasped. The pain was so intense he could hardly breathe. The only thing he knew for certain was that this woman could kill him without breaking a sweat and he needed to get away from her.

'Brother call, pain stop.' She ground her heel to the left, then to the right. Leo screamed.

Suddenly the foot was gone. Leo had three seconds of relief, then she slammed it down, catching him hard in the kidneys.

The pain bloomed with a savagery that almost made him wish for death.

He heard his phone ring. The blonde answered it. 'Yes. Is here.'

She put the phone to Leo's ear. He heard Pat's voice: '... harm a hair on his—'

She put the phone to Leo's lips. 'Say words.'

'Pat ...' Leo managed. 'Pat ... she—'

The blonde took the phone away and listened. She laughed and hung up.

She knelt down beside Leo, brought her lips close to his ear. He caught traces of peppermint on her breath. For the rest of his life that smell would make his balls shrivel.

'I go,' she said. 'Tell Pat, make deal.' She flicked his nose with her forefinger, stood up and left.

Leo curled up and pressed his face into the ground. He was still there when Eddie arrived.

'Leo! Oh my God. Leo!'

Darkness gathered around; it was welcome.

'Leo! Oh my God. Leo! Hold on, hold on …'

Darkness beckoned, drawing in, faster now.

Darkness was good.

59

Christopher Dodd, known to his friends as Triple D, was streaming a film on his laptop when he felt the faint tickle of a draught on the back of his neck.

Uneasy, he muted the film and slipped his headphones off.

The flat was in near darkness, the only light from a small desk lamp on the floor next to the sofa he was sitting on. Triple D sat perfectly still, but his hand drifted under the cushion for his gun.

He listened. He heard the traffic on George's Street, buses, taxis. Laughter from the people dining on the terrace at l'Gueuleton across the street, the chitter-chatter of a busy night in the city. It all sounded perfectly normal.

It was possible, of course, that a draught meant nothing: the building was old, the windows single-glazed and not entirely well-fitted. But he had drawn all the curtains earlier in the evening and locked the doors.

So where had the draught come from?

Slowly, carefully, he moved the laptop to one side and got to his feet, carrying the gun low by his right hip. The flat was small, no more than four rooms. A narrow hall, a kitchen, bedroom, bathroom and this, the living room, each one stacked floor to ceiling with boxes of contraband and stolen goods. Triple D was a fence, a thief, a hoarder and a collector; every square inch of space was used.

He crept out into the hall and to the front door. It was exactly as he'd left it earlier that evening after he had taken a delivery kung-po chicken. Locked, chain securely across.

He shook his head, annoyed. He was getting paranoid. Maybe it was time to take a break, skip on over to Liverpool for a few weeks and visit his sister, catch up with some of the heads. Lay low until he was certain things were safe.

But what about the draught?

'Fuck this,' he said aloud. He placed his eye against the peephole. The landing was in total darkness. This bothered him, as there was usually a low-level emergency light on twenty-four seven. He stared into the blackness for a few seconds, unsure of what to do. The couple across the hall had come in an hour before; he'd heard them talking and laughing on the landing.

He put the gun on top of a stack of carboard boxes, undid the chain and the deadbolt, opened the door and stepped into the darkness.

Silence. No sound from the adjacent flat; no music, no television. They were in; he hadn't heard them go back out.

His skin prickled with unease as he backed into his flat and relocked the door. He reached for the gun and came away empty, right before someone knocked him unconscious with the butt of his own weapon.

When he came to, he was back on the sofa, and he was barefoot, his hands and feet bound with tape. His head ached, and everything was blurred.

'You are difficult man to find,' the blonde woman said.

Triple D shook his head, but was sorry he did so when it felt like his brain would explode. He narrowed his eyes as much as he could without closing them, and she came a little more into focus. Thin, blonde, dressed head to toe in black, sitting on one of his kitchen chairs, his gun on her lap.

'How did you get in? The door was locked from the inside.'

'Yes.'

Corrine had turned on the overhead lights. He wished she hadn't; he didn't want to know what she looked like, he didn't want to see her smile, he didn't want to see her dead eyes.

And he really didn't want to see the grey case open on the table behind her, the contents gleaming in the light.

Triple D was a lot of things, but he wasn't stupid.

'Y'don't need to hurt me – I'll tell you everything.'

And he did, everything he knew, even things he didn't know but had only guessed at. When he finished talking he was bathed in sweat, even though Corrine hadn't laid a finger on him.

It didn't matter, of course, he was a dead man talking; but like all cornered rats, he held out hope of escape.

Right up until the last moment.

*

When Corrine was finished she went directly to Castleknock, where Duchy was expecting her.

'Explain it to me again.'

'He and other were paid to kill Arthur. You are right. Is connected.'

'To Stanley?'

'Yes.'

'I knew it,' Duchy said. 'Didn't I tell you, I knew it. But I'm gonna need proof.'

Corrine reached into the inside pocket of her jacket, removed a phone and a plastic bag and set them down on the glass-top coffee table.

Duchy leaned forward and looked at the bag. 'What's that, then?'

Corrine lifted the bag to the light; Duchy could see that it contained a recently severed index finger.

'Is that a finger?'

'For phone activation.'

Duchy stared at her, impressed.

She opened the bag and used the bloody digit to unlock Triple D's phone. Once open she passed it directly to Duchy, who immediately began scrolling though the lists. There were a lot of calls.

'It appears our chap was a busy man.'

His thumb flipped, then stopped as a slow grin spread across his face. 'Gotcha,' he said.

60

Gradually Leo became aware of sounds: there were voices, some raised, others hushed and urgent, though he could not figure out the sequence of the words used. The pain quickly followed, filtering through the haze as the blood moved through his veins and his nerve endings fired.

He tried to speak, but his tongue refused to make the correct movements and, besides, he wasn't sure he wanted to include himself in the cacophony above him, nearby, in the distance … whatever.

He tried to drift on the blackness a little longer, but the voices kept calling him home.

'I think he's awake.'

Hands then, under his neck, under his armpits, pulling, dragging. Pain accelerating.

'Unnngh,' he said. He opened his eyes and found himself staring into a moving light.

'Can you hear me?' the light said.

'Yes.'

'What's your name, son?'

'Leo.'

'Okay, Leo.' As the light moved, he registered shadows behind it. 'We're going to try move you—'

He drifted; when he came back the man was gone. He smelled a familiar aftershave and tried to be sick again.

'You're hurting him.'

'I'm not.'

'He needs to be in a hospital. I can't believe you sent them away.'

'He's not safe in a hospital.'

'Why? Why is he not safe? You know who did this, don't you, Pat? Pat, answer me, what is going on? What have you done?'

'Me?'

The incredulity in Pat's voice made Leo want to laugh, but the pain soon took care of that. He opened his good eye. 'Eddie?'

Her frightened face swam in and out of focus. He reached for her and tried to sit up at the same time; neither move was successful.

'Oh, Leo, steady, steady now, you've had a right going-over, so you have.'

He let his head slump forward onto his chest. A going-over …

'Here.'

He felt Eddie's knees under his neck, her hands on either side of his face, warm and slightly rough, smelling strongly of the tobacco she used for her rollie cigarettes. If he died right here and now, he thought, it would be a good passing.

'All right, Bosco, hold your head up a little and take a sip of this. Not too much now.'

He tried, he really did. Some water ran into his mouth; the bulk of it dribbled down his chin. He coughed, spluttered. His balls burned. ''Kay,' he said, turning his head to one side. 'Okay.'

Eddie put the glass down and examined him closely.

The expression on her upside-down face told Leo everything he needed to know. 'That bad?'

'How many fingers am I holding up?' She raised her right hand.

Leo squinted with his one working eye. 'Two.'

'And now?'

''Sake, Eddie.'

'All right, I think your brain's in one piece even if the rest of you is not doing so well. What the hell, man, what the actual hell?' Without warning, she burst into tears.

Leo put his hands on either side of his body and tried to push himself up. Immediately his back spasmed and the pain rushed up through his nerve-endings so fast he almost fainted and had to lie back down.

'Ah, now.' Eddie was distraught. 'Ah, now.'

A second wave of nausea proved too much; he turned his head and vomited. Somewhere in the distance he heard footsteps come towards him.

Leo concentrated on his breathing, tried to take slower breaths, riding the waves of pain, seeking the troughs, trying to stay there a little longer each time. He risked opening his eyes again. 'Patrick,' he said.

'Leopold.' Pat was squatting by his side, looking worried.

'He needs to be in a hospital,' Eddie said. 'He puked; he probably has concussion.'

'We've discussed this,' Pat snapped. 'Leo, do you think can you walk?'

'I don't know.'

'Help me get him up.'

'Jesus Christ, Pat, are you mad? Look at the state of him.'

Leo wanted to tell Eddie not to be scared, but the words were gone before he could grasp them.

One, two, three. Oh, the count was for him. He gritted his teeth and tried to help.

Eddie was under his shoulder, then Pat on the other side.

'Use your feet,' Pat said.

He attempted to coordinate them a little. He felt he was doing his best under the circumstances.

Outside, the cold air revived him a little. The sky was streaked crimson. 'Shepherd's delight,' he mumbled.

Pat opened the door of the Jeep and between him and Eddie they managed to wedge Leo onto the front seat. Eddie strapped his seatbelt on and patted his chest. There was blood all over her shirt. 'Oh, Bosco' she said softly. 'I warned you.'

'S'okay, be okay,' Leo mumbled. 'I'm sorry 'bout your shirt. Sorry 'bout that.'

Pat got behind the steering wheel. 'Shut the door, Eddie.'

Eddie closed the door and stood watching until they drove away. She walked back inside Bocht, sat down at a table and called her girlfriend.

'Dom?' She tried to control her voice, but the earlier adrenaline had worn off and she couldn't stop the tears. 'Dom, will you get Fanny and come collect me?' She put her hand to her face. 'No, I'm not okay, no. Please, Dom, come get me and bring me home.'

61

The rain had started mid-morning and carried on from there. Up in the office, Celestine lay on her pallet under her sleeping bag, neither sleeping nor watching the television. Something was happening to her, something bad. She did not feel well. She could not remember her numbers or the rhymes Yulia had taught her to say when she was afraid; there was no space in her head for such things since the man hit her and made her mouth bleed.

For most of the night she thought about her situation.

Yulia promised her nobody would ever hurt them again. But the man had hurt her; the man had frightened her very badly. The two things did not tally, and she was very unhappy about this.

Very unhappy.

The man had been good to her; he had brought her food.

The man had hit her in the face, made blood come in her mouth.

Frightened her.

Yelled at her.

What if someone hurt Yulia this way? What if someone made her mouth bleed?

Yulia had promised no one would hurt her.

Yulia had been wrong.

Shortly before dawn she formed a plan of sorts. She would leave this place; she would leave and find Yulia.

That seemed the most efficient decision she could make.

Leave.

Find Yulia.

Very good.

How?

What did she know about the place they had been taken to first? It was old and made of stone. It was cold, yes. There were dogs, big ones that looked like bears. There was a bad man with black hair. There was a lane too; it was bumpy.

But first she would need to deal with the man here. The man was not a good man.

He was a bad man.

In a strange way it calmed her to think of him like this. It made sense. She had known bad men in her life before; they did not surprise her.

But she could surprise them.

Oh yes.

Yulia had told her she should not think about such things any more. But Celestine remembered pain; she remembered fear. She remembered standing in a tin bath in the middle of the kitchen, with blood streaming down her legs, the private space between her legs burning like it was on fire. She remembered Yulia washing the blood from her body, from her hair. She remembered how the tears streamed down Yulia's face. Celestine had been frightened then, thinking Yulia was angry with her. But later Yulia said she was not angry with her at all: she said she was angry with herself.

Celestine did not fully understand why this should be, but it was better than the alternative.

'He deserved it,' Yulia told her when Celestine surprised the man who tried to hurt her again. Yulia was very pale and was biting her lower lip when she took Celestine by her shoulders and looked into her eyes. 'Listen to me, he deserved it.'

Celestine did not disagree.

Then she was being bundled into her only coat and they left, carrying a bag each. They hitch-hiked their way into the nearest town, where Yulia said she had a 'contact', whatever that was. In a noisy café, drinking cola, Yulia said, 'Remember what I say, Celestine. None of this was your fault. There are bad men everywhere.'

None of it was her fault.

The man was a bad man and none of *this* was her fault. There are bad men everywhere.

Decision made, she waited.

In the end she did not have to wait long before she heard the door roll up and the van drive in. She got up and crept out of the office, but instead of going downstairs she snuck around the corner and crouched behind a stack of pallets, out of view from the ground floor or the landing.

The van's engine shut off and the door dropped back into place. The van door slammed. She heard nothing for a while, then the occasional sound of something being moved, a series of coughs.

Silence.

Her legs were beginning to cramp: she desperately wanted to move them.

Still nothing.

Head down; be good.

Head down.

The metal steps rattled; they squeaked under the man's weight. She heard him step out onto the mezzanine, heard him open the office door, heard him call her name.

She pressed her body tight against the outer wall of the office, the wood panels so badly warped she could almost see the outline of his legs through the joists. A spider ran across her hand; it had soft legs, tickle tickle. She watched it scuttle under the pallets and disappear.

The man said more words; they sounded angry.

His movements were faster now; back out onto the mezzanine.

She heard the metal railings as he leaned his weight on them to scan the floor below. Moving as stealthily as possible, Celestine stood up and slid her body to the right until she saw him standing with his back to her.

She inhaled, lowered her head and began to run.

He heard her, of course – metal is unforgiving to stealth. But when he turned she saw it was a different man, a younger man. A man who did not understand her plan; he did not understand her commitment.

He braced his body as she reached him, raising a hand to strike her. He made a strange, startled sound when she leaped. He was bigger, stronger, but she had the element of surprise and, more importantly, she had momentum. It took him a split second to realise what was happening, but by then it was too late, not even enough time to call out as Celestine caught him sailing past and they both spun through the air and dropped to the factory floor thirty feet below.

62

Leo had no idea where they were going or for how long they drove, but at some point the Jeep stopped, and he heard Pat pull up the handbrake.

When he opened his eyes – correction, eye – he saw a set of electronic gates in the headlights, opening inwards. They passed through the gates into a secluded courtyard, surrounded by apartments, most of them in darkness; the lights picked out shrubs against red brick walls.

Pat parked in a space marked 'reserved', got out and came around to his side. He opened the door, flooding the interior with freezing air.

'Can you walk?'

'I don't know.'

'It's not far, but there are a few steps.'

Leo half fell, half slithered out of his seat, managed to get his legs under him and stood shivering with his back propped against the metal. By necessity he allowed Pat to help him as he shuffled across the courtyard at a snail's pace towards a set of concrete steps leading to a second-floor landing.

Up they went. The pain was so bad he had to stop halfway up and cling to the handrail, gritting his teeth.

'Come on.' Pat's voice was steady in his ear. 'Nearly there.'

'She kicked my balls up into my stomach.'

'Nearly there,' Pat repeated.

Determined, Leo put one foot in front of the other. At the end of the walkway, Pat unlocked a door and helped him inside. He led Leo down a hall, opened another set of double doors and into an L-shaped living room.

Leo leaned heavily on the doorjamb, breathing hard, feeling like he was going to be sick. Pat put on a few lamps and came back to lower him onto a dark red velvet sofa. Once down, Leo groaned and released the breath he'd been holding. He let his head fall forward, sweating now despite the cold.

Still the pain kept coming, though thankfully it wasn't as sharp as it had been back at Bocht. To try and take his mind off it, he studied his surroundings.

It was a decent-sized room, two windows, plain, sturdy furniture, beige carpet and cream walls, generic prints: efficient and utterly charmless. Pat was tricking about with the heating, jabbing buttons in a panel on the wall with impatience.

'Who owns this place?'

'I do.'

'You live here?'

'No, I don't.'

Case closed, then.

Satisfied with his work, Pat removed his jacket and went through another door and began clattering around what Leo assumed was a kitchen. He heard the sound of a fridge opening and the clink of ice against glass. Pat returned carrying two tumblers. From an ornate wooden globe, he pulled out a bottle of Town Branch bourbon. He perched on the arm of a beige armchair, poured two healthy measures and held one out. 'Drink this.'

'I don't—'

'Drink it, it's medicinal.'

Leo's hands shook badly when he reached for the glass, leaving him to wonder if his nerves were damaged in some way. Part of him hoped that's all it was. Another part was fear. He had been beaten before, he knew what came next, and so he feared it.

That fear shattered his resolve.

He raised the glass of amber liquid to his lips, breathing in the sweetness of it; he took a sip and immediately started coughing and spluttering.

'I said drink it, don't gargle it.'

He tried again; this time it went down easier.

Too easy.

Familiar.

Liquid gold.

'Where do you hurt?'

'Pick a card, any card.'

Pat put his glass on the table and went down the hall to one of the other rooms. He returned and handed him four tablets.

'What are these?' Leo squinted at them with his one working eye, unable to make out the tiny printed letters.

'They'll take the pain away, help you sleep.'

'But what are they?'

'Zimmos.'

'Zimwhats?'

'Zimmos. Don't worry, they won't kill you.'

'Where did—?'

'Stop asking me questions, will you? Just take them. You need them right now.'

Leo looked down at the tablets. He wanted to refuse, hand them back, get up and go home, but even as he thought about moving, his balls delivered another pulsing ache, so he tossed the tablets into his mouth and chased them down with the rest of the bourbon. Pat refilled the glass immediately.

They sat, sipping their drinks in companionable silence like two old chums at the end of a bar on a quiet winter's evening. Occasionally Pat checked his phone, tapping replies that needed a frown or a scowl to complete. For a while, Leo watched him, until all but the sharpest pain had dulled; what remained settled into a manageable discomfort and utter exhaustion.

He could no longer hold his head up. 'Pat?'

'What?'

'Who was that woman?'

Pat glanced over, his eyes in shadow. 'Stop talking, Leo. Try get some rest.'

'She wanted you to know she had me. Why?'

'Rest. We'll talk tomorrow.'

Leo stretched out on the sofa and let the drugs do their work. Pat rolled a joint and smoked it. At some point he fetched a blanket from a press in the hall and put it over Leo and removed his shoes. Leo's breath slowed.

He dreamed of his mother, pictured her standing by the cooker in the old house on Sheriff Street, her auburn hair curled high on her head, sweaty tendrils loose about her neck. She was upset, puffy and red in the face, heavily pregnant and ready to pop any second. Who was she carrying? Had to be Liam. When she looked at him, her mouth moved as though she was talking, but he could hear no sound. He looked out the window; Eddie was standing on the footpath. She had a skipping rope in her right hand and her knees were bleeding.

When Leo woke he was alone, but there was a glass of water on the coffee table by his head and some more tablets. He moved slightly, and the pain struck immediately.

This time he didn't hesitate in taking them.

It hurt like hell, but he managed to ease his body upright, feeling every muscle and fibre scream in protest. Gingerly he touched his face and discovered unfamiliar territory: lumps, bumps, splits and swellings. The pain was a rolling, dull fogbank that sought out every nook and cranny and found them.

The blinds were still down, but enough of a weak wintery light filtered through to suggest it was morning. Slowly he got to his feet and tested his balance. There was some strength in his legs, so, using that, he shuffled to the kitchen.

It was spotless: unused pans hung from hooks over a gleaming hob; the presses held generic crockery and a small amount of dried food items and some instant coffee. The fridge was similarly stocked: bottled water, hard cheese, UHT milk and little else.

He drank water from the sink, backtracked to the living room and searched the rest of the apartment. The first door down the hall opened into a bathroom: clean, though the shower had been recently used, and the towel thrown across the radiator was damp to the touch.

Urinating was interesting – if you called blood-streaked urine interesting – but at least the plumbing was working, to a degree.

He opened the mirrored door of a cabinet over the sink; it held toothpaste, mouthwash, a number of toothbrushes still in plastic wrappers, a variety of gauzes and plasters, and bottles of tablets.

He shut the door and stared at his reflection. He was not a pretty sight: his left eyebrow was split, his eye below sealed shut, the skin around it fat and shiny like a well-fed leech; and the rest of his face was a mess of dried blood, split skin, swelling and bruising.

He washed as carefully as he could, using the corner of a towel to clean the dried blood from his nostrils. He rinsed his mouth with the mouthwash, wincing and spitting streams of pink streaks onto the porcelain. When he was done he helped himself to another few tablets from a bottle prescribed to – he checked the label on the bottle – Miss Jean Kirkland, and swallowed them with some more tap water.

The bedroom was as impersonal as the living room. One standard double bed, undisturbed, made up with a plain maroon duvet matched by a maroon mat on a sisal carpet. Two bedside lockers, a slide-door wardrobe, mostly empty except for a fluffy white dressing gown that had obviously been lifted from a Jury's Inn. Leo limped over to the window and looked down into the courtyard. Pat's Jeep was gone.

He stared at the vacant reserved space, thinking, trying to work out the last twenty-four hours. He'd learned that Pat, and not Frank, had killed their Uncle Niall; Liam was in rehab; a woman with blonde hair had given him the hiding of a lifetime. And here he was sitting in a strange flat looking like the Elephant Man with only his older, slightly psychotic, brother to rely on. Oh, and he was taking drugs prescribed to a lady called Jean.

Nope, his stock was not exactly rising.

A little while later he heard keys in the front-door lock and he inched his body down the hall in time to see Tommy enter, carrying a brown paper bag in one hand and a holdall in the other. He stopped dead when he saw Leo.

'Shit. Your face.'

'You should see the other guy.'

Tommy didn't even crack a smile. He handed Leo the brown bag and carried on walking towards the living room. Leo limped after him and sat gingerly on the sofa to open the bag. It held a doughnut and a Styrofoam cup of what he guessed was coffee. The tough spud had even packed a straw: how thoughtful.

Tommy pulled down the window slats and scanned the street below. 'There's fresh clothes too.'

Leo put down the coffee, unzipped the holdall and pulled out a navy tracksuit and a polo shirt. He started to laugh, and when he did he found it really difficult to stop, despite the pain it caused.

'What's so funny?' Tommy demanded, when Leo finally managed to get a hold of himself.

'This is … you are … all of it. It's … ridiculous. The whole situation …' He started to laugh again but thought better of it. He tossed the clothes back into the bag. 'I need to see if Eddie is okay.'

'Pat said you're to stay here.'

'Why?'

'Ask him.'

Leo felt a sudden rush of blood to his head. 'Are you going to try and stop me if I leave, Tommy?' He took a breath, gathering the strength to make his exit look good. On the way down the hall he made a quick diversion and snagged the rest of the painkillers from the bathroom.

He walked out of the apartment and into the cold bright light of the morning, and hobbled down the steps as fast as his swollen testicles would allow.

63

Leo collected his car from the flats and drove directly to Eddie's home. He parked behind Fanny and got out, very slowly, and hobbled up the short drive to the door of the ground-floor flat Eddie shared with Dom. Before he reached it, the door was flung open and Dom, Eddie's girlfriend, came rushing out. She looked furious.

'Get away,' she said, closing the door behind her. 'Eddie is sleeping. Now get away.'

'Excuse me?'

'Get away from here.'

'I need to see Eddie. I need to see if—'

'No.' Dom put both hands up as though to push him. 'You will stay away from her.'

'Look, if this is about yesterday …'

'Yes, it is about yesterday, and other days. You are bad person, bad luck, bad …' she waggled her fingers '… bad energy.'

'What are you talking about?'

'Eddie try for so many times to help you. She say always you are … misunderstood.' Here she curled her lip. 'You are *victim* of bad things, bad blood. But she is wrong about you; she is blind to you.'

'Dom, listen to me. What happened yesterday was not my fault.'

She laughed, but there was no humour in it. 'Of course not. Nothing is ever your fault. You destroy your life, but not your fault, you break relationships, but is not your fault, you do stupid things, drink, drugs, not your fault. And if Eddie get hurt, also not your fault. A pattern, yes?'

'You don't understand, I never saw that woman before in my life, she wanted me to—'

'Ahhh!' She threw up her hands. 'I don't care, I don't care at all. Bad people?' She pointed at him. 'You are bad people. I told Eddie this a long time ago, but Eddie, she has a big heart.'

'I'm not bad people, Dom.'

'You have bad blood, like your father.'

'You don't know my father.'

Dom came right into his face, her eyes blazing. She was tiny compared to him, but right at that moment she looked mad enough to lift him up over her head and physically fling him out onto the street.

'I know men like him. I know men like you. You are your father's son,' she said, through bared teeth. 'You break, you destroy, you use, you are a … *cabrón*.'

Leo did not know what that was exactly, but he doubted it was complimentary.

'I'm sorry,' he said. 'I never meant to upset Eddie.'

'This I believe,' Dom said. 'But she is upset, and is your fault. You say Eddie is your friend? Then do this. If she is your friend, you will break with her, you will leave her alone. She is good person, she have a good life. I will kill you myself if anything happen to her.' She balled the fingers of her right hand and shook a fist in his face.

Leo looked over her head towards the flat. He thought he caught a glimpse of someone moving behind the frosted glass of the front door, but no one appeared, and after a moment he turned and made his way back to the car.

Dom was right, of course she was. Until he found out what the hell was going on he had no right to put anyone else in danger.

He took some more of Jean's magical tablets, dry swallowed

them, put the car in gear and started to drive. He kept driving until he turned into the tree-lined avenue of The Elms where he parked Bellisa behind – surprise surprise – Pat's Jeep.

He felt dizzy as he climbed the granite steps to the front door. Dizzy and unwell. He managed to ring the doorbell and straighten up, though the sweat was pumping from his pores.

Frank answered the door.

'Leo? Your face.'

'You should see the other guy,' Leo said, and fell forward in a dead faint.

64

Stonewall could not sleep. His leg ached, and no matter which way he tried to position his body, he could not get comfortable, so shortly before dawn he got up, dressed and left the farmhouse.

It took him an hour to reach the small enclave of houses, off the main road and sequestered behind high walls. A pack of mongrels and lurchers ran towards the car, barking and yipping. The dogs were no great threat but were an effective alarm. Lights came on, doors opened here and there, eyes watched the car as it cruised slowly by, passing abandoned toys, cars on concrete blocks, sulkies, washing lines, more dogs, this time chained to rings hammered into the ground. Serious dogs who did not bark but watched him with deadly intent.

Her house was the last house, built on the bend of the cul-de-sac so her front windows faced back the way he had come. There was a light on, and he wondered if she was already aware of his presence.

He parked on a patch of scrub grass and climbed out, making sure he was visible to all and sundry. He was kin, of a sort. But that connecting line had long been watered down, and his welcome was not assured.

She opened the door as he was halfway to it. 'Well,' she said, wrapping a man's cardigan around her body. 'They said you were coming, and here you are.'

She stepped aside, and he entered the little house, removing his shoes inside the door. 'Who said I was coming?'

'Them who'd have you join them.'

Stonewall felt his entire body shiver.

'Go on down to the kitchen,' she said. 'I have the kettle on.'

Her kitchen was much as he remembered it. Bright yellow walls covered in photos of children, grandchildren, great-grandchildren, nieces, nephews, cousins, sisters, brothers. He recognised his own father and mother among them; one of him standing with his hands clasped tightly together, wearing his Holy Communion suit; a black and white photo of Chester and his wife, standing on a pier somewhere, Chester squinting out from under a peaked cap, his face not yet lined as it was when he died. He scanned the walls again.

There was no photo of Mariposa. Not a single one.

The table was old and took up one-third of the kitchen. It was covered in an oilskin tablecloth that was bright red with pineapples on it. The curtains on the window were made from the same cheery design. The cupboards were old-fashioned, the cooker ancient. It was like stepping back in time through a portal.

'Sit down, Francis.'

Stonewall sat, turning his body to one side to accommodate his leg. He watched her make the tea, leaves of course, marvelling at how precise and assured her movements were for a woman of her years. For what could she be now? Eighty-five? Eighty-six?

'Now.' She filled a little metal strainer and dropped it straight into the teapot before she closed the lid. He knew the tea would sit for three minutes before a single drop was poured.

'Will you have a biscuit?'

'No, thank you.'

She ignored him and fanned some biscuits out on a plate before him, custard creams, exactly as she had done before.

Finally, she put out the cups and saucers and sat down facing him with a contented sigh. 'Well,' she said. 'Let me have a look at you.'

He brushed his hair back and let her see where the bullet had almost scalped him and sat perfectly still as she looked him over. There was no sympathy in her eyes, no sorrow either. Only professional curiosity. For a brief moment she reminded him of Corrine.

'A bad business,' she said at last.

'I was lucky.'

'Lucky?' She barked an incredulous laugh. 'Indeed and you were not.'

'Lucky to be alive, I mean.'

'Even that,' she said levelly, 'was not down to luck alone.'

'No.' He tried to rearrange his hair again. 'Probably not.'

'Leave it,' she said, taking his hand and placing it on the table. 'Let them see you as you are.'

When the tea was ready, she poured it, adding a squirt of honey to hers from a plastic container.

They drank in silence. Beyond the kitchen window the night stars began to fade as dawn approached over the horizon.

'It's been a long time, Francis,' she said finally. 'I thought you'd forgotten us.'

'No, not forgotten.'

'Then why have we not seen you in these parts?'

'I … was caught up in things.'

'Snared, is it?' Her eyes seemed to twinkle.

'If you like.'

'Some animals will chew their own legs off to escape a snare. You only had to lose a patch of hair.'

'I lost more than that.'

'Ah, Arthur, rest him.'

'Rest him.'

Arthur, squeezing the back of his neck. Arthur, with the stupid love bite and the stupid happy grin. A lump formed in the back of Stonewall's throat. If he'd been asked to explain its presence he would not have been able to do so, but it was there.

'Musha,' she said, reading his emotions as easily as she read her tea-leaves. 'He knows how you really felt.'

'I need …' Stonewall hesitated and looked down at his hands, pressing his fingers into the oilcloth to keep from making a show of himself in front of her.

She surprised him by reaching across the table, putting her hands over them. Her skin was warm, soft, the back of her hand laced with thick blue veins. He could almost see the blood pump through them under her thin skin.

'I need to know—'

'You have the look of a haunted man. Is that so?'

He lowered his head, unable to meet her gaze. 'It's Chester. He won't give me a minute's peace.'

'His spirit is restless,' she agreed. 'I feel him too, hear his lament.'

'I don't know what to do or think. I have …' he touched his fist to his chest '… I have doubts.'

'Doubts?'

He shook his head. 'I heard Arthur die. I heard the last rattle in his chest. I could do nothing, move nothing. All I could do was lie there and die myself. I thought, this is it, it's over. Then I woke up again. But it's not the same: it's all changed. I live, and I do not live.'

'You *are* haunted, Francis,' she said softly. 'You already know the truth.'

He lifted his great ruined head and stared at her with open sorrow.

'You know,' she repeated. 'At night, when they whisper in your ear, they're trying to warn you, they're trying to make you listen. Why won't you listen?'

'It can't be.'

She removed her hands, sat back and sighed.

'When I was a child,' she said after a while, 'I loved horses. Oh, mad about them, I was. I pestered my father to buy me a pony of my own. I never let up, day and night, any chance I got. In the end he gave in and two days later arrived home with the most beautiful palomino pony you could ever imagine. Now, my father was a great horseman. Ach, what he could do with them you'd scarce believe your eyes. But I was a child and I had my own notions.'

She winked, and Stonewall smiled. He realised, sitting here in the warm kitchen, he had missed his great-aunt more than he'd allowed himself to admit.

'Every free minute I had I spent with this creature, feeding him, talking to him, brushing his hair.' She closed her eyes, face pink with pleasure. 'His mane looked like spun gold and I loved him so much it hurt.' She glanced at him. 'It physically hurt.'

He nodded.

'But when it came to riding the beast, well, that's where I had a problem. This pony didn't want to be ridden. He didn't want to do any work at all. Every time I tried, he'd stop short, put his head down, and off I'd go.

'After a while my father noticed I didn't ride him much and wanted to know why. Of course, I didn't tell him why, but my father was not a stupid man. Sez he to me, "Bábóg, I know you love that animal, but he doesn't respect you because he doesn't fear you. Fear and respect go hand in hand." She waved a hand. 'And sure I took not a bit of notice. I spent months trying to win that pony's heart, months. But the next time I rode him he tossed me off again.'

She crossed her arms over her chest, hugging herself as though suddenly cold.

'Late autumn it was, I remember the chestnuts were starting to fall. I went down to the stable to fetch the pony, determined that this was the day I'd ride him at last. I was carrying a saddle my uncle had given me, because I thought if I can learn to ride in it, I'll have a better chance of staying on.'

'And did you?'

She shook her head. 'I never got the chance to put it on him. I opened the stable door, called his name and the next thing two hooves lashed out.' Her eyes widened. 'He would have caught me right in the chest, but I was carrying the saddle like this.' She held her arm out. 'It took some of the force. Not all, mind; he broke my collarbone in three places.'

She took his hands again.

'When I got home from the hospital the pony was gone, and I knew better than to ask where. But you know the worst part? Worse than the pain in my collarbone? Worse than losing the pony? My father didn't speak to me for weeks.'

'Why?'

'Because I didn't listen, Francis. I didn't heed his warnings and it near cost me my life.'

She gripped his fingers, gently bouncing them up and down. 'You can love a thing with all your heart, Francis, but it can kill you stone dead. Do you understand?'

He nodded, afraid to speak.

'All right, then. Drink your tea before it gets cold.' She smiled at him. 'Have a biscuit, sure I only got them in for you.'

65

Stefan woke up and knew straight away something was wrong. He got out of bed, put on a quilted robe, fixed his daytime toupee to his head and left the bedroom.

Mariposa wasn't in her room and her bed had not been slept in, which was odd, because she had definitely come back the night before. He had mixed several cocktails for her before retiring to bed shortly after two a.m.

Also, the room seemed … he looked around him … empty.

He went into the narrow walk-in wardrobe that separated her bedroom from the bathroom and found nothing but hangers and empty shelves. He backed out and stood with his hand on his chest, feeling his blood pressure ding with alarm.

This was all wrong.

He hurried downstairs, heading directly to her office. He found her burning papers in the fireplace, dressed in the same clothes she had been wearing the night before.

'Mariposa, what's going on?'

She glanced up, and Stefan got a genuine fright when he saw her. Her face was white, her eyes fully painted, her lips fire engine red. She looked like something from a horror show.

'Mariposa?'

'Ah, there you are.' She tossed another sheet of paper on the fire and watched it smoulder and catch flame. 'I wasn't expecting you to be up so soon.'

'What time did you get up?'

'Oh, several times ago.'

She was drunk, or high. Her voice had the distinctive purr it carried when she was flying, like Icarus, too close to her own personal sun. Stefan looked around, spotted the bottle of gin on her desk, next to a glass. It was two-thirds empty.

Uh-oh.

'What's the matter? What's happened?'

'I've been thinking about lions, Stefan.'

'Lions?'

'Hmmm, yes, lions. King of the jungle, the males, at any rate. Lazy, though; they let the females do all the work and they saunter in and take the lion's share.' She tittered, tossed more paper on the fire.

'Mariposa, what's wrong? What's happened?'

'The lion roared, Stefan. He saw the kill and he roared.'

'I don't understand.'

'Duchy came over last night.'

'He did?'

'Yes, not long after you'd gone up to bed.'

'What did he want at that hour?'

'Oh, I called him. I wanted to trade on my own turf.'

Stefan gathered his gown tightly. 'Is this about—?'

'I offered to agree to his terms, buy him and the fat slug out.'

'I see.'

'Do you know what he said?'

Stefan had a vague idea, but he played along. 'I have no idea.'

'He laughed, he laughed at me.' She went to her desk, yanked open a drawer, gathered more papers and came back to the fire. 'It was a lie, you see, a ruse.'

'A ruse?'

'He never had any intention of letting me keep Lakeside.'

Stefan's legs got shaky. 'But this is our home.'

'Home, yes, home. Home is where the heart is. Home is where you lay your hat.'

'What?'

She looked at him, her dark eyes suddenly keen and sharp. 'Did you know Stonewall was planning to leave?'

'No, I had—' Stefan stopped and frowned. He had never heard Mariposa refer to her bother as anything other than 'Francis' before. There was danger here; he had to be careful. 'Leave? Leave Dublin?'

'Leave Ireland, darling. Leave me.'

'No! I had no idea.' God, he thought, all those acting classes, wasted. 'None.'

'Arthur probably knew. I'll bet he did. It's the sort of thing he'd know, don't you think?'

She flung the rest of the papers on the floor and walked over to a large watercolour painting of a boggy landscape and rolled it to one side, revealing the wall safe. She opened it. 'Here.' She threw a solid bundle of money on the desk. 'Take that and go treat yourself. Have lunch, a facial, whatever tickles your fancy.'

Stefan stared at the money. Whatever had happened, this was bad. She wanted him out of the way and that never ended well. 'I don't want anything, Mariposa.'

'Then that's what you'll get.' She picked up the bottle of gin and refilled the glass on her desk. 'That's what I got, a big fat nothing for my troubles.'

'Where are all your clothes?'

'My clothes?'

'Your wardrobe is empty.'

She supped her drink and eyed him slyly over the rim of her glass. 'Snoop, did you?'

'I was looking for you.'

She waggled a finger. 'No, you snooped. You're a snooper.'

'Mariposa, for God's sake, I can see you're upset. Please talk to me.'

'All right, here's the scoop, Mister Snoop. Duchy's going to sell this house out from under me.'

'He can't do that.'

'The *family* makes the decisions now. The blood family.' She snorted. 'Blood.'

'Jesus.' Stefan put his hand to his throat. If Duchy sold the mansion, he'd be out of a job, homeless. He'd have to start again with next to nothing and he was too old to do so, too old and too frightened. The world was not a kind place to small, weak-chinned men in toupees. 'Mariposa—'

'Make money on my sweat, on my labour.'

'What are we going to do?'

'Take the day off, Stefan.'

She waved him away and went back to burning papers in the fire. Terrified, Stefan hurried upstairs and began to pack.

66

Agatha helped Yulia to dress. Her clothes were too big on the younger woman, but at least they were clean and her hair had been freshly washed. Her injuries were not as bad as they had initially looked and she said the painkillers helped.

Agatha was glad of that.

Her external injuries would at least heal.

They had a late breakfast and walked across town to Dorset Street, to speak with a woman who might be able to help them. Initially Yulia did not want to go – she had even cried – but Agatha was firm.

'We need help,' she told her terrified niece. 'If we're going to find Celestine, we need help. We cannot do this alone.'

The office was at the top of an old narrow building overlooking a church. The woman waiting for them was tall, broad, with a flat face and intelligent eyes. Her desk was narrow and covered in paperwork. Three of the office walls were lined with filing cabinets.

'Thank you for seeing us,' Agatha said, almost bowing, for this woman's reputation was something close to legendary.

'Sit, sit,' the woman said.

They sat.

'This is my niece, Yulia.'

The woman looked at Yulia with some curiosity. She gave a very brief smile. 'You escaped your captors, yes?'

Yulia nodded.

'How?'

She lifted her head, tightened her jaw. 'My eyes.'

'She has a condition called anisocoria.' Agatha explained. 'The pupil on one remains dilated at all time.'

The woman peered across the desk.

'So I see, interesting.'

'When she arrived in this country, she was wearing coloured contacts. When she was attacked, she removed one and this is how she escaped.'

'I made many cuts,' Yulia said, holding her arms up. 'Much blood and I can dislocate my arm.'

'How?'

'I did as a child.' She shrugged. 'In an accident. It is not difficult to do.'

'Clever.' The woman leaned back in her chair with a thoughtful look on her face. 'I know of this place, of course. I hear many rumours.'

Yulia said something in Serbian to Agatha, the words fast and urgent.

'What is it?'

'She said they sent her sister away; she does not know where.'

The woman nodded. 'I understand. It is possible she was sold on.'

'Sold?'

'These people, they think people are property.' Her face darkened. 'Commodities to be bought and sold.'

Yulia looked sick. 'Celestine is a child.'

The woman shrugged and pressed a button on her desk. A few moments later a big red-faced man with bushy eyebrows entered the room.

'My husband,' the woman said. 'This is Oleg Taktarov.'

'Like bear,' Oleg said, offering his hand. Agatha shook it. Yulia did not. Seeing Oleg, she seemed to shrink into her chair with fear.

'Oleg has contacts all over the country.' The woman leaned forward and linked her fingers. She looked directly at Yulia. 'If your sister surfaces anywhere, we will find her. I give you my word.'

'I do not know your name,' Yulia whispered, darting a terrified look at Oleg.

The woman smiled. 'I am Livia. Taktarov.' She smiled at Oleg. 'Like bear, but much more dangerous.'

67

Celestine opened her eyes. She was lying on her side on the factory floor. Her head hurt, she couldn't move her right arm and her legs felt numb.

Moaning softly, she used her left arm to push her body over onto her back, where she lay for a minute, breathing slowly and deeply as she had learned to do many years before when pain was inflicted upon her. After a while she wiggled her toes, stretched her calf muscles, pulled her legs up and lowered them again. It took several minutes, but gradually she gained enough control to sit up.

The man was lying close by, crumpled and very still. A large pool of blood had spread out from under his head and she could see parts of his skull were broken. She was glad he was turned away from her. She did not want to see his face.

Getting to her feet was a complicated affair. The right side of her body had taken the brunt of the fall, but when she stood, neither leg seemed willing to move in the right direction, forcing her to swing them out to either side to propel herself forward. Climbing the stairs to the office took a long time with many rest breaks, but eventually she managed, collected her things and came down again, on her bum this time, dropping onto each step like a toddler.

The factory door was locked, but she knew the man had opened it from inside the van. She searched his body for the keys and found them in the front pocket of his jeans. There were a number of keys on the ring and a small electronic fob. She used it to open the factory door and leaned on the wall as it slowly rose.

Celestine pushed off the wall and stepped outside into the cold, damp air. She raised her head towards the sky, saw nothing but grey clouds, dark and ominous.

She had to find Yulia. Yulia would know what to do.

With renewed determination, she tucked the sleeping bag under her one working arm and hobbled along the driveway, heading towards the sound of distant traffic. Nobody saw her go; nobody noticed this bloodied and bruised child leave the business park and limp away.

68

Leo came around to a familiar sound: his father was yelling.

'Who are you to decide what I can and can't know?'

'I made a decision, Dad—'

'It's not up to you.'

Leo put his hands under him and sat up. He found he was in Frank's study, on the Chesterfield sofa with the same blanket over him that had been on Liam the day before. Pat was standing between him and the desk, with his jacket off, shirt sleeves rolled up to his elbows.

'What happened?'

'Welcome back,' Pat said. 'Idiot.'

'How long was I out?'

'Half an hour.'

Leo groaned, pulled the blanket off and swung his feet onto the ground. His head felt heavy and muzzy, his body like it had been hit by a truck and run over by a steamroller.

Focus. He looked around. Three walls of books, French doors overlooking the lawns, fireplace, Frank's big desk with the leather inlay. Bit crowded, though, what with him, Frank, Sean, Pat *and* Tommy all gawking at him.

'Are we having a committee meeting?'

'You're a bloody idiot.' Pat was angry, Leo could see that, but he heard the definite sound of relief under it. He was almost touched.

'We're trying to decide what the hell to do with you,' Frank said.

'I have an idea.' Leo got shakily to his feet. 'Why don't you tell me what's going on?'

'Stay out of it,' Pat said.

'Stay out of what, that's the question.'

Nobody answered. Leo pressed his finger to his lumpy face and winced.

'Are you all right?' Frank asked. 'He should he in a hospital.' This was directed towards Pat, who shook his head.

'Too risky, we need to move him to—'

'I'm standing right here!'

All eyes turned towards Leo. The shout had cost him, but it had to be done.

'I'm standing right here,' he repeated, lowering his voice a little. 'Tell me what's going on. I have a right to know.'

'Duchy Ward,' Pat said after a moment. 'He has a price on Liam's head.'

'Who?'

'He's an ex-jailbird, says Liam killed his brother, Arthur Ward.'

'Did he?'

'Of course not.'

'Then why would he think that?'

'Because Arthur Ward was seeing Marcy Dunne.'

'Who?'

'Liam's ex-girlfriend.'

'Ah.' Leo sensed this was supposed to be an explanation of sorts, but it didn't cut the mustard. Also, his legs stopped working and he had to sit down again. 'Why did that woman attack me?'

'Duchy Ward wants me to pay the so-called price on Liam. When I said no he decided to up the stakes. You're … collateral damage.'

'Collateral damage.'

'I'm sorry, I didn't think he'd go after you.'

Leo smiled, then frowned. He hadn't meant to smile. His skin felt odd, tingly. 'Is he right?'

'Who?'

'This man. Did Liam kill his brother?'

'No, he never touched him. Well, he had a fight with him,' Pat said, glancing at Frank, who looked fit to be tied. 'A punch-up in front of a room full of witnesses.'

'Right.'

'And … he did threaten to kill him.'

'In public?' Frank snapped.

'He didn't *do* it,' Pat countered. 'He was just mouthing off.'

'Well, then.' Leo clapped his hands together. 'That's perfect. That's what we'll say.'

'To who?'

'Ducky Ward.'

'Duchy.'

'Yeah, him.'

Tommy snorted a laugh. 'What are you going to do? Rock up to Duchy Ward's house and demand he stop?'

'I'm going to talk to him, yes.'

'You can't be serious.'

'I've never been more serious,' Leo said with giddy calm. 'I'm not a brave man, but I have people who I care about and that woman nearly killed me. I'm not going to wait for her to come back and finish the job.' He squinted at Pat. 'I'm not going to wait for her to make someone else collateral damage.'

'He's right,' Frank said. 'This has gone on long enough.' He stood up and gave Pat a meaningful look. 'Too long. You say he came to the site?'

'Yes.'

'Then let's return the favour. Where do we find this fucker?'

'I don't know,' Pat said softly. 'We'd need to talk to Marcy Dunne.'

'Liam's ex?' Frank asked.

He nodded.

'Okay, where do we find her?'

'She's a hairdresser; she works over in Swords.'

'Where exactly?'

'A place called Vanilla Topping, she's working today.'

'How do you know?'

Pat shrugged, looking a little uncomfortable.

'He's been keeping tabs on her,' Leo said, grinning. 'He's like a super spy.'

'Is he okay?' Frank asked, squinting at Leo, who waved. 'What's wrong with you – why are you grinning like a gibbon?'

'Pat gave me drugs; they're very good.'

'He did what?'

Pat grabbed his jacket from the back of a chair and put it on. He glanced at Tommy. 'You got your piece?'

Tommy patted his lower back.

To Frank, Pat said, 'Keep him here and—'

'Nope.' Leo got to his feet. Well, he got there on his second attempt. 'She broke me up, Pat, she broke me up. I'm going.'

'You can barely stand.'

Leo grinned and took the pills from his pocket. He shook the bottle. 'A few more of these and—'

Frank came from behind his desk and snatched them out of his hand. 'Give me those.' He tossed them onto the open fire.

Leo watched them burn with a sad little sigh. 'They were very good.'

'Let's go,' Pat said.

They went.

69

Duchy heard a car horn beep outside, leaned backwards in his chair and glanced out through the window in time to see his sister's Volvo pull up beside his wife's Toyota Yaris.

'Right,' he said to Murray, who was sitting on the other side of his desk, cap in hand. 'There's Sylvia now, she's early.'

Murray got to his feet. 'Are you really going to do this?'

'It's no less than she deserves.'

'Stonewall is going to have a fit.'

'You leave Stonewall to me.' Duchy stood up. 'Go and get the girls. We'll send them up north, the lot of them, sell them on as a job lot. And Murray, we're done with that business, do you hear me?'

Murray felt sick to his stomach handing the women over – avoiding their pleading stares, their cries for help. He knew the buyers were no good, that the girls would end up scattered across the various small ugly brothels that popped up like a bad mushroom in every town in the country. But what could he do about it, he was only one man?

He checked his watch. It was almost twelve-thirty and he hadn't heard from Rally, which was starting to bother him, unless he was off somewhere blowing off steam after his … mission. Still, it wasn't like him to be out of touch for so long.

Cally tapped on the door and poked her head around it. 'Sylvia's here. Oh, Charlie, are you off, then? I thought you might like to stay for a bite of lunch? It's only shepherd's pie, not much, but plenty to go round.'

Murray smiled warmly. He liked Cally: she was the only one who called him by his first name, the only one who bothered to treat him like he was part of the family. 'Cheers, Cally, my love, but I've got to get going. No rest for the wicked, eh?' He gave her a quick peck on the cheek and walked out into the hall, where he found Sylvia at the foot of the stairs, unwinding a silk scarf.

'All right, Sylvia.'

'What are you doing here?'

'Tying up a few odds and ends.'

She raised her hands and fluffed out the ends of her hair. 'He's told you, has he? About Lakeside?'

'That he's putting it on the market, yeah,' he said. 'You're going to handle the sale?'

'The agency will. It should never have let it go on as long as it did.'

'Well, Arthur liked the place.'

'Arthur wanted a private club.' She wrinkled her nose with distaste. 'What it became was nothing to do with him.'

Murray said nothing, but his expression must have because Sylvia rattled on.

'He was too soft on that woman and look how she treated him. I could never understand what he saw in her; he was so handsome when he was young – he could have had anyone.'

And did, Murray thought, but he let that slide. Sylvia had a particular blind spot for both her bothers, even when they were kids she'd defend them to the point of blatant stupidity. It suited her to think Mariposa was a bad egg: there was none so blind as those who did not want to see.

'Well,' he said, 'I'll be off, then.'

He went to walk past her and was surprised when she caught his arm.

'I don't want any unpleasantness, Murray. Make sure she keeps away.'

'That's not up to me.'

'She should know her place.'

'Her place?'

'Look, she's my sister-in-law and I—'

'Love the bones of her, do you?'

Her mouth twisted into a sour little plum. 'Do you think this is easy for me?'

'I don't know.' Murray shrugged her hand off. 'You don't seem too cut up about it.'

Sylvia narrowed her eyes. 'You know this is a family decision.'

'I'm family, Syl; my opinion wasn't asked for.'

'You know what I mean.'

'Yeah,' Murray said, 'I understand. It's a two-tier system.'

He put his hat on and walked out the door before he said something he would later regret.

70

The sound of car horns woke Celestine. She groaned and tried to pull the damp sleeping bag tighter around her body. Beyond the lip of the overpass, the rain beat down, steady and relentless, as the day brought with it a bank of freezing fog.

Exhausted, she dozed for a while, slightly comforted by the sound of traffic passing overhead. But it wasn't long before the cold became too much to bear and so, shivering and trying to clamp her teeth together, she leaned on the concrete behind her and forced her body upright.

Movement brought pain so shocking she almost collapsed. Her legs felt like they were on fire and her right wrist was so badly swollen she could not use it at all. Digging through the plastic bag, she selected one of the T-shirts Yulia had bought her and tried to fashion a sling with it, wrapping the T-shirt around her neck and sliding her useless arm into the gathered material.

It was a poor effort, but it would have to do.

Slowly, she rolled the wet sleeping bag and hoisted it under her good arm. She left the shelter of the bridge and stood in the rain, looking down the embankment. In the distance she saw the spire of a church in the distance. In her country, a church meant sanctuary. Slowly, painfully, she picked her way carefully down the slippery bank, one aching footstep at a time, until she reached the road and set off, she hoped, in the direction of sanctuary.

Cars and lorries passed her; some slowed but none stopped. In no time at all she was soaked through to her underwear and had blisters on both feet.

Her wrist throbbed uncontrollably.

Still she walked.

The plastic watch had broken in the fall so she had no idea what time it was. At some point the light began to fade and the passing cars put on their headlights. Before dusk the rain looked as though it might stop, but a fresh bank of clouds came looming over the hills, bringing another downpour with them.

Celestine no longer cared about being wet. Her feet, in her cheap runners, were bleeding.

Eventually she reached the outskirts of a town and found the church. She hobbled up to the double doors, but they were locked and no one came when she hammered on them with her fist. Exhausted, Celestine sat for a few moments, letting her head hang down as far as it would go to relieve the strain in her neck and shoulders. It was getting harder and harder to keep going. She was exhausted, hungry and thirsty. She wanted to lie down and sleep for a little while, but it was too cold and the rain was relentless.

She dragged herself to her feet and went back out onto the road.

By the time she reached the town centre she was staggering. People saw her. Some stood and watched; others gave her a wide berth. A man got in her way and said something to her, but his face was blurred and she could not understand him. Over his shoulder she saw a brightly lit shop with a jazzy red and white sign above the door. She pushed him away and lurched towards it.

Electronic doors parted. She stumbled inside and stood dripping on the mat, gasping for breath. The sleeping bag was so heavy she could barely carry it.

Her strength was failing.

People were staring at her, some with faces of concern, some of disgust. Behind the counter a man with hair like candy floss wagged his finger at her and pointed towards a sign Celestine could not read.

She ignored him and went stumbling down the aisles, past bread, past jars of pasta sauces, past rows and rows of cleaning products, past the freezer section, past the fish counter, past shoppers with trolleys who saw her at the last minute and reeled away.

Past cereals and dry goods, past … no. She stopped dead and stood swaying as she found what she was searching for. In a dreamlike state she reached for the six-pack of cola, tore the plastic open and downed the first can in several long, gulping swigs. It hit her empty stomach hard and she burped so loudly a young boy standing nearby with his mother burst out laughing.

The mother did not laugh; she took one look at Celestine, grabbed the boy's hand and hauled him away, looking back over her shoulder as she walked.

Celestine opened a second can and drank this one a little slower: she was still terribly thirsty, but trying to control herself. She put the sleeping bag down at last and the open can beside it, reached for a big bag of popcorn on the next shelf and ripped it open with her teeth. Smaller bags fell out onto the floor. She chose one, opened it again using her teeth and upended the bag into her mouth, spilling kernels everywhere.

A pale man wearing a badge and a walkie-talkie on his belt came around the corner and jerked to a stop. His eyes went very wide when he saw her. Celestine tossed the empty bag over her shoulder and drank the rest of the second can, burped again and wiped her mouth with the back of her hand.

The man looked at the mess and walked towards her, talking loudly. He reached for her, but Celestine slapped his hand away, bent down and dug into the plastic bag. She found the flowers, pulled them out and offered them to the man as payment.

The man looked at the flowers, then looked at her a little more carefully. He took the walkie-talkie from his belt and spoke to someone, listened and nodded. He glanced at Celestine and waggled his fingers, indicating she should follow him. Taking the cola and the popcorn with her, Celestine did exactly that.

Five minutes later, Celestine was sitting in a small overcrowded office. The man with the badge had fetched a heater and put it on for her and had given her a towel to dry her hair. Steam rose from her clothes. After a while she put her head down on the desk and fell asleep.

A short time later someone shook her shoulder. She tried to open her eyes, but it was next to impossible. She heard a woman speaking and someone shook her again.

The man with the badge had been joined by a dark-haired woman in a blue uniform. The woman had a stern, serious face, but her eyes when she looked at Celestine seemed kind.

After more talking, the woman tapped Celestine on the shoulder and beckoned her to follow her. Celestine got up and trudged through the shop, half asleep, half crippled. People stared; she didn't care. The heat had woken the pain in her arm and now it throbbed so badly it made her feel light-headed.

Outside, the rain had finally stopped. The air smelled country fresh and the street lights gleamed. The woman put Celestine in the back of a car and got in the front, taking her hat off as she did. She picked up a walkie-talkie of her own and spoke to someone. Celestine fell asleep again.

71

Pat found a parking spot a few doors down from the hair salon. He shut off the engine and was undoing the seatbelt when Leo grabbed his hand and shook his head.

'Stay in the Jeep.'

'Why?'

'Because I don't want to scare her.'

'Really? Have you seen your face?'

'Pat.'

'Fine.'

Leo got out and walked back up the road, moving slowly, with great concentration. He pushed open the glass door and was immediately overwhelmed by the heat and noise. He shook his head, felt sweat break out all over and a warning hum in his ears.

A small man in impossibly tight red jeans approached him. 'Can I help you?'

'I'm looking for Marcy.'

The man smiled but only with his mouth; his eyes were full of suspicion. 'Do you have an appointment?'

'No. I don't want … I need to talk to her for—'

'Listen, pal, no offence, but you don't look so good.'

'Actually, I need to sit down for a—'

When Leo opened his eyes again, he was lying on the floor with both his legs up on a chair. Various people were gathered around him, all concerned faces. A woman with wraps of tinfoil in her hair leaned a little closer. 'You okay, hun?'

'I think so.'

'Don't get up; stay there for a minute until the blood goes back to your poor head.'

'I heard an awful smack,' another woman said.

'He's fierce pale, isn't he?'

'Was he in an accident do you suppose?'

'Look at his poor face.'

'Could be low blood sugar, I read about that recently.'

Embarrassed, Leo tried to sit up and somehow managed to kick the chair over; the women scattered like hens.

'Sorry, sorry!'

'Take it easy, take it easy.'

The guy in the red jeans helped him sit down on a different chair. 'Kelly, go get him some water, there's a love.'

Someone pressed a paper cup of water into his hands; it was delicious and cool and perfect.

'Thank you.' Leo looked up and found he was staring into the face of the prettiest woman he had seen in years, a really pretty woman with long, incredible silver hair. 'You look like an elf,' he said.

'Great,' she said. 'What I've always wanted to hear.'

'I'm sorry.' He put his hand to his head and felt a fresh bump in his hairline. 'I can't seem to stop being a complete stupid eejit at the moment.'

She took pity and sat down next to him. 'You look pretty bad.'

'You should see the other guy.'

She frowned. Leo sighed and decided to retire that line for good.

'J'Pree said you were looking for Marcy before you keeled over.'

'Yeah, I … I'm sorry, did you say "J'Pree"?'

She nodded.

'Okay,' Leo thought, keep it together. 'Yes, I'm looking for Marcy Dunne.'

'Why?'

'I need her help.'

Kelly looked sceptical. 'With what?'

'She knows … knew … a man. I'm trying to find him. Well, not him, his brother.'

'Yeah? What's your name?'

'Leo.'

'Leo what?'

'Kennedy.'

Her face instantly darkened. 'Any relation to Liam Kennedy?'

'He's my brother.'

Kelly got to her feet. 'I think you should leave before I call the guards.'

'Please … Kelly, is it?' Leo took another mouthful of water. 'My brother is an idiot. I don't know what went on between him and Marcy, but I'm fairly certain that whatever she said about him is correct and I'm not here to defend him or cause trouble for her, I swear.' He looked up into her incredible eyes. 'Please, I need help. I wouldn't be here if I didn't. I mean, look at the state of me.'

Kelly thought about it for a moment. 'All right, but if you try anything stupid—'

'I promise … I won't.'

'All right, wait here.'

She went to the rear of the salon and walked up a spiral staircase. Leo sipped his water and tried not to notice everybody was watching him.

Kelly came back a minute later, accompanied by another beautiful woman who also did not look at all happy to see him.

'This is him,' Kelly said, folding her arms across her chest.

'What do you want?' Marcy said.

'Is there somewhere we can talk in private?'

'No.'

Leo put the water down on the floor by his feet and stood up. Marcy and Kelly looked ready to take flight or to fight.

'Listen, Marcy. Whatever my pig-headed brother has done, I'm sorry about it.'

'Sorry, yeah.' She looked up at him. Her eyes were huge, doe-like, but right now they were also furious. 'I've heard all that before. Sorry is just a word with him.'

'Marcy, I need your help.'

'With what?'

'I'm trying to find a man called Duchy Ward.'

'How should I know where he is?' She snorted and shook her head. 'You think I'd be involved with someone like that?'

'You were seeing Arthur Ward.'

'So?' She snorted again. 'Arthur's nothing like Duchy. Have you seen him?'

'No.'

'He's gross.'

'I see.'

'Going on about giving me a job, as if.'

'He offered you a job?'

'Running Arthur's old club. Said I'd be a natural. I told him I wanted nothing to do with him or any of the rest of them. Not after what I read in the papers.'

Leo blinked. 'Club?'

'Arthur owned a private members' club. Lakeside.' Her expression softened a little. 'Thought he was cock of the walk, he did. He liked rubbing shoulders with them stupid toffs.' Her eyes watered and her lip trembled. 'He was daft like that, a real big soft eejit.'

'Where is this place?'

'Out in the middle of nowhere. Cavan. By a big lake.' Her face soured. 'If you're looking for Duchy you can find him that way.'

'That's brilliant, Marcy, I really appreciate this.'

'Yeah? Then you can do me a favour.'

'Anything.'

'You tell Liam to stop calling me, stop calling my mam, stop sending flowers, stop, just stop.'

'I'll make sure he gets the message, loud and clear.' He cleared his throat. 'He's gone to rehab.'

'Good for him.' She put her hands on her hips and as she did Leo noticed for the first time the soft swelling underneath her shift.

'You're pregnant.'

She glared at him. 'What business is that of yours?'

Leo held up his hands. 'None, none at all. Congratulations on the … on the … foetus.'

She gave him a look that didn't need any translation. 'I've got to get back to work. Make sure you pass that message on. Loud and clear, yeah?'

She turned and went back upstairs. Leo gave J'Pree and Kelly an apologetic wave, left the shop and went back to the Jeep.

'Well?' Pat asked.

'You ever hear of a club called Lakeside?'

'Yes.'

'Ever been there?'

'Once. It's not my scene.'

'Let's go.'

72

Mariposa stood at the window of her office and watched Murray drive away with the sobbing girls in the van. She smoked her cigarette and lit another. She still had not slept and her nerves were more than a little frazzled, but she liked the manic energy coursing through her veins, it felt more authentic than the usual tamped-down carapace she had been forced to wear for so long.

No, if it was to be war, let it be war and her go into it fully prepared for battle. It was high time she was free from this family and now, with Dolan's money, she would finally have financial freedom and would never have to look at Duchy Ward's pasty face again as long as she lived.

The house was now empty and Stefan was nowhere to be seen. She assumed he had taken her advice and cleared off to town, but whether he had or he hadn't was of no concern to her any longer. A clean cut, that's what this was, no room for stragglers.

The Wards. When she thought about them she wondered how she had managed to tolerate them as long as she did. Even thinking of Duchy's smug ugly face made her sick. The state of him the night before, strutting around *her* lounge, drinking *her* drink: pontificating, preening, issuing decrees like a puffed-up little emperor. She'd laughed in his face. Oh, he hadn't liked that, no he hadn't like that at all, she could tell. He'd wanted her to beg, cry, plead for mercy.

Fool.

He didn't know her at all.

She stubbed her cigarette out, put on her coat, grabbed her handbag and went downstairs. She reapplied her lipstick in the hall mirror before she opened the great front door.

Her car was parked on the gravel, full of her bags and whatever else she could fit into the little two-seater. She had taken every cent from the safe.

A white heron flew overhead and landed in the lake. She watched it ruffle its feathers and step around the edge of the water on its spindly legs.

So, Duchy and Sylvia thought they could take Lakeside, did they? She pictured their faces and laughed.

She should have done this years ago.

Her heels crunched on the gravel as she walked around to the stables and grabbed the petrol can she had refilled the day before at the Circle K garage. Cackling and muttering under her breath, she lugged it back around to the front of the mansion and into the lounge, where she tossed and spilled it across the furniture and the heavy drapes.

She drained what remained on the stairs, making sure to coat the runner liberally.

When every last drop was emptied, she tossed the can aside, lit a cigarette with Arthur's lighter and tossed that into the lounge. She heard a 'whomp', then a 'whoosh', as she made for the door.

The curtains were already alight as she started the engine. Laughing like a maniac, Mariposa put the car in gear and shot off down the drive as the first of the windows blew out.

By the time Duchy and Sylvia arrived thirty-five minutes later, the fire had spread to the second floor and black smoke billowed from several windows.

'Oh my God,' Sylvia said. 'Oh my God!'

Duchy got out of the car and stared in disbelief.

'That crazy bitch,' he said. 'That stone-cold crazy bitch. I'm going to kill her.'

73

Mariposa drove straight to the farmhouse. The dogs were in the courtyard; she could hear them barking as she got out of the car.

She walked down the hall and entered the kitchen.

Empty.

She looked out the back window and saw Francis talking on the phone by one of the sheds. Watching her brother, the set of his body, Mariposa felt a prickle of unease. She tapped on the window and waved and got a start when Francis turned his head towards her. He looked worse than ever before, thinner, gaunt, sickly almost, a word she would never have associated with her brother.

Quickly Mariposa put on the kettle, poured herself a glass of water and took a seat at the kitchen table. She felt underneath it until her fingers closed in on the gun Francis always kept there. She heard the back door open and close again, and waited.

He entered the kitchen. 'What are you doing here?'

'I can't stay long, Francis, I'm leaving.'

'That so?'

'Francis, look at me.'

He sat down awkwardly, dragging his bad leg into position with his hands and looked at her.

'I know things have been difficult lately, I … I haven't been there for you as much as I should.'

'And how much is that, Mariposa?'

She tried to smile, but there was something so cold in his expression it died on her lips.

'We don't need these people, Francis, we can go away, we can make a fresh start in another country. I know you've been thinking about Canada—'

'A fresh start?' Stonewall laughed. 'With you?'

'I have money coming, we can go wherever—'

'Look at me.'

She met his gaze.

'I'm going to say two names, sister. I want you to tell me what they mean to you.'

'We don't have time for—'

'Conor Stanley, Lorcan Stanley.'

The colour drained from Mariposa's face. Even her lips went white. She shot to her feet. 'Francis, whatever you've heard—'

'Sit down. I won't ask you again.'

She sat, rigid and breathing hard, heart racing.

'You killed Arthur. I want to hear you say it.'

'Francis, please—'

'Say it.'

'All right.' Under the table she snapped open her handbag. 'I … killed Arthur.'

Stonewall exhaled. He made a queer face, sucked in his cheeks, blew them out again. 'Did Chester ever put a hand on you?'

It was such an unexpected question Mariposa was momentarily speechless. 'What?' she finally managed to say.

'Did Chester force himself on you, like you said? You said he raped you. Did he?'

'Why are you asking me about that? Why now after all these years?'

'I killed him. I strangled him, heard the bones break in his neck.'

'He was a hard bastard, Francis; he beat us black and blue.'

'Did he rape you, Mariposa?'

She raised her head defiantly. 'I won't dignify that with an answer.'

Stonewall surprised her by chuckling. 'No, of course he didn't. He was a hard man, but he was no pervert.' He leaned back, resting the back of his head on the chair, and closed his eyes. 'You lied to me; you've been lying to me my whole life.'

'I protected you – I protected us. He was a bastard, Francis, and he was going to sign over this house to Belle and her ragtag crew, did you know that? He'd leave us on the street with nothing.'

'It was his to sign over to whoever he wanted,' Stonewall roared, making Mariposa flinch. 'This was his house.'

'He deserved it, after how he treated us.'

'And did Arthur too deserve to die? What did I do to deserve this?'

'Francis, listen to me—'

'Oh he was a stupid man with drink taken,' Stonewall conceded. 'Never knew when to keep his trap shut. But you knew the type of man he was when you married him. So something changed.'

Stonewall looked down. 'She was different – he told me so himself. I didn't believe him at the time, but now …' He looked at her. 'Why was she different?'

'She was pregnant – he got the slut pregnant.'

'That's all?'

She glared at him, suddenly furious. How like a man to dismiss something so crucial. Arthur had never pretended to be anything other than what he was, a charming, feckless, cheating bastard. All true. Of course, a child changed things, a child changed everything. How could she explain the anger and hurt the child caused her? The humiliation? How could she make him understand?

She couldn't.

'Francis, I swear to you, I didn't know you'd be in the car.'

Stonewall laughed mirthlessly. 'You've ruined me.'

'Francis, I'm sorry. I can't change the past, if I could, I would do it in a heartbeat.'

'The past.' Stonewall gave her the same lopsided, humourless grin. 'You're a palomino pony, Mariposa.'

She wrinkled her forehead in confusion. 'I don't know what you're talking about.'

'Tell me something, what were you going to do when you got Dolan's money? What was your great plan?'

She startled badly. 'How do you know about Dolan?'

'Did you really think you'd get away with it?'

'How do you know about him?' she repeated, dread building.

He shook his head again, mockingly this time. 'It's over, Mariposa, there's no money coming. Best thing you can do is run, run away before Corrine gets to you.'

'I'm your sister, Francis, your flesh and blood.'

'You had everything you needed; you would have been taken care of.'

She was genuinely speechless. 'Taken care of? *Taken care of?* Do you hear yourself, Francis? I don't want to be taken care of.'

Stonewall slammed his hand on the armrest. 'Then what do you want, Mariposa?'

'Respect!'

'What?'

'How about some respect. How about what was promised to me. All my life I've been treated like dirt: first father, then Chester, then Arthur, then Duchy, now you. Well, I'm not going to sit here and beg for scraps. I'm owed, Francis, I'm bloody owed.'

He got to his feet, huge and furious. Mariposa opened her handbag, her fingers slipping around the butt of the pistol resting on top of the bundles of money she had taken from the safe.

'I think we can both agree I've paid, Mariposa, I've paid in full.'

'My God,' she laughed. 'Will you listen to yourself? The martyr speaks.'

There was a single electronic beep from one of the cameras, a sign indicating someone had driven over the cattle grid at the end of the lane. Moments later, a beige Tiida drove into view, driven by Corrine.

'You're too late,' Stonewall said, watching the car swing into the front garden.

'Are you going let her take me?' Mariposa was incredulous. 'Francis?'

Stonewall looked at her, then looked away. 'You made your choice, Mariposa. I've made mine.'

'You should have told me about Canada,' she said quietly, raised the gun and shot him.

74

Pat, Tommy and Leo travelled in Pat's Jeep. Sean and Frank were in Sean's Audi right on their bumper when they pulled up to the gates of Lakeside.

'They're open,' Pat said. 'That's not right.'

He got out of the car and went back to confer with Frank. While they waited, Leo let the window down, hoping the cold air would help clear his head.

'You smell that?' Tommy said.

'It wasn't me.'

'No, smoke.'

Leo leaned out a little. The spud was right: he could smell smoke too.

'Maybe they're having a bonfire.'

'Lot of smoke for a bonfire.'

Pat came back. 'We're going in.'

They drove through the gates and down a long, sweeping drive with a badly neglected orchard on one side and a small lake surrounded on three sides by willow trees on the other. The smell of smoke grew stronger.

They rounded the last bend and saw why.

The mansion was ablaze.

The two cars pulled up and all occupants got out.

'What the hell's going on?' Frank asked, gazing at the inferno. The flames had reached the roof and several sections had collapsed inwards.

'You reckon anyone is in there?' Leo asked.

'If they are, they're goners,' Tommy said as the flames rose ever higher.

*

They were still standing there when a taxi drove up behind them and a pink-faced man wearing a pretty obvious toupee hopped out from the back and ran forward, screeching at the top of his lungs. They stared as he dropped to his knees and howled.

'What's up with him?' Frank asked no one in particular.

'Maybe he's a member?' Sean said.

'Hey,' Pat called. 'We're looking for Duchy Ward – you know where we can find him?'

The little man noticed them for the first time. His eyes widened in alarm. 'Why?'

'What's your name?' Frank asked.

'Stefan. I'm the manager. Oh my God, what's happened here? Where's Mariposa? Oh my God!'

'Who's Mariposa?'

'She's my boss. Oh my God, I knew she was upset … but this is … this is … I never thought she'd do something like this.'

'Do you know where we can find Duchy or not?'

'I don't know where he is. I don't know where anything is or isn't anymore.' He started to wail, flinging his hands out to the sky, like he was in *Platoon* or something. 'My clothes! My art! Oh, that bitch, she could have given me more notice. That miserable bitch!'

Another car pulled up behind them, a dented Opel Corsa. This time a big man dressed in black got out. 'Holy shit,' he said. He looked at Stefan. 'Are the girls in there?'

'I don't know, I don't know anything!'

'Who are you?' Frank asked.

'Doug.'

'You work here?'

'I did,' he said, nodding towards the burning building.

'You know where we can find Duchy Ward?'

He looked at the burning building. 'Maybe at the farmhouse.'

'The farmhouse?'

'Yeah.'

'Where's that?'

'I don't know, but Stefan does.' He nodded this time to the wailing man, who instantly stopped wailing.

'Shut up, Doug.'

'Nah, man.' Doug squared his shoulders. 'Naw, I'm done shutting up. I'm done acting like I don't see shit, like I'm … I'm …'

They waited. But apparently Doug was done trying to find an example.

'If Mariposa did this, she's probably gone to the farmhouse.' He glared at Stefan, who had grown decidedly paler. 'She's a mean bitch, so be careful.'

'Is she blonde? Wears black?' Leo asked.

'Nah, that's Corrine. She's a mean bitch too.'

'You don't need to tell me,' Leo said, grimacing.

'She do that to your face?'

'Yeah.'

'You're lucky you're still breathing.'

'I don't feel very lucky.'

'I used to be a good guy,' Doug said, looking at the flames. 'I used to be able to sleep at night. Not anymore.'

'You'll be able to sleep plenty from now on,' Stefan said nastily. 'You're fired!'

Doug laughed. 'Fired from what? The place is nearly ash.'

'Hey!' the taxi driver yelled out the window, 'are you going to pay me or not?'

'I'm homeless!' Stefan yelled back, sliding towards the drive. 'Have you no pity?'

Pat caught Stefan by the arm, stopping the little man from slipping away any further. 'Don't go anywhere,' he said, 'because you and me are about to have a serious talk.'

'About what? I don't know anything.'

Stefan wiggled, but Pat's grip was vice-like.

'Where can we find this farmhouse?'

'I can't help you.'

'Try.'

'Doug, make him let me go.'

'You just fired me.'

'You stupid bloody oaf!' Stefan yelled, his toupee beginning to slide to the left. 'I'll have your guts for garters.'

The smack Pat gave him knocked the toupee right off his head. He bent to retrieve it and put it back on, his cheek flaming red, his eyes brimming with tears of humiliation and rage. 'You can't do this,' he said, and it occurred to Leo that he really believed what he was saying, which was incredible under the circumstances.

'Yeah, we can.'

'Pat,' Frank said.

'What?'

'Pay the taxi man what he's owed and let's get the hell out of here.'

75

The drive from Lakeside to the farmhouse took less than thirty minutes, but in that time, Stefan had gone from vicious, to docile, to snivelling, to openly weeping, and Leo was sick to the teeth of listening to him.

'You don't understand the position you're putting me in,' he wailed. 'They'll kill me for this. You're dealing with some very dangerous people.'

'I'm going to kill you if you don't shut up,' Tommy said, turning around in the passenger seat, his intentions perfectly clear when he raised his fist.

Stefan shrank back against Leo. 'It's not fair,' he blubbed. 'I was doing my job.'

'Just following orders, eh?' Leo said, trying to push him off.

'Exactly!' Stefan said, not realising what Leo meant.

Leo looked disgusted. 'You kept women as slaves, you sold them! What the hell's wrong with you?'

'I took care of them!'

'So you're a compassionate slaver,' Pat said, glancing in the rear-view mirror.

Stefan started snivelling again. 'None of this is my fault.'

'Oh, shut up.'

When they reached the farmhouse, they were surprised to find they were not the only ones paying a visit that day. There were three people, a man and two women, bent down between a Volvo and a beige Tiida with its windscreen blown out. There was a two-seater Mercedes parked a few feet away from that. The older of the women was a big-boned blonde in an ill-fitting red pantsuit, and the younger woman, also blonde, was dressed in black.

'That's her!' Leo yelled, startling everyone in the Jeep, even Pat. 'That's the woman who attacked me at the restaurant.'

'That's Corrine. You can't let her see me,' Stefan said, trying to duck down out of sight behind the seats. 'Please—'

'Oh, for—'

'She's most likely armed,' Pat said to Tommy, who rested his own gun on his lap.

Seeing the weapon caused Leo to instantly regret his insistence that they speak to Duchy Ward at all. What the hell had he been thinking?

Pat swung the Jeep into the yard and cut the engine. Sean stopped at the top of the lane where he and Frank could see the action from a safe distance.

'Now what?' Leo asked.

Pat let his window down a few inches. 'Hey, Duchy, what's going on?'

'This is private property, Kennedy. You need to leave, right now.'

'I don't think so. We need to talk.'

'Are you mad? Can you not see I have a situation here?'

'I can see that.'

'Then get the hell out of here.'

'Liam didn't kill your brother!'

The top of Duchy's head appeared over the roof of the Tiida.

'This is a volatile situation, Kennedy; you need to leave.'

'I'm going nowhere until I have assurances that my family is safe.'

'Pat, ask him what happened to the windscreen of that car,' Leo mumbled.

'What happened to the car?'

'Family dispute.'

'Oh yeah?'

'Will you get out of here?'

Pat said nothing for a moment, then: 'My brother's going to need compensation.'

'What?' Duchy yelled.

'What?' Leo said. 'No I don't, I don't want anything to do with this man.'

'What's he talking about?' the heavy-set blonde asked. 'Who are these people?'

'You have no business here,' Duchy roared. 'Get going.'

'I'm going nowhere,' Pat repeated. 'I'm going to get out now and we are going to talk.'

'Don't do it, Pat,' Leo said, 'seriously.'

'Be quiet.'

Pat opened the driver's door and stepped out. 'Cover me, Tommy.'

Tommy got out of the passenger side of the Jeep and, using the door as a shield, pointed the gun towards Corrine, who had her own weapon drawn.

Stefan made a strange sound in the back of his throat, until Leo elbowed him to stop.

Corrine aimed her gun right at Pat's chest. 'Turn around. Lift your coat.'

Pat lifted the ends of his coat and turned around in a slow circle.

'Come forward. Slowly.'

Pat walked up to the Volvo, his hands wide. 'What's going on here?'

'My sister-in-law has lost her mind,' Duchy said.

'Your sister-in-law?'

'She set me up, your brother too. Bitch wanted me to kill him.'

'Wait, are you saying this Mariposa woman killed Arthur?'

'Not personally, but she was behind it. Behind a lot of things, I've since discovered.'

'But why?'

Duchy pulled a face. 'Who can explain the vagaries of the female mind?'

He glanced at the heavy blonde, who curled her lip. 'You need to make her pay, Duchy, all right? An eye for an eye.'

Pat pinched the bridge of his nose. 'Look, I need assurances from you that my family is off-limits. I don't want a war, Duchy, but if you push me, war is what you'll have.'

'My war is not with you.' Duchy glanced towards the cottage. 'But blood calls for blood.'

'Then my family is off-limits?'

Duchy looked at him. 'Sure.'

'Your word.'

Before Duchy could respond, the front door of the cottage opened and two huge monsters came racing towards them.

Duchy leaped up onto the Volvo with surprising agility for a man of his years. Pat clambered up next, followed in a flash by Corrine. Sylvia wasn't so agile: the dogs hit her full force and took her to the ground.

She screamed and they tore her flesh.

'Sylvia!' Duchy leaped off the roof, landed awkwardly and started kicking at the dogs, giving Sylvia a chance to crawl away; she was bleeding heavily and disorientated, in shock, her suit filthy and torn.

'Tommy!' Leo yelled. 'Shoot them, Tommy!'

'I can't risk hitting someone.'

The Audi roared into the yard. Frank leaped from the passenger seat and waved his arms. The dogs ran around to his side of the car, leaping at the door and scoring the paint with their nails. Duchy grabbed Sylvia and flung her into the back seat and scrambled in beside her.

'Get in!' Sean yelled to Pat.

Pat slid off the roof and dived in after Duchy, who was trying to help Sylvia.

'Come on!' Pat held his hand out to Corrine, who hesitated.

It was her undoing.

The door of the cottage opened again, and everyone ducked as the business end of a handgun appeared in the gap. The shot clipped Corrine and sent her spinning off the roof and onto the ground. The dogs abandoned Frank's attempts to distract them and raced around the car towards her as Pat leaned out to grab the back of her jacket.

'We're going to die.' Stefan was weeping into his sleeve. 'She's going to kill us all.'

Tommy aimed carefully and got off a round.

76

Mariposa whistled. Within seconds both dogs appeared at a charge and back into the house. She slammed the door and retreated to the rear of the cottage, ducking into the little room off the kitchen to check the cameras. The attack had drawn the Audi out of the lane and now all she needed to do was get one of the vehicles from the shed and make her getaway.

Cushla nuzzled her hand. He was bleeding from where the bullet had grazed his chest, but otherwise seemed unharmed.

'Good boy, good boy.' She patted his huge head. It was amazing what weeks of feeding could accomplish: she had thought they were indifferent to her, but now she saw they would lay down their life to protect her.

She checked the camera and noticed with some alarm that Corrine was no longer visible from where she had fallen. She'd shot the bitch and the dogs had mauled her – surely there was no way she could have survived. She hurried into the kitchen where Stonewall lay slumped in the armchair, his breathing ragged.

She pulled open the drawers, searching for keys, and found a set to the Scania, the same lorry Murray had used to traffic Yulia and the others into the country. Excellent, she thought, if anyone tried to stop her she'd simply run them over.

She scooped the keys up and turned around as Stonewall rose from his chair with the fireside poker in his hand and lunged for her.

He struck her across the side of the head as hard as he could.

Mariposa spun, staggered and fell. Stonewall dropped the poker, pitched forward and toppled down beside her.

'Brother,' Mariposa whispered. 'Brother, I ...'

She made a strange hiccupping sound, then another and then she grew quiet and quieter still.

The dogs whined. Stonewall took Mariposa's hand in his and dragged his body next to hers. He looked into her eyes as his breathing became shallow and his heart slowed. The dogs snuffled and licked his face, their combined breaths hot on his skin. He thought he saw Chester standing in the shadows, wearing his peaked cap pushed back too far on his head and the same faint smile of puzzlement on his face as on the day Stonewall had sought him out and hung him from the rafters. Stonewall watched his grandfather until his sight grew dim and his chest ceased to rise or fall.

77

When the guards arrived at the farmhouse that same evening they were met with an eerie silence. The courtyard gates were standing wide open, and there was blood all over the front yard.

They found Mariposa and Stonewall in the kitchen where they had fallen. They discovered cameras aplenty, but no recordings and no sign of phones or computers of any kind. They also found a small, near hysterical man locked in a shed with several lorries and vans and a number of empty filing cabinets.

'Place has been cleared out,' one of the detectives said to DI Maken, who arrived two hours later.

'Who was the guy in the shed?'

'He said his name is Stefan Millibrand and that he was kidnapped at gunpoint from his place of employment earlier today.'

'Who kidnapped him?'

'He said it was his employer.' He looked down at his notebook. 'Mariposa Ward? Who we have identified as the dead woman.' The detective noted Maken's sceptical face. 'I know, but I ran his name. He's so clean, he squeaks.'

'Where is he now?'

'Gone to the hospital. He told us he had a heart condition and that he was in shock.'

'So, what happened here?'

'Family feud, apparently. Millibrand said there was bad blood between the siblings.'

Maken looked around. Mariposa and Stonewall were lying under protective covers. He thought about the day he'd met her at the hospital, how strange and difficult she had been, but how vital.

He watched the forensics team work for a while. Then he got into his car and left, none the wiser, but troubled. Deeply troubled. Nothing about this scene sat right with him, nothing at all.

78

'You sit yourself down there.' Sergeant Samantha Quinn pointed to a chair. 'I'll be with you in a jiffy.'

Celestine sat, although her legs were so short her feet did not reach the floor fully. She had spent the night in the police station, sleeping in a cot in a back room. The woman with the kind eyes came back in the morning and brought a change of clothes for her to wear. They were a little big, but they smelled nice and were very soft, as though they had been washed many times.

In an office down the hallway, Samantha was talking to Duty Sergeant David Ross. 'I haven't a clue, David. I thought she was a runaway at first, but now I'm not so sure.'

'What's she in for?'

'She was in a supermarket, eating popcorn and drinking cola. She tried to pay for it with this.' Samantha put the bag on his desk.

David opened it and caught the unmistakable smell of cannabis. He put his hand in and withdrew a big sticky flower that had been somewhat squashed. 'Where the hell did she get this?'

'I have no idea. And that's the other thing: I don't think she speaks.'

'What, English?'

'I don't think she speaks at all.'

'Probably putting it on. Wouldn't be the first.'

'Maybe so.' Samantha shifted her weight from one bum cheek to the other. 'I don't think she understands a word I'm saying either.'

'That complicates things.'

'We need to call social services, get Evette down here this morning for an assessment. And she'll need to get that arm looked at properly.'

'All right, I'll make the call. What are you going to do with her until then?'

'Is the vending machine working?'

'I think so.'

'I'll see if I can get her to give me some idea of where the hell she came from. She's got a lot of old injuries, poor kid.'

She walked back up the hall. 'Right, come on, you.' She waggled her fingers at Celestine, who slid off the chair and trailed after her like a bedraggled puppy.

'Okay.' Samantha opened the door of interview room one and ushered her in. 'Sit down there now, good girl.'

Celestine sat. Samantha looked her over with a critical eye. She couldn't have been more than thirteen or fourteen, and her hair was matted and unkempt. From the look of her, she'd been sleeping rough, which explained the sleeping bag, but not the plastic bag full of cannabis. There were old scars under her left ear, as though her skin had been sanded away at one time.

Samantha, who had two children of her own, felt a surge of protectiveness for the poor little mite. 'Right, you hold on there now. I just need to go and make a call and I'll be back in a few minutes, okay? I'm going to get a doctor to look at that arm for you too, okay?'

Celestine did not respond.

'Right.'

Samantha closed the door and went down the hall. She made all the calls she needed to make and returned half an hour later with a cup of sugary tea and a chicken and stuffing sandwich from the shop across the street.

Celestine was curled up under the table with her sleeping bag, fast asleep. Samantha put the food and drink on the desk and left quietly. The interview could wait another hour.

By the time the social worker came, it was after midday. Samantha welcomed Evette and together they tried to talk to a groggy Celestine. It was impossible.

Clearly the girl could hear them and understood some of what was going on, but she made no effort to communicate, shutting down completely when Evette tried some rudimentary sign language.

'Where did she come from?' Evette asked out in the hall, having tried and failed to engage Celestine for a third time.

'I have no idea, she just turned up in the supermarket yesterday.'

'With a big bag of high-grade grass.'

'It's a mystery.'

'Right.' Evette looked at her watch. 'Well, I suppose the best thing I can do is see if I can get her into the residential home. Not sure if they have any space but I'll give it a shot.'

'She'll need that arm seen to.'

'I'll bring her to A&E, get it X-rayed.'

They shook hands, and within half an hour Celestine was on the move again. This time she managed to stay awake.

The hospital people were nice to her; they X-rayed her arm and bandaged it up, gave her a clean, working sling and painkillers. A different doctor examined her legs and took blood from her arm. It stung a little, but he gave her a lollipop afterwards. By the time it was all done it was dark outside again and she was sleepy.

They left the hospital and went for a drive in Evette's untidy car, stopping outside a brown single-storey building where Evette seemed to know many of the people.

Inside she limped along after Evette, trailing down one long corridor after another before they finally stopped outside a door with the number fifteen on it. Evette unlocked it, turned on the light and stepped back.

It was a small room with a single bed, a desk, a wardrobe and a lamp. There was a yellow and blue duvet on the bed and two pillows in the same stripy material. Evette showed her where the bathroom was down the hall. Three stalls and three sinks. Evette gave her a plastic bag with a toothbrush, a comb and a small bar of soap wrapped in paper. She stayed in the bathroom until Celestine had washed her face and brushed her teeth. None of it was easy using only one hand, but she managed.

Back in her room Evette once again tried to communicate, but Celestine was exhausted and wanted to lie down. Evette put on the lamp and turned the main light off. She said some more words and left, closing the door softly behind her.

When she was gone, Celestine got out of bed and went back to the bathroom to check the windows. They were barred from the outside. She walked back up the corridor the way they had come in, but the double doors were locked.

Celestine went back to her room, got into bed and fell into a deep sleep.

*

At the station, Samantha Quinn was about to finish her shift when the phone on her desk rang. She snatched it up. 'Quinn.'

'Oh good, you're still there.'

'Hey, Evette, everything okay? How's our mystery girl?'

'She's okay. Look, the reason I'm calling is because I went through her old clothes before I put them into the laundry here and I found something interesting.

'Oh yeah?

'It's a postcard of a donkey wearing a straw hat. I think it's in Connemara.'

'Wearing a hat?'

'And get this, it's addressed to a local business park.'

Samantha sat up a little straighter. 'Shoot me the address, will you?'

Evette read it out. Samantha asked her to repeat it, said she'd look into it and hung up.

It wasn't far from there, eight miles tops. She could stick her nose in on the way home, have a little look.

What harm could it do?

79

Murray saw the lights flashing the second he turned the corner, clocked the guard standing at the gate of the business park, checking the ID of everyone who entered or left. Murray, canny as always, drove past the main gate, keeping to the same speed.

Half a mile up the road, he pulled into a lay-by and made a call. 'The fuzz are all over the grow house. I think—'

'Murray?'

'Oh, Cally. Sorry, love, I was looking for Duchy.'

'Oh, Murray.' She began to sob. 'What's going on?'

'What do you mean?'

'I'm at the hospital.'

'What? Why?'

'Duchy and Sylvia were savaged by dogs. The doctors think Sylvia might lose the use of her arm.'

'Dogs?' Murray narrowed his eyes, staring at the green nothingness beyond his windscreen. 'Did you say dogs?'

'I don't understand. What's going on? Do you know who owns dogs like this? Were they pets belonging to someone? Nobody will talk to me.'

'No,' Murray said. 'Not pets. Look, I've got to go, Cally. I'll talk to you later, yeah?'

He hung up, put the van in gear and took the long way back to the main road to avoid being noticed.

By the time he made it to Dublin, the guards were waiting at the garage to speak to him, and he knew before they said a single word that Rally was dead.

80

Celestine slept and slept and slept. People came, lots of different people, to see her. The first woman, the police officer, came with another man, older than her. They showed her photographs of different people. Celestine looked at them and said nothing, though she recognised the bad man with the dogs and the man who brought her and Yulia into Ireland.

On the fourth day, the woman who ran the place, a very short woman called Jodie, who smiled a lot, knocked on her door and waved, indicating she should follow her. Celestine unfolded herself from the bed and trudged down the hall, suspecting another barrage of questions she could not understand from people she did not know.

Jodie led her into a room just down from the kitchens. A woman was waiting inside, a tall woman with a broad face and shrewd eyes. Jodie and the woman spoke briefly and after a moment Jodie patted Celestine on the back and left the room.

The woman looked at Celestine, who stared at the floor.

'Does your arm hurt?' the woman asked, and Celestine looked up, her eyes widening in surprise.

'That's right,' the woman said. 'I speak Serbian – in fact I speak a lot of languages.'

Celestine continued to stare.

'Does it hurt?'

Celestine shook her head.

The woman nodded. 'I can see you are very brave, very ... resilient.' She leaned forward and lowered her voice. 'Like your sister, Yulia. She is very brave too.'

Celestine held herself very still, kept her expression blank. She did not know this woman, did not have any reason to trust her. She might work for the men, she might work for government: she might be very bad indeed.

'My name,' the woman said, 'is Livia Taktarov. Tomorrow morning you are going to find a way out of this place, unseen, and you will walk down the hill quickly and without attracting any attention to yourself. A van will pull up and you will get into it; the van will be grey and have a ladder attached to the roof. The driver of the van is a man named Oleg. Oleg is a good man and you can trust him.'

Celestine said nothing – she didn't dare to breathe. Was it a trap? Was it a trick?

The woman, Livia, took a phone from her pocket, made a call and passed the phone to Celestine, who took it with hesitation. She held it to her ear.

'Celestine?'

Celestine started to tremble. It was Yulia.

'Celestine, listen to this woman, do what she says. I will see you soon. I love you. I love you. Please, do as she says.' She hung up.

Celestine handed the phone back to Livia.

'Can you do what I ask?' Livia said.

Celestine nodded.

'Good girl,' Livia said and stood up. She opened the door and called Jodie back.

'Well? How'd you get on?' Jodie asked, looking hopeful.

'I'm sorry,' Livia said. 'She doesn't understand me either.'

'Oh dear.' Jodie glanced at Celestine. 'Oh dear, that's a shame.' She sighed. 'So sad. I don't know what to do with her really – she must be so lonely.'

'I'm sure things will improve,' Livia said and gave Celestine a nod and left.

The next morning, shortly after breakfast, Celestine waited until Jodie was busy in the kitchen and simply walked out the front door and down the street. She had gone several hundred metres when a grey van with a ladder on the roof pulled in and a red-faced man with huge eyebrows said, 'Do you need a lift?'

Celestine got into the passenger seat and closed the door. The man checked the mirrors and pulled out again.

Long, slender arms came from behind and encircled Celestine's body.

'I have you.' Yulia's voice was soft in her ears. 'I have you, you're safe, you're safe.'

Celestine leaned back into her sister's arms and closed her eyes.

81

Leo woke up and groaned. A week had passed since the chaos at the farmhouse and still he felt like someone had driven over his body in a combine harvester.

He took two over-the-counter generic painkillers (God, how he missed Jean's wonderful tablets) and went downstairs. He knew Oleg was already in the kitchen, because he could hear Guns N' Roses being played at a decibel level most teenage boys would balk at.

'Good morning!' Oleg said when saw him. 'Coffee is on.'

Leo turned the radio down a little and poured himself a half measure of Oleg's coffee. The Russian liked it strong enough to stand on.

Oleg peered at him. 'You look better, less like piece of shit.'

'Good to know.' He took a sip of the coffee and winced. Tar, this was coffee-flavoured tar.

'I bring paper.'

'I see that,' Leo said, making no move to reach it. 'They're still going on, are they?'

'A little, not as much as before.'

The redtops were having a field day with the happenings at the farmhouse and Lakeside. The papers were full of stories about

Stonewall, Duchy, Mariposa, Murray and Rally. It was the stuff tabloid editors dreamed of. Of course the guards were playing their cards close to their chests, but it was clear they weren't really buying what happened as a simple murder-suicide. They wanted to talk to Liam again, but with him in rehab, they'd have to wait.

Leo had been to see his brother the day before. The kid was doing okay – not great, but okay. He had, Leo knew, a long road of recovery ahead of him and he vowed to help him in every way he could.

Things were strained between him and Eddie and he felt low about that. The thing that bothered him most was … he felt Dom was right. Not about everything – he did not believe he was a bad man at heart, but trouble seemed to sniff him out at every turn. He would never have forgiven himself if Corrine had hurt Eddie, and Eddie couldn't forgive him for inviting his family back into his life.

Several days after the fracas at the farmhouse he took Bellisa and drove out to Woodlawn Cemetery where his mother was buried. He placed a bouquet of pink carnations – her favourite – on her grave and sat for a while to talk to her. Niall was buried in the plot beside her, good old Uncle Niall. Leo twisted his body so he didn't have to look at the headstone and didn't have to read the inscription. Beloved brother, beloved uncle. Beloved.

Lies, Leo thought. Nothing but lies.

On the drive back to Bocht he wondered what deal Pat and Duchy Ward had struck, for the two men had spent some time in deep conversation at the farmhouse before Duchy took his sister to the hospital. He wondered if Corrine was alive, and hoped she was, though he also hoped he never laid eyes on her again. He wondered why Pat and Tommy had taken Stefan to the shed and spent so long in there with him. He wondered a lot of things, but knowing Pat, wondering was probably as close as he would get to anything resembling the truth.

Whatever Pat was up to, it was best if he didn't know. It might be best if he concentrated on food for the future. Food was safe, food was uncomplicated.

Maybe he'd sleep at night, maybe not.

'What time did Nadia say she was coming in?'

'Ten.'

Leo looked at the clock; it was only ten past nine. He sipped his coffee and thought about the day's menu and tried not to think about Nadia.

*

Across town in an office that could have done with a plant pot or two, Pat Kennedy sat down, unbuttoned his jacket and leaned back in his chair with the faintest of smiles on his lips. 'I appreciate you taking the time to see me, minister.'

Ivan Dolan sighed. 'All right,' he said. 'Cut to the chase and tell me what you want.'

Pat leaned down, lifted a duffle bag from the floor and placed it on the desk.

Ivan looked at it as though it might explode at any moment. 'What's that?'

'Open it.'

Dolan stood and unzipped it slowly. He looked inside and frowned. 'I don't understand.'

'Towel-rail, phone, knife, blood-stained towels,' Pat said. 'I was … fortunate to be able to procure them from an independent source.'

Dolan looked at him. 'These are from the … incident.'

'That's right.'

'And you're just giving them to me, is that it?'

Pat Kennedy smiled. It was a pretty good attempt at affable, but if Leo had seen it he would have assumed the worst for this was a predatory smile, the smile of someone who has the upper hand and knows it.

It was the smile of a barracuda.

Acknowledgements

My thanks, as always, to my editor Ciara Considine for her insights and patience, and to the incredible team at Hachette Ireland.

Thanks also to my agent Faith O'Grady of Lisa Richards Agency.

To my friends and family for putting up with me from one end of the year to the other, much love.

To the readers, bookshop owners and book lovers who I like to think of as my tribe, my eternal gratitude for your continued support. To Jordan and Andrew, my deepest abiding love, for now and for always.